最讓人發毛的

鬼話英文

Spooky
English

CONTENTS 目錄

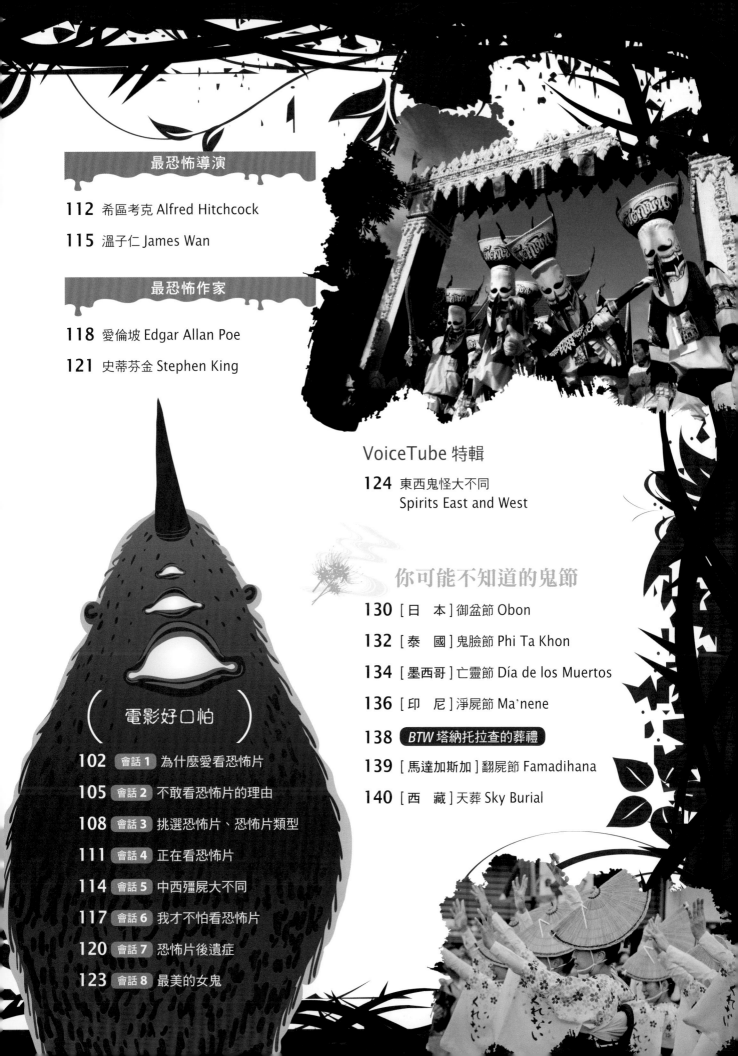

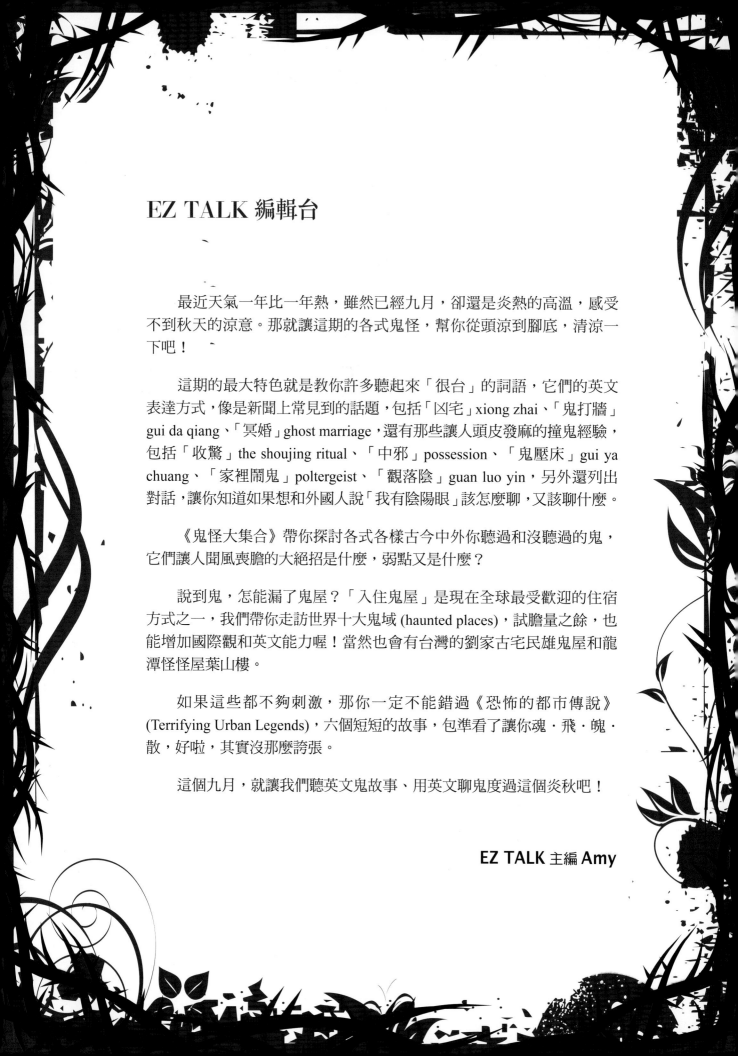

EZ TALK 編輯台

最近天氣一年比一年熱，雖然已經九月，卻還是炎熱的高溫，感受不到秋天的涼意。那就讓這期的各式鬼怪，幫你從頭涼到腳底，清涼一下吧！

這期的最大特色就是教你許多聽起來「很台」的詞語，它們的英文表達方式，像是新聞上常見到的話題，包括「凶宅」xiong zhai、「鬼打牆」gui da qiang、「冥婚」ghost marriage，還有那些讓人頭皮發麻的撞鬼經驗，包括「收驚」the shoujing ritual、「中邪」possession、「鬼壓床」gui ya chuang、「家裡鬧鬼」poltergeist、「觀落陰」guan luo yin，另外還列出對話，讓你知道如果想和外國人說「我有陰陽眼」該怎麼聊，又該聊什麼。

《鬼怪大集合》帶你探討各式各樣古今中外你聽過和沒聽過的鬼，它們讓人聞風喪膽的大絕招是什麼，弱點又是什麼？

說到鬼，怎能漏了鬼屋？「入住鬼屋」是現在全球最受歡迎的住宿方式之一，我們帶你走訪世界十大鬼域 (haunted places)，試膽量之餘，也能增加國際觀和英文能力喔！當然也會有台灣的劉家古宅民雄鬼屋和龍潭怪怪屋葉山樓。

如果這些都不夠刺激，那你一定不能錯過《恐怖的都市傳說》(Terrifying Urban Legends)，六個短短的故事，包準看了讓你魂‧飛‧魄‧散，好啦，其實沒那麼誇張。

這個九月，就讓我們聽英文鬼故事、用英文聊鬼度過這個炎秋吧！

EZ TALK 主編 Amy

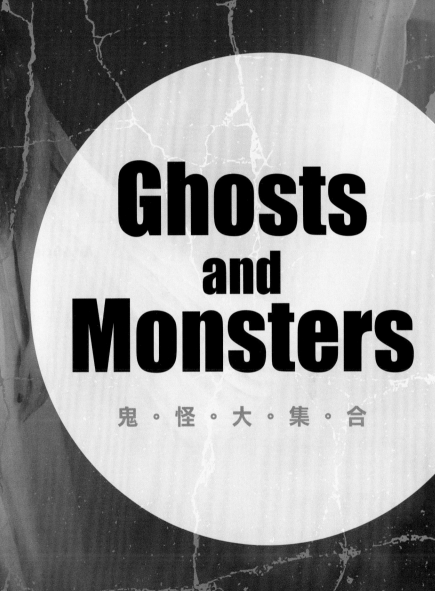

Ghosts and Monsters

and

Monsters

鬼。怪。大。集。合

鬼魂與靈魂
Ghosts and Spirits

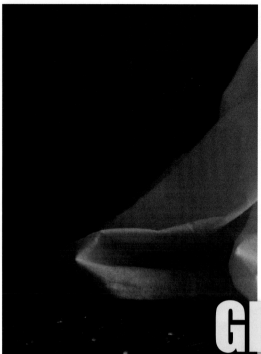

🎧 002 Vocabulary

1) **afterlife** [ˋæftɚˏlaɪf] (n.) 來世

2) **underworld** [ˋʌndɚˏwɝld] (n.)（首字母常大寫）陰間，冥府

3) **lunar** [ˋlunɚ] (a.) 陰曆的，按月球的運轉測定的

4) **entertainment** [ˏɛntɚˋtenmənt] (n.) 娛樂

5) **eternity** [ɪˋtɝnəti] (n.) 永遠，（似乎）無止盡的時間

6) **reference** [ˋrɛf(ə)rəns] (n.) 提及，參考書目

7) **Testament** [ˋtɛstəmənt] (n.)（首字母大寫）聖經舊約，聖經新約

8) **defeat** [dɪˋfit] (v./n.) 擊敗，戰敗

9) **discourage** [dɪsˋkɝɪdʒ] (v.) 勸阻，阻擋

10) **sighting** [ˋsaɪtɪŋ] (n.) 目擊，目睹

11) **era** [ˋɛrə] (n.) 歷史時期，年代

12) **account** [əˋkaʊnt] (n.) 記述，報導

13) **haunted** [ˋhɔntɪd] (a.) 鬧鬼的；**haunted house** 即「鬼屋」；動詞為 **haunt** [hɔnt] 指「（鬼魂）經常出沒」

14) **carry out** [ˋkæri aʊt] (phr.) 完成，執行，進行

15) **firsthand** [ˋfɝstˋhænd] (a./adv.) 第一手的；親自地

16) **witness** [ˋwɪtnɪs] (n./v.) 目擊者，證人；目擊，證明

🎧 001 An ancient belief 古老的信仰

Belief in ghosts is as old as mankind itself. In ancient cultures all around the world, people believed that the human soul left the body at the time of death and entered the [1]**afterlife**. But if spirits go to live in the afterlife, why would they appear to the living in the form of ghosts? In Chinese tradition, the gates to the [2]**underworld** open during Ghost Month—the seventh month of the [3]**lunar** calendar—allowing the spirits of the dead to visit the world of the living for food and [4]**entertainment**.

　自從有人類以來，就存在鬼魂的信仰。在世界各地的古文化中，人們相信在死亡之際，人的靈魂會離開身體，進入來世。但靈魂若是到來世生活，又為何要以鬼魂的形式出現在人間？中國傳統認為，陰間大門會在鬼月，也就是農曆七月開啟，讓往生者的靈魂到人間覓食和作樂。

In Christian tradition, the souls of the dead go to Heaven or Hell, where they remain for [5]**eternity**. No wonder there are only two clear [6]**references** to ghosts in the Bible. In the Old [7]**Testament**, 🅛🅖 **Saul, King of Israel**, asks the ghost of Samuel for advice in [8]**defeating** the Philistines; and in the New Testament, Jesus has to persuade people that he's not a ghost after he rises from the dead. Yet while the Church [9]**discouraged** belief in ghosts, there were so many [10]**sightings** over the centuries that their efforts had little effect.

基督教傳統認為，死者的靈魂會上天堂或下地獄，並永遠留在那裡，因此聖經中只有兩處明確提到鬼魂也就不足為奇了。在舊約中，以色列的掃羅王向撒母耳的鬼魂請教如何打敗非利士人；在新約中，耶穌復活後要說服大家他不是鬼魂。不過，儘管教會阻止人民相信鬼魂，但千百年來仍有許多看到鬼魂的傳聞，可見教會的控制成效不彰。

Ghosts enter the modern[11]era 傳入現代的鬼魂

Ghost stories had long been popular with **LG Victorian** readers, but it was the work of Scottish writer Catherine Crowe that brought belief in ghosts into the modern era. In *The Night Side of Nature*, published in 1848, she collected [12]**accounts** of ghost sightings and [13]**haunted** houses from all over Europe. What made Crowe's book different from other collections of ghost stories was the fact that she [14]**carried out** careful research, requiring at least two [15]**firsthand** [16]**witnesses** for each account included.

鬼故事長久以來一直深受維多利亞時代的讀者歡迎。但將鬼魂信仰帶入現代的，是蘇格蘭作家凱瑟琳克羅的作品。她在 1848 年出版的《自然的夜界》中，收錄歐洲各地看到鬼魂和鬼屋的報導。克羅的書和其他鬼故事選集的不同之處在於她精心進行研究，所收錄的每篇報導，都至少有兩位第一手目擊證人。

字母童書的 G 以狄更斯故事當中的小氣鬼 Scrooge 和鬼魂 Marley's ghost 表現。

🎧 004 Vocabulary

1) **spiritualism** [ˋspɪrɪtʃuəˏlɪzm] (n.) 通靈，招魂論

2) **awareness** [əˋwɛrnɪs] (n.) 意識，認識，了解。**raise awareness** 即「使進一步了解，喚起…意識」

3) **supernatural** [ˏsupəˋnætʃərəl] (a.) 超自然的，靈異的

4) **movement** [ˋmuvmənt] (n.)（社會）運動，活動

5) **interpret** [ɪnˋtɝprɪt] (v.) 解釋，闡述

6) **rap** [ræp] (v./n.) 敲打；扣扣聲

7) **séance** [ˋseɑns] (n.) 降神會

8) **medium** [ˋmidɪəm] (n.) 靈媒

9) **fraud** [frɔd] (n.) 騙子，詐欺，騙局

10) **investigator** [ɪnˋvɛstɪˏgetə] (n.) 調查者，研究者，偵探

11) **transparent** [trænsˋpærənt] (a.) 透明的

12) **location** [loˋkeʃən] (n.) 所在地，地點，位置

13) **tragic** [ˋtrædʒɪk] (a.) 悲慘的，不幸的

14) **get rid of** [gɛt rɪd əv] (phr.) 排除，擺脫

15) **cleanse** [klɛnz] (v.) 清洗，淨化

16) **incense** [ˋɪnsɛns] (n.) 香

17) **exorcism** [ˋɛksɚˏsɪzəm] (n.) 驅魔，招魂；動詞為 **exorcise** [ˋɛksɚˏsɪz]

🐌 Language Guide

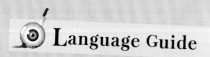

Fox sisters 福克斯家三姐妹

Maggie Fox（1833~1893）和 Katie Fox（1837~1892）堪稱現代靈媒的始祖，十幾歲起展現她們的通靈能力，能透過敲擊聲組成的密碼與鬼魂溝通。兩人的大姐 Leah Fox（1831~1890）曾經協助她們發展事業，在上流社交圈內舉辦降神會、首開先河收費表演通靈術。儘管 Maggie 和 Katie 晚年公開招認只是在裝神弄鬼，但相信及研究鬼魂的風氣，早已隨她們的聲名遠播而大開。

🎧 003 The rise of [1] spiritualism 通靈的崛起

While Crowe's book did much to raise public [2]**awareness** of the [3]**supernatural**, it was an event on the other side of the Atlantic that turned belief in ghosts and the afterlife into a new religious [4]**movement** called spiritualism. In the spring of 1848, when the Fox family of New York State was kept up by strange noises in their house, sisters 🔊 **Maggie and Katie** discovered the source was a ghost, and that they could communicate with him by asking questions and [5]**interpreting** the [6]**rapping** sounds that he made.

雖然克羅的書推波助瀾使大眾對超自然有進一步的認識，在大西洋的另一邊發生的事件則興起了一場將鬼魂和來世的信仰發展成通靈的新宗教活動。1848 年春季，紐約州的福克斯家因住家發出奇怪聲響夜不成眠，瑪姬和凱蒂兩姐妹發現聲音的來源是鬼魂，而且她們能透過提問並解讀鬼發出的敲擊聲來跟鬼溝通。

The ghost claimed that he was a salesman who'd been killed by the house's former owner, and when human bones were discovered in the basement, the sisters' story spread across the country. They began traveling from town to town holding [7]**séances**, where they communicated with other spirits using the same method. As their fame as [8]**mediums** grew, many others found that they could also contact spirits, and a new religious movement was born. Instead of church, members attended séances, where mediums helped them talk to dead relatives and receive guidance from the spirit world.

那個鬼魂自稱是銷售員，是被那棟房子的前屋主所殺，屍骨在地下室被找到後，這對姐妹的故事傳遍全國。她們開始周遊各個城鎮，舉辦降神會，以同樣的方式跟其他鬼魂溝通。隨著她們的靈媒聲望越來越高，也有許多人發現自己能跟鬼魂溝通，於是新的宗教運動就此誕生。信徒不上教堂，而是參加降神會，靈媒在集會上幫他們跟死去的親戚溝通，接受來自靈界的指引。

Are ghosts real? 真的有鬼魂嗎？

When ghosts at séances went from rapping on tables to moving objects and even appearing before audiences, many began to suspect that the mediums were just performing tricks. Clubs and societies were formed to investigate the existence of ghosts, and while a number of mediums turned out to be [9]**frauds**, some [10]**investigators**—including doctor and author 🔊 **Arthur Conan Doyle** and scientist 🔊 **Pierre Curie**—actually became believers. This tradition continues today on popular shows like *Ghost Hunter* and *Ghost*

Adventures. Although no solid proof has been found yet, it's hard to prove that ghosts *don't* exist.

當降神會上的鬼魂不再敲打桌子，轉而移動物品，甚至出現在群眾眼前，許多人開始質疑這是靈媒在耍把戲。於是有人成立會社和協會調查是否有鬼魂存在，儘管有些靈媒證實是騙子，但也有些調查者成了信徒，包括醫生兼作家亞瑟柯南道爾和科學家皮耶居里。這種傳統持續至今，甚至以此製作成受歡迎的電視節目，例如《靈異前線》和《靈異探險》。雖然尚未找到可靠的證據證明鬼魂存在，但也難以證明鬼魂不存在。

Properties of ghosts 鬼魂的特性

When ghosts can be seen to humans, they usually have a white, [11]**transparent** appearance, but may also look just like they did in real life. Some walk around in a normal manner, while others float through the air. Ghosts are almost always dressed, usually in clothing from the period they lived in. They may use words or gestures to communicate with the living, or may not even notice them at all. Some ghosts appear to living relatives to deliver warnings or advice, and others haunt specific [12]**locations**, usually where they died violent or [13]**tragic** deaths. Ghosts called poltergeists—"noisy ghosts" in German—make loud noises and throw objects around.

人看到的鬼魂通常外表是白色、透明的，但也可能看起來就是祂們在世的模樣。有些鬼會正常走路，有些則飄浮在空中。鬼魂幾乎都有穿衣服，通常穿著生存時代的衣服。祂們可能會用言語或手勢跟生者溝通，也可能根本不理會活人。有些鬼魂出現在活著的親戚眼前，給他們警告或建議，另一些鬼魂則在特定地點出沒，通常是祂們慘遭暴力或不幸而喪生的地方。源自德文的騷靈，意思是「喧鬧的鬼」，會發出巨大的噪音和到處扔東西。

[14)]**Getting rid of ghosts** 驅鬼

Most ghosts 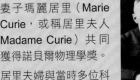 **mean humans no harm**, but living in a haunted house can still be a scary experience. Sometimes getting rid of a ghost is as simple as asking it to leave. If the ghost is a dead loved one, just tell it that it's all right to **move on**. Another way to get rid of a ghost is to [15)]**cleanse** the space with [16)]**incense**, candles and prayer. For ghosts that are particularly stubborn or evil, an [17)]**exorcism** may be necessary.

大部分鬼魂無意傷害人類，但住在仍是可怕的經歷。有時驅鬼的方式就只是要求他們離開這麼簡單而已。如果鬼魂是死去的親人，只要請祂放下並離開就好。另一種驅鬼方式是用焚香、蠟燭或禱告淨化空間。對於那些特別頑固或邪惡的鬼魂，可能有必要舉行驅魔儀式。

魔鬼
Demons

 Vocabulary

1) **suffering** [ˈsʌfərɪŋ] (n.)（身體上的）痛苦，（精神上的）苦惱，令人痛苦的事

2) **troublesome** [ˈtrʌbəlsəm] (a.) 令人煩惱的，製造麻煩的

3) **Christianity** [ˌkrɪstʃiˈænəti] (n.) 基督教（包含天主教、新教等）

4) **Satan** [ˈsetən] (n.)（固定大寫）撒旦，魔鬼

5) **misfortune** [mɪsˈfɔrtʃən] (n.) 厄運，不幸，災難

6) **tempt** [tɛmpt] (v.) 引誘，吸引

7) **Biblical** [ˈbɪblɪkəl] (a.)（常為大寫）聖經的

8) **rebellion** [rɪˈbɛljən] (n.) 叛亂，起義

9) **pagan** [ˈpegən] (a.) 異教的，多神教的，非基督教的

10) **worship** [ˈwɝʃɪp] (v./n.) 拜神，做禮拜

11) **possess** [pəˈzɛs] (v.)（鬼神）附身；名詞為 **possession** [pəˈzɛʃən] 附身，著魔

12) **scratch** [skrætʃ] (n./v.) 抓痕，刮痕；抓傷

13) **sulfur** [ˈsʌlfɚ] (n.) 硫磺

005 What are demons? 魔鬼是什麼？

A demon is generally defined as an evil spirit that causes pain and [1]**suffering** to humans. The term comes from the word *daemon*, which the ancient Greeks used to describe nature spirits that were neither good nor evil. In most cultures, however, demons are [2]**troublesome** rather than helpful, and many are evil. In [3]**Christianity**, all demons are evil servants of [4]**Satan** who bring [5]**misfortune** and [6]**tempt** people to sin.

魔鬼的定義通常是會造成人類痛苦的邪靈。demon 一詞源自古希臘文 daemon，形容既非善也非惡的自然神靈。但在大部分文化中，魔鬼通常是帶來麻煩而非幫助，其中有許多是邪惡的。在基督教中，所有魔鬼都是撒旦的邪惡屬下，會帶來不幸，並引誘人類犯罪。

The [7]Biblical history of demons 聖經中的魔鬼史

When the ⑥ **angel Lucifer** led a [8]**rebellion** against God, he was thrown out of Heaven and became Satan. From that time on, Satan ruled over Hell and the other fallen angels, who became demons. As Christianity spread, all [9]**pagan** gods, goddesses and spirits were turned into demons and people were no longer allowed to [10]**worship** them. During the Middle Ages, people began to believe that demons appeared in different forms, sometimes human, sometimes animal, and sometimes part human, part animal. They also believed that demons could not only tempt people to sin, but also [11]**possess** their bodies and make them perform evil deeds.

天使路西法帶頭反叛上帝時，被逐出天堂並成了撒旦，此後撒旦統治地獄和其他墮落的天使，祂們都變成了魔鬼。隨著基督教的傳播，所有異教的男神、女神和幽靈都變成了魔鬼，且不再允許人們膜拜祂們。在中世紀，人們開始相信魔鬼會以不同形式出現，有時是人類，有時是動物，有時半人半獸。他們也相信魔鬼不但會引誘人犯罪，也會附在人身上，導致他們做出惡行。

Demons in modern times 現代的魔鬼

Belief in [11]**possession** by demons continues to this day. When someone becomes possessed by a demon, their personality and behavior may change completely. The demon may take complete control of their body and speak through them in strange voices or languages they don't know. The person may also start shaking violently and swear or spit at people who come near. Sometimes, [12]**scratches** or bite marks may appear on the person's body, or the smell of [13]**sulfur** may fill the room.

魔鬼附身的信仰持續至今。人被魔鬼附身時，其個性和行為可能會完全改變。魔鬼可能會完全控制被附身者的身體，並透過人體以奇怪的聲音或被附身者也不懂的語言說話。被附身者也可能會開始劇烈搖晃，並朝靠近他的人咒罵或吐口水。有時被附身者的身體上可能會出現抓痕或咬痕，或整個空間會充滿硫磺味。

How to get rid of a demon 如何驅魔

Catholics believe that exorcism is the only way to remove a demon from someone who is possessed. When possession by a demon has been confirmed, a specially trained priest is sent to perform the exorcism. After the victim is tied down to prevent harm to himself or others, the priest holds up a cross and commands the demon to leave in the name of Jesus Christ. The priest also makes the sign of the cross over the person and may sprinkle him with holy water and read passages from the Bible. If the demon is a powerful one, more than one exorcism may be required.

天主教徒相信驅魔儀式是趕走附身魔鬼的唯一方法。有人被確認附身時，他們會派受過特殊訓練的神職人員舉行驅魔儀式。他們會將受害者捆綁起來，以防止他對自己或他人造成傷害，然後驅魔師舉起十字架，以耶穌基督之名命令魔鬼離開。驅魔師也會在被附身者身上畫十字符號，並可能在他身上灑聖水，讀聖經中的幾段文字。魔鬼若是法力強大，可能需要多舉行幾次驅魔儀式。

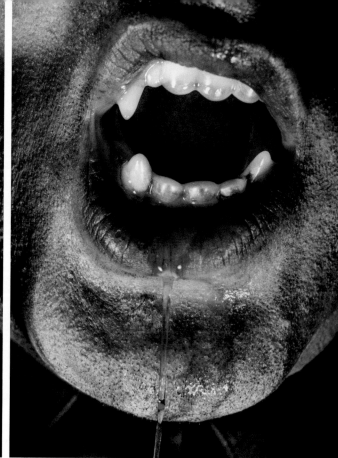

吸血鬼
Vampires

🎧 008 Vocabulary

1) **undead** [ʌn`dɛd] (a.)（傳說中）死而不僵的，活死人的

2) **folklore** [`fok.lor] (n.) 民間傳說，字尾的 **lore** 是「口頭傳說」的意思

3) **corpse** [kɔrps] (n.) 屍體

4) **grave** [ɡrev] (n.) 墓穴，埋葬處

5) **mysterious** [mɪs`tɪrɪəs] (a.) 神祕的

6) **plague** [pleɡ] (n.) 瘟疫，鼠疫

7) **culprit** [`kʌlprɪt] (n.) 罪魁禍首

8) **graveyard** [`ɡrev.jɑrd] (n.) 墓地

9) **decay** [dɪ`ke] (n./v.) 腐爛

10) **stake** [stek] (n.) 木樁，棍棒

11) **explanation** [.ɛksplə`neʃən] (n.) 解釋，說明；注意動詞的拼法為 **explain** [ɪks`plen]

12) **infectious** [ɪn`fɛkʃəs] (a.) 有感染力的

13) **build up** [bɪld ʌp] (phr.) 積聚，慢慢增加

14) **plump** [plʌmp] (a.) 豐滿的，鼓起的

🎧 007 Everyone's favorite scary creature
大家最愛的可怕生物

Unless you've been 🅛🅖 **living under a rock**, you know what a vampire is. These [1]**undead** monsters who survive by drinking human blood are everybody's favorite scary creature. They're not only popular around Halloween, but can be found in books, movies and TV shows any time of the year. The public thirst for vampires is almost as endless as vampires' thirst for blood. But where do vampires come from?

> 除非你是與世隔絕，否則應該都知道吸血鬼是什麼。這種活死人怪物靠飲人血維生，是大家最喜愛的可怕生物。他們不只在萬聖節時流行，一年到頭也都能在書、電影和影集中看到。大眾對吸血鬼的渴望，猶如吸血鬼對血的渴求一樣永無止境。但吸血鬼是從哪裡來的？

MORT DU CHOLERA

The vampires of Slavic legend
斯拉夫傳說中的吸血鬼

The word vampire has Slavic origins, so it's not surprising that vampires can be traced back to Eastern European [2]**folklore**. In the early 18th century, stories began appearing about [3]**corpses** climbing out of their [4]**graves** at night and drinking the blood of the living. When villages were struck by [5]**mysterious** [6]**plagues**, the deaths were often blamed on vampires, and teams of vampire hunters were formed to find the [7]**culprits**. These teams dug up graves at the local [8]**graveyard**, and when they found corpses with certain signs—like blood around the mouth or lack of [9]**decay**—they "killed" them with a wooden [10]**stake** through the chest.

vampire 一詞源自斯拉夫語，因此吸血鬼可追溯到東歐民間傳說也不足為怪。18 世紀初，屍體在夜間從墳墓中爬出並吸活人血的傳聞開始出現。村子裡爆發神祕的瘟疫時，村民往往將死因歸咎於吸血鬼，並組織吸血鬼獵殺隊尋找罪魁禍首。獵殺隊會在當地墳場挖掘墳墓，只要在屍體上發現某些跡象，比如嘴邊有血跡或屍體未腐爛，就會用木樁刺穿胸部，「殺死」屍體。

But were these actual vampires, or are there other [11]**explanations**? The plagues supposedly caused by vampires may have been [12]**infectious** diseases only later discovered by medical science. And the "signs" the vampire hunters used? As corpses decay, gases [13]**build up** in the chest, and the resulting pressure can cause blood to leak from the mouth and give the body a [14]**plump**, almost healthy look.

但那些真的是吸血鬼？還是有其他解釋？號稱由吸血鬼造成的瘟疫，可能是後來經由醫學科學發現的傳染病。那吸血鬼獵殺隊發現的「跡象」呢？屍體腐爛時，會有氣體在胸部累積，所產生的壓力可能導致血液從嘴滲出，讓屍體看起來豐滿，像是完好的狀態。

Language Guide

live under a rock 與世隔絕

當你發現一個人對外界發生的事漠不關心，大家都知道的事，他都沒聽說過，會驚愕地問他：「你是山頂洞人嗎？」live under a rock 就是形容一個人最近發生的重大事件渾然不知。

A: Who are the Kardashians? Is that the name of a band or something?
卡戴珊家族是誰啊？這是樂團的名字還是啥？

B: You don't know who the Kardashians are? Have you been living under a rock?
你不知道誰是卡戴珊家族？你是山頂洞人嗎？

© Zharov Pavel / Shutterstock.com

小說《德古拉》原型弗拉德三世（Vlad Dracula）的雕像，及他出生的城堡，位於羅馬尼亞的 Sighisoara。

009 The vampires of modern [1]fiction
現代小說中的吸血鬼

In the 19th century, **LG Gothic** writers in England were [2]**inspired** by Slavic folklore to write vampire stories of their own. But unlike the bloody undead corpses they were based on, these new vampires were [3]**charming**, attractive and [4]**aristocratic**. John Polidori's 1819 novel *The Vampyre* tells the story of Lord Ruthven, a mysterious [4]**aristocrat** who drinks the blood of beautiful young women. But most famous is Bram Stoker's *Dracula* (1897), which was said to be inspired by Vlad Dracula, a 15th-century Romanian prince famous for [5]**torturing** his enemies. Stoker's Count Dracula, who could turn into a bat and [6]**infect** others with his bite, became a model for all the [1]**fictional** vampires that followed.

19 世紀時，英國的哥德派作家受到斯拉夫民間故事的啟發，自編吸血鬼故事。但跟故事所本的血淋淋不死屍體不同的是，他們新編造出來吸血鬼迷人、有魅力，散發著貴族氣息。約翰波里道利的 1819 年小說《吸血鬼》敘述神祕的貴族盧希梵爵士啜飲美少女的鮮血。但最有名的是伯蘭史杜克的《德古拉》（1897 年），據說靈感來源是 15 世紀的羅馬尼亞王子弗拉德三世，他以刑求敵人聞名。史杜克的德古拉伯爵會變身成蝙蝠，咬過的人也會變成吸血鬼，成了後來所有虛構吸血鬼的原型。

Vampires in film and television
電影和影集中的吸血鬼

Ever since Bela Lugosi played Count Dracula in 1931's *Dracula*, Hollywood—and the American public—has been [7]**obsessed** with vampires. Over the years, Dracula has appeared in more films than any character [8]**other than** Sherlock Holmes. Perhaps most famous in the role was English actor Christopher Lee, whose Dracula movies of the 1960s and '70s made the image of vampires with [9]**fangs** and long [10]**capes** part of the popular culture on both sides of the Atlantic.

010 Vocabulary

1) **fiction** [ˈfɪkʃən] (n.) 小說，虛構；形容詞 **fictional** [ˈfɪkʃənəl] 為「虛構的，小說的」

2) **inspire** [ɪnˈspaɪr] (v.) 賦予⋯靈感，激勵

3) **charming** [ˈtʃɑrmɪŋ] (a.) 迷人的，有魅力的

4) **aristocratic** [əˌrɪstəˈkrætɪk] (a.) 貴族的，儀態高貴的；名詞 **aristocrat** [əˈrɪstəˌkræt] 為「貴族」

5) **torture** [ˈtɔrtʃər] (v./n.) 刑求，折磨

6) **infect** [ɪnˈfɛkt] (v.) 傳染，感染

7) **obsessed** [əbˈsɛst] (a.) 著迷的，入迷的；動詞為 **obsess** [əbˈsɛs]

8) **other than** [ˈʌðər ðæn] (adv.) 除了

9) **fang** [fæŋ] (n.) 獠牙，毒牙

10) **cape** [kep] (n.) 斗篷，披肩

11) **slayer** [ˈsleər] (n.) 屠宰者

12) **saga** [ˈsɑɡə] (n.) 長篇故事，傳說，冒險故事

13) **dreamy** [ˈdrimi] (a.) 夢幻的，迷人的

貝拉盧戈西在 1931 年電影《德古拉》的扮相。

© Anton_Ivanov / Shutterstock.com

自從貝拉盧戈西在 1931 年的電影《德古拉》飾演德古拉伯爵後，好萊塢和美國大眾就此迷上吸血鬼。多年來德古拉出現在電影的次數只有福爾摩斯能相匹敵。飾演德古拉最有名的或許是英國演員克里斯多福李，他在 1960 年代和 1970 年代的德古拉電影中，打造出獠牙和長斗篷的吸血鬼形象，成了大西洋兩岸的流行文化。

But late in the 20th century, vampires became younger and more romantic. All it took was Tom Cruise and Brad Pitt playing vampires in 1994's *Interview with a Vampire* to prove the creatures could be sexy. And in the popular TV show *Buffy the Vampire* [11]*Slayer*, which ran from 1997 to 2003, the title character falls in love with a handsome vampire named Angel. But what really turned vampires into romantic figures in the popular imagination was the *Twilight* [12]*Saga*, the book and film series about teenager Bella Swan and her romance with [13]**dreamy** vampire Edward Cullen.

但在 20 世紀末，吸血鬼越變越年輕浪漫。這都要歸功於湯姆克魯斯和布萊德彼特在 1994 年的《夜訪吸血鬼》飾演的吸血鬼，證明了這種生物也能有魅力。1997 年到 2003 年放映的熱門電視影集《魔法奇兵》中，劇名角色巴菲愛上了英俊的吸血鬼安傑爾。但真正將普羅大眾想像中的吸血鬼變成浪漫角色的，是長篇小說和電影系列《暮光之城》，敘述青少女貝拉史旺與夢幻般的吸血鬼愛德華庫倫之間的浪漫愛情故事。

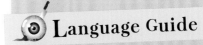

Language Guide

Gothic fiction 哥德派小說

始於 18 世紀的哥德派小說融合恐怖、神秘、靈異、魔幻、羅曼史，稱得上是現代恐怖電影的始祖，故事場景多發生在哥德式建築（如廢棄城堡、修道院、古老宅邸）是一大特色。英國小說家瑪麗雪萊（Mary Shelley）的《科學怪人》（*Frankenstein*）是這種文體的早期代表。19 世紀中期，這類小說出現越來越多腥羶色的內容，難登大雅之堂但廣受歡迎，對 19 世紀末維多利亞時代英國文學影響極為深遠。珍奧斯汀（Jane Austen）、愛倫坡（Edgar Allan Poe）、狄更斯（Charles Dickens）、王爾德（Oscar Wilde）的作品都能看到哥德派的痕跡。

近代吸血鬼名著

The Vampire Chronicles《吸血鬼紀事》

作者 Ann Rice 以《吸血鬼紀事》系列聞名，電影《夜訪吸血鬼》*Interview with a Vampire* 是由該系列第一本小說改編拍攝，為美國超自然（supernatural）文學的代表作家，全球暢銷上億冊，文壇地位無可取代。

Southern Vampire Mysteries《南方吸血鬼謎案》

作者 Charlaine Harris 出身美國南方，長期致力於奇幻推理小說的創作，其中以《南方吸血鬼謎案》系列最受歡迎，一共出了 13 本，曾創下全系列同時登上《紐約時報》暢銷榜的空前紀錄。HBO 廣受歡迎的系列影集《嗜血真愛》（*True Blood*）就是以此部小說改編。

BTW

Twilight《暮光之城》

作者 Stephenie Meyer 寫這部暢銷系列作品之前，完全沒有寫作經驗，儘管評價兩極，但因內容充滿少女情懷，廣受青少女喜愛，小說馬上被改拍為賣座的系列電影，被媒體譽為「J.K. 羅琳第二」。

[011] [1)]**Characteristics of vampires 吸血鬼的特徵**

Modern vampires are usually described as being tall and thin with good looks and pale skin, although some may look no different than normal humans. If you're not sure, hold up a mirror—vampires don't have [2)]**reflections**. They're also afraid of the sunlight, and don't have shadows. Vampires suck blood from their victims with hollow fangs, which only appear when they [3)]**feed**. If you're bitten by a vampire, you'll either die or turn into a vampire yourself. Some vampires also have supernatural powers, like the ability to turn into animals or ⑥ **read people's minds**.

現代吸血鬼的外型描述通常是高瘦、帥氣、皮膚蒼白，不過有些可能看起來跟正常人類無異。你要是不確定的話，可以拿鏡子照他，因為吸血鬼沒有鏡中倒影。吸血鬼也怕陽光，也沒有影子。吸血鬼會用中空的利牙吸取人血，而利牙只有在吸血時才出現。要是被吸血鬼咬到，不是死就是變成吸血鬼。有些吸血鬼也有超能力，比如會變成動物或有讀心術。

How to get rid of vampires 如何驅離吸血鬼

Most vampires are afraid of crosses, garlic and sunlight, so carrying a cross or garlic with you when you go out at night is a good way to keep them away. But these methods may not work on more powerful vampires. Although vampires live forever, they can be killed. The easiest way is to catch them asleep in their [4)]**coffin** during the day and drive a wooden stake through their heart. They can also be killed by cutting off their head or burning them to ashes.

大部分吸血鬼怕十字架、大蒜和陽光，所以夜間外出時可攜帶十字架或大蒜，是驅離吸血鬼的好方法。但這些方法對法力較強大的吸血鬼來說可能沒用。雖然吸血鬼是長生不死，但還是有殺死他們的方法。最簡單的方法是在白天趁他們在棺材裡睡覺時，用木樁刺穿他們的心臟。砍斷他們的頭或把他們燒成灰也能殺死他們。

[012] **Vocabulary**

1) **characteristic** [ˌkærəktəˈrɪstɪk] (n.) 特徵，特性

2) **reflection** [rɪˈflɛkʃən] (n.) 影子，映照出的影像

3) **feed** [fid] (v.) 進食，片語 **feed on** 即「以⋯為食」

4) **coffin** [ˈkɔfɪn] (n.) 棺材

5) **bedbug** [ˈbɛd.bʌg] (n.) 臭蟲，一種以動物（尤其是人類）血液為食的寄生昆蟲，常寄生於床板，會分泌惡臭液體

6) **leech** [litʃ] (n.) 血蛭

7) **murderer** [ˈmɝdərɚ] (n.) 謀殺犯

Are vampires real? 真的有吸血鬼嗎？

Although most people agree that the vampires of legend aren't real, they *do* exist in nature. A variety of creatures, from fleas and mosquitoes to [5]**bedbugs** and [6]**leeches**, survive by sucking blood from animals and humans. And then there's the vampire bat, which [3]**feeds on** large animals—and sometimes humans—by making small cuts in the skin with their sharp teeth and licking up the blood.

雖然大部分人認同吸血鬼的傳說不是真的，但自然界確實存在吸血生物。從跳蚤、蚊子到臭蟲和血蛭等各種吸血生物，都是靠著吸取動物和人類的鮮血維生。還有吸血蝙蝠，牠們以大型動物為食，有時包括人類，牠們會用利牙在皮膚上咬破一小洞後舔舐血液。

But there are also people who call themselves vampires. While they may not have supernatural powers, they do drink human blood—but only from willing victims. Some of them even dress up like vampires and get together for blood-drinking parties. And there have also been a number of [7]**murderers** who acted like—and even believed they were—vampires. A German man named Fritz Haarmann killed at least two dozen people, mostly by biting their necks, in the early 20th century. And an American man named Richard Chase, also known as the Vampire of Sacramento, murdered and drank the blood of six people in the 1970s. Maybe we should be afraid of vampires after all!

但也有人自稱是吸血鬼，他們或許沒有超能力，但確實會喝人血，不過是喝自願獻血者的血。有些人甚至打扮成吸血鬼的樣子，聚在一起辦飲血派對。也有一些殺人犯以吸血鬼的手法行凶，甚至自認為就是吸血鬼。20 世紀初，有個名叫弗里茲哈爾曼的德國人至少殺害 20 多人，大部分手法就是咬受害人的脖子。還有位名叫理查蔡斯的美國人，也被稱為沙加緬度吸血鬼，在 1970 年代殺害六人，並喝受害人的血。也許我們還是應該對吸血鬼心懷恐懼！

Language Guide

read one's mind 讀心

用來表示像一個人肚裡的蛔蟲，能看透他的想法。

A: Why has Sharon been acting so moody lately?
莎朗最近怎麼陰陽怪氣的啊？

B: I don't know. I can't <u>read her mind</u>.
不知道。我又不是她肚裡的蛔蟲。

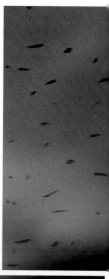

死神

The Grim Reaper

🎧014 Vocabulary

1) **grim** [grɪm] (a.) 無情的，殘忍的，陰森的

2) **reaper** [`ripə] (n.) 收割者，收割機

3) **saying** [`seɪŋ] (n.) 格言，諺語

4) **inevitable** [ɪn`ɛvɪtəbəl] (a.) 不可避免的，必然（發生）的

5) **representation** [ˌrɛprɪˌzɛn`teʃən] (n.) 代表，描繪；動詞 **represent** [ˌrɛprɪ`zɛnt] 「描繪，表示」

6) **mythology** [mɪ`θɑlədʒi] (n.) 神話，神話學

7) **ravage** [`rævɪdʒ] (v.) 蹂躪，摧毀

8) **ghastly** [`gæstli] (a.) 可怕的，死人般的

9) **skeleton** [`skɛlɪtən] (n.) 骨骸

10) **cloak** [klok] (n.) 斗篷，披風；形容詞為 **cloaked** [klokt] 包封的，掩飾的

🎧013 Gods of death 死神

As the [3]**saying** goes, nothing is certain but death and taxes. Since it's an [4]**inevitable** part of life, man has been making [5]**representations** of death since the beginning of history. In Greek [6]**mythology**, death was a god named Thanatos, son of Nyx, the goddess of night. Usually [5]**represented** as a young man with wings, he led the souls of the dead to the shore of the river Styx, which separated the world of the living from the world of the dead. And in LG **Norse mythology**, beautiful goddesses called Valkyrie chose which soldiers would die in battle and led them to LG **Valhalla**.

常言道，沒有什麼事是既定的，除了死亡和繳稅。由於死亡是人生中無可避免的事，因此人類從開天闢地以來就不斷創造死亡的代表形象。在希臘神話中，死神塔納托斯是黑夜女神妮克斯的兒子。塔納托斯的代表形象通常是帶著翅膀的年輕男子，祂帶領死者的靈魂到冥河岸邊，冥河是生死兩界的分界線。在北歐神話中，美麗的女武神瓦爾基麗會在戰役中選擇哪些戰士會死，然後帶他們到英靈神殿。

VALKYRIE

希臘神話中引領死者亡靈到冥河岸的塔納托斯（Thanatos）

Death gets scary 越來越恐怖的死神

The image of death began to change in the 14th century, when Europe was [7]**ravaged** by the Ⓛ **Black Death**. This plague, which was carried into Europe by the fleas on black rats, ended up killing 30-60% of the population. In Europe's cities, piles of corpses lay on every street corner, and the fear of death was everywhere. Artists began painting death as a [8]**ghastly** figure, at first as a dancing [9]**skeleton**, and later in a dark [10]**cloak** leading his victims to their fate. Although this figure wasn't called the Grim Reaper until the 19th century, "the Grim" was a nickname for death at the time of the Black Death.

死神的形象在 14 世紀開始改變，歐洲此時正遭到黑死病肆虐。這場瘟疫是由黑老鼠身上的跳蚤傳進歐洲，最終造成三成到六成人口死亡。當時在歐洲各城市中，每個街角都堆著屍體，到處散發著死亡的恐怖氣氛。藝術家開始將死神描繪成陰森恐怖的形象，一開始是跳舞的骨骸，後來穿上黑色斗篷，引領受害人走向生命終點。雖然這種形象要等到 19 世紀才被稱為猙獰收割者，但「猙獰」其實是黑死病蔓延時的死神綽號。

中古歐洲黑死病疫區到處可見臉戴防疫面具、身穿斗篷的醫生。

🎧(016) Vocabulary

1) **distinguishing** [dɪ`stɪŋgwɪʃɪŋ] (a.) 明顯的；動詞為 **distinguish** [dɪ`stɪŋgwɪʃ]「區別，識別」

2) **hood** [hʊd] (n./v.) 兜帽

3) **scythe** [saɪð] (n.) 長柄大鐮刀

4) **blade** [bled] (n.) 刀刃

5) **attach (to)** [ə`tætʃ] (v.) 使附著，連接

6) **encounter** [ɪn`kaʊntɚ] (n./v.) 偶遇，遭遇（困境）

7) **skull** [skʌl] (n.) 頭骨，頭顱

8) **destination** [ˌdɛstə`neʃən] (n.) 目的地，去處

9) **circumstances** [`sɝkəmˌstænsɪz] (n.) 情況，情勢

🎧(015) Characteristics of the Grim Reaper
猙獰收割者的特徵

The Grim Reaper's most [1])**distinguishing** feature is a long black cloak with [2])**hood** that covers most of his face. In his hand, he carries a [3])**scythe**—a long wooden pole with a curved [4])**blade** [5])**attached** to the top. The scythe is traditionally used to harvest crops at the end of the summer, but the Grim Reaper uses his to harvest people's souls at the end of their lives. Few people have had a close [6])**encounter** with the cloaked figure and 🄛 **lived to tell the tale**. But among those who have, some describe his face as a [7])**skull** with glowing red eyes, and others say they saw only darkness inside the hood.

死神最明顯的特徵是穿著長長的黑色連帽斗篷，兜帽幾乎罩住整個臉。他的手上拿著大鐮刀，長長的木柄頂端嵌著彎刀。鐮刀一向是在夏季末用來收割農作物，但死神在人將死之際，用鐮刀收割其靈魂。很少有人跟死神近距離接觸的體驗，並得以活下來講述這個故事。而其中有些人形容死神的臉是有著發光紅眼睛的骷髏頭，有些人則說他們看到的兜帽裡只有黑暗一片。

Can death be cheated? 可以騙過死神嗎？

You may think the Grim Reaper is evil, but he's actually just doing his job. You could even say it's important work. He ends the suffering of the old and sick, and helps keep the population under control. But what if you're not ready when death comes for you? Is it possible to cheat the Grim Reaper? In 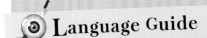 **Ingmar Bergman**'s classic film *The Seventh Seal*, a knight buys time by challenging him to a chess game, but loses the game—and his life—in the end. And in *Final* [8]***Destination***, when the characters cheat death by staying off a flight that crashes, they all end up dying under mysterious [9]**circumstances**. The Grim Reaper, it seems, always gets his soul.

　　你可能覺得死神是邪惡的，但祂其實只是善盡職責，甚至可以說那是重要的工作。他讓受苦的老人和病人結束生命，幫忙控制人口。但你若是還沒準備好迎接死亡呢？有可能騙過死神嗎？在英格瑪柏格曼的經典電影《第七封印》中，一名騎士跟死神比賽下棋以換取時間，但最後輸了比賽，也輸掉性命。《絕命終結站》中有幾個角色避開即將墜毀的班機以騙過死神，但他們最後都死於神秘事件。看來死神總是能收割到他要的靈魂。

電影《第七封印》海報

圖片來源：網路圖片
電影《第七封印》中，騎士與死神對弈的畫面。

狼人

Werewolves

萊卡翁王（King Lycaon）被宙斯變成狼。
（版畫家：Hendrick Goltzius（1558~1617））

🎧 018 Vocabulary

1) **transform** [trænsˋfɔrm] (v.) 改變，改觀

2) **feast** [fist] (n.)（宗教上的）祭日、節日，盛宴

3) **widespread** [ˋwaɪdˋsprɛd] (a.) 普遍的，廣泛的

4) **accuse** [əˋkjuz] (v.) 指控，指責

5) **confess** [kənˋfɛs] (v.) 承認，供認，招供

6) **ointment** [ˋɔɪntmənt] (n.) 藥膏

7) **guilty** [ˋgɪltɪ] (a.) 有罪的

8) **shapeshift** [ˋʃepˋʃɪft] (v.) 變身

9) **on purpose** [ɑn ˋpɝpəs] (phr.) 故意，別有目的

10) **hereditary** [həˋrɛdəˏtɛrɪ] (a.) 一代傳一代的，遺傳的

11) **hideous** [ˋhɪdɪəs] (a.) 可怕的，醜陋的

12) **upright** [ˋʌpˏraɪt] (a.) 直立的，豎的

13) **poisonous** [ˋpɔɪzənəs] (a.) 有毒的

🎧 017 Ancient werewolves 古代的狼人

The idea of werewolves, men who [1)]**transform** into wolves, can be traced back to ancient times. In the 5th century B.C., Greek historian 🄛 **Herodotus** wrote about a tribe in what is now the Ukraine who turned into wolves for a few days each year. And several centuries later, the Roman poet 🄛 **Ovid** told the story of King Lycaon, who fed human meat to Zeus at a [2)]**feast** to see if he was really a god. As punishment, Zeus turned Lycaon and his sons into wolves.

人類變身成狼人的概念可追溯至古代。西元前五世紀，希臘歷史學家希羅多德寫過現今烏克蘭有個族群每年有幾天會變成狼人的故事。幾個世紀後，羅馬詩人奧維德講述過萊卡翁王的故事，他在一場盛宴中將人肉獻給宙斯，看他是否真的是神。於是宙斯懲罰萊卡翁王，將他和他的兒子們都變成狼。

Werewolves of Europe 歐洲的狼人

Belief in werewolves later became [3)]**widespread** in areas where wolves were common. In 16th century France, a man named Giles Garnier, known as the Werewolf of Dole, was [4)]**accused** of killing and eating at least four children. After [5)]**confessing** to turning himself into a wolf with a magical [6)]**ointment**, he was found [7)]**guilty** and burned at the stake. And then there's German farmer Peter Stumpp, the Werewolf of Bedburg. Caught by a group of hunters, who said they saw him [8)]**shapeshift** from wolf to human form, he confessed to killing and eating dozens of people.

狼人的信仰後來在常見到狼群的地方廣為流傳。16 世紀在法國時，有個人名叫基爾斯卡尼爾，也被稱為多勒狼人，他被指控殺害並吃掉至少四名兒童。他供認自己使用能變身狼人的魔法藥膏後，被判定殺人罪，並被綁在木樁上燒死。還有德國農夫彼得史唐普，又稱為貝德堡狼人。他被一群獵人抓到，獵人說他們看到他從狼變成人，史唐普也供認殺害並吃掉幾十人。

Characteristics of werewolves 狼人的特徵

There are generally two types of werewolves: some change shape [9]**on purpose** by magical means; others, for whom the condition is either [10]**hereditary** or caused by a bite from another werewolf, are transformed on nights when the moon is full. Both types of werewolves kill and eat humans and animals and then return to human form at dawn. They usually have no knowledge of what they did the night before, but if they're injured in wolf form, the injury will remain when they become human again. Some who have seen werewolves describe them as large, [11]**hideous** wolves, others as half wolf, half man—covered with fur, but walking [12]**upright** like a human.

狼人通常有兩種類型：有些狼人可以刻意施魔法變身；有些狼人則是因為遺傳或被其他狼人咬過，在月圓之夜時會變身成狼人。這兩種類狼人都會殺害並吃掉人類和動物，然後在黎明時恢復人形，而且通常不知道自己在前一晚做了什麼，但他們如果在變身成狼人時受傷，那麼在恢復成人形後會留下傷口。有些見過狼人的人形容他們是巨大、可怕的狼，有些人則形容是身上覆蓋著毛皮的半狼半人，但能像人一樣直立行走。

How to get rid of werewolves 如何驅離狼人

Just as vampires dislike garlic, werewolves dislike wolfsbane—a [13]**poisonous** plant related to the buttercup—so carrying some with you can help keep the werewolves away if you plan on taking a late night walk in the woods. But if you want to kill a werewolf, the best way is with a silver bullet. One shot is enough to send them to their grave. If you don't have any silver bullets, chopping off their head or removing their heart will also 🅛 **do the trick**. You can also kill them by normal means when they're in human form, but that would be murder.

就跟吸血鬼怕大蒜一樣，狼人則怕附子草，那是一種毛茛科的有毒植物。所以你若是想在深夜到森林散步，可以隨身攜帶附子草好驅離狼人。但你若想殺狼人，最好的方法還是用銀製子彈射殺，一槍便足以讓他們斃命。你若沒有銀子彈，砍斷狼人的頭或挖掉他們的心臟也行得通。你也可以趁他們變回人形時以一般殺人方式下手，但這就構成凶殺罪了。

buttercup 毛茛

wolfsbane 附子草

木乃伊

Mummies

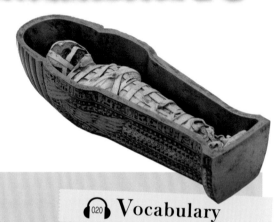

🎧 Vocabulary

1) **preserve** [prɪˋzɝv] (v.) 保存，保藏。名詞為 **preservation** [prɪzɝˋveʃən]
2) **substance** [ˋsʌbstəns] (n.) 物質
3) **deceased** [dɪˋsist] (a.) 亡故的
4) **involve** [ɪnˋvɑlv] (v.) 包含
5) **embalm** [ɪmˋbɑm] (v.) 用藥物進行防腐處理
6) **sarcophagus** [sarˋkɑfəgəs] (n.) （古埃及）石棺
7) **tomb** [tum] (n.) 陵墓，墳墓
8) **possession** [pəˋzɛʃən] (n.) 所有物，財產
9) **pharaoh** [ˋfɛro] (n.) （古埃及國王）法老
10) **pyramid** [ˋpɪrəmɪd] (n.) 金字塔
11) **curse** [kɝs] (n./v.) 詛咒
12) **invade** [ɪnˋved] (v.) 入侵
13) **excavate** [ˋɛkskə͵vet] (v.) 挖掘（墓穴），發掘（古物）
14) **archeologist** [͵ɑrkɪˋɑlədʒɪst] (n.) 考古學家
15) **revenge** [rɪˋvɛndʒ] (n./v.) 報仇
16) **potentially** [pəˋtɛnʃəli] (adv.) 可能地
17) **reverse** [rɪˋvɝs] (v.) 反轉

🎧 (019) What are mummies? 木乃伊是什麼？

Since ancient times, there have been records of dead bodies being [1]**preserved**, sometimes by nature (very dry, or very cold climates), and sometimes by the use of special chemicals. Both natural and manmade mummies—as these preserved bodies are called—have been found on every continent, but the mummies of ancient Egypt are the most famous. Indeed, the word mummy comes from the Arabic *mumiyah*, which means "bitumen"—one of the [2]**substances** used to create mummies.

自古以來就有屍體保存的紀錄，有時是大自然保存下來（在非常乾燥或寒冷的氣候下），有時是利用特殊化學物保存。每個大洲都發現過自然形成和人造的木乃伊——木乃伊意指保存的屍體——但古埃及的木乃伊是最有名的。事實上，木乃伊一詞源自阿拉伯語的 mumiyah，意思是「瀝青」，是用來製作木乃伊的其中一種物質。

The Egyptians began creating mummies over 4,000 years ago, believing that [1]**preservation** of the body after death was necessary for the [3]**deceased** to live well in the afterlife. This process [4]**involved** removing all the organs—except for the heart, which was the center of thoughts and emotions—[5]**embalming** the body with oils and other substances, wrapping it in linen bandages and laying it in natural salts to dry. Finally, the mummy was sealed in a special coffin called a [6]**sarcophagus** and buried in a [7]**tomb** along with the [8]**possessions** they would need in the afterlife. The wealthier the person, the fancier the tomb. The Egyptian rulers, called [9]**pharaohs**, had the fanciest tombs of all: the [10]**pyramids**!

埃及人四千多年前就開始製作木乃伊，他們相信死後保存屍體可以讓死者在來世過得好。製作過程包括移除所有內臟——除了心臟，因為那是思想和情緒的中心——用油等其他物質塗抹大體，再用亞麻繃帶包

裏，然後放於天然鹽中吸乾水分。最後會把木乃伊密封在特殊的石棺中，連同死者在來世所需的隨身物品一起埋入墳墓。死者生前越富有，墳墓就越奢華。埃及的統治者，法老王的陵墓是最奢華的，也就是金字塔！

The [11]curse of the pharaohs 法老王的詛咒

So how did mummies go from being embalmed Egyptians to being undead monsters? After  **Napoleon** [12]**invaded** Egypt in the early 19th century, European scientists began [13]**excavating** the tombs of the pharaohs, and some had curses at the entrance to keep people away. Most famous was the curse of **King Tut**. After British [14]**archeologist** Howard Carter discovered the tomb of the young pharaoh Tutankhamun and removed its treasures, the members of his team started dying mysterious deaths one by one. This inspired authors of horror fiction, who began writing stories about mummies **coming to life** and seeking [15]**revenge** against the people who robbed their tombs.

那麼木乃伊是怎麼從不腐敗的埃及人變成不死怪物？拿破崙在 19 世紀初侵略埃及後，歐洲科學家開始挖掘法老王的陵墓，有些陵墓會在入口下詛咒以防止外人入侵。最有名的是圖坦卡門王的詛咒。自從英國考古學家霍華德卡特發現年輕法老王圖坦卡門的陵墓，並拿走裡面的寶藏後，他的掘墓團隊中開始有人一個接一個神祕地死去。這件事成了作家寫恐怖小說的靈感來源，包括木乃伊死起回生並向盜墓者尋仇的故事。

Characteristics of mummies 木乃伊的特徵

Brought back to life by curses cast by ancient Egyptian priests, mummies are said to have supernatural powers. Because mummies are undead, they're almost impossible to kill. Most weapons have no effect on them, and they can [16]**potentially** live forever. A touch from a mummy is enough to kill its victim, who will fall ill and quickly turn to dust. Mummies also possess great strength, and some can transform into clouds of sand or insects. Because mummies are dry and covered by bandages, they can be destroyed by fire. But the best way to **get a mummy off your trail** may be to [17]**reverse** the curse by returning the treasure you stole to his tomb.

據說經由古埃及祭司施咒而復活的木乃伊擁有超自然力量。由於木乃伊是不死之身，所以幾乎無法殺死。大部分武器對他們無效，而且他們可能可以永生。被木乃伊碰到一下就足以致死，會病倒並迅速變成骨灰。木乃伊也擁有強大的體力，有些能變成一團沙塵或昆蟲。由於木乃伊是乾屍，被繃帶包裹著，因此可以被火燒毀。但不讓木乃伊找上你的最好方式，或許就是歸還從陵墓中盜出的寶物，才能免於詛咒。

喪屍
Zombies

021 Haitian zombies 海地喪屍

When slaves were brought from Africa to work on the sugar 1)**plantations** of Haiti, they brought their religious beliefs with them, and these beliefs became 2)**voodoo**, a religion of spirit worship and magic. Some voodoo priests use their magic for good, and others for evil. Haitian folklore tells of evil priests using their magic to create zombies—from the African word *nzambi*, meaning "spirit of the dead"—which are corpses brought back to life to do the priests' 3)**bidding**. These zombies have no will of their own, and are used by their creator to do evil deeds or serve as their personal slaves.

奴隸從非洲被帶到海地的甘蔗田工作時，也帶來了宗教信仰，這種信仰變成巫毒教，也就是崇拜神靈和魔法的宗教。有些巫毒教祭司利用魔法做好事，但有些是做壞事。在海地的民間傳說中，有邪惡的祭司會用魔法製造出喪屍，zombie 一詞源自非洲語 nzambi，意思是「死者的靈魂」，起死回生的屍體會聽從祭司的命令。喪屍沒有自己的意志，並被創造者利用來做壞事，或被當成私人奴隸。

The zombie 4)apocalypse 喪屍末日

Why are the zombies we see in movies like *World War Z* and TV shows like *The Walking Dead*—5)**swarms** of rotting corpses hungry for human flesh—so different from their Haitian cousins? We have director 🅛🅖 **George Romero** to thank for that. In his 1968 film *Night of the Living Dead*, a group of people in a Pennsylvania farmhouse are attacked by hungry corpses, and turn into zombies one by one as they

022 Vocabulary

1) **plantation** [plæn`teʃən] (n.) 農園，大農場

2) **voodoo** [`vudu] (n.) 巫毒教，魔法

3) **bidding** [`bɪdɪŋ] (n.) 命令，召喚

4) **apocalypse** [ə`pakə͵lɪps] (n.) 世界末日，大災難

5) **swarm** [swɔrm] (n./v.)（如蟲蟻般）大批，成群；蜂擁，群集

6) **sequel** [`sikwəl] (n.) 續集

7) **descend (into)** [dɪ`sɛnd] (phr.) 淪為

8) **spell** [spɛl] (n.) 符咒，咒語

9) **potion** [`poʃən] (n.) 液狀的魔藥，藥水

10) **radiation** [͵redi`eʃən] (n.) 輻射，放射

11) **virus** [`vaɪrəs] (n.) 病毒

12) **stumble** [`stʌmbəl] (v.) 蹣跚而行

13) **groan** [gron] (v./n.) 呻吟

14) **treat** [trit] (n.) 令人愉悅的事物

15) **outrun** [aʊt`rʌn] (v.) 跑贏，逃脫

16) **rip** [rɪp] (v.) 撕裂，扯破

17) **chunk** [tʃʌŋk] (n.) 大塊，厚片

get bitten. They weren't called zombies in the film, but they were in the [6]sequel *Dawn of the Dead*, in which the whole country [7]descends into a zombie apocalypse. These two films, and the following four sequels, were so popular that flesh-eating zombies have become part of the popular culture.

《活死人之夜》1968 年版海報

為什麼《末日之戰》等電影和《陰屍路》等影集裡的喪屍，都是腐爛的屍體成群結隊，嗜食人肉，跟海地的喪屍很不一樣？這都要拜導演喬治羅梅洛所賜。在他 1968 年執導的電影《活死人之夜》中，賓州一群人在農舍遭飢餓的屍體攻擊，被咬到的人一個個變成喪屍。在這部電影中他們不叫喪屍（zombie），但在續集《活人生吃》已經如此稱呼，片中整個國家淪為喪屍末日。這兩部電影和接下來的四部續集因為太受歡迎，所以吃人肉的喪屍也成了流行文化。

Characteristics of zombies 喪屍的特徵

Zombies may be created in a variety of ways. Haitian zombies are brought to life by magic [8]spells or [9]potions, and modern flesh-eating zombies are usually created by something like [10]radiation or a [11]virus. Whatever you do, don't get bitten by this type of zombie. If you do, you'll die and turn into a zombie yourself within a few hours. Your original personality will be gone, your flesh will start to rot, and all you'll be able to do is [12]stumble along [13]groaning and looking for people to eat. Human brains will become your favorite [14]treat.

喪屍可以各種不同方式打造出來。海地的喪屍是由魔咒或魔藥打造而成，現代的吃人喪屍則通常是經由輻射或病毒之類的東西造成。不管怎樣，你都不要被這種喪屍咬到，否則會死掉，然後在幾小時內變成喪屍。你會失去原本的人性，肉體會開始腐爛，你能做的就只有一邊呻吟、一邊蹣跚而行，尋找人類當食物。人腦會成為你最愛的美食。

Getting rid of zombies 驅離喪屍

Although zombies are strong and violent, they don't move very fast, so it's easy to [15]outrun them. In swarms, however, they're very dangerous. Before you know it, they'll surround you and start [16]ripping out [17]chunks of your flesh. Since zombies are already dead, you can't really kill them. But because their movements are controlled by the brain, you can stop them by destroying their brains or chopping off their heads. So if there are zombies around, be sure to carry a gun, a sword or a baseball bat at all times.

雖然喪屍強大而暴力，但他們的動作很慢，所以很容易逃離。但出現一大群喪屍時就很危險了，轉眼之間，他們會包圍你，開始把你身上的肉一塊一塊挖下來。由於喪屍本來就是死的，你無法真正殺死他們。但由於他們的行動是由大腦控制，你可以藉由毀掉他們的大腦或砍掉他們的頭來阻止他們。所以如果有喪屍在附近，務必隨身攜帶槍械、刀劍或球棒。

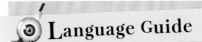

女巫
Witches

 023 What are witches? 女巫是什麼？

When asked what a witch is, most people will describe an ugly old woman in a black dress and a tall, pointed black hat. She may be holding a broom and have a black cat by her side, and her long nose is probably covered with [1]**warts**. She also has magical powers, which she uses to [2]**cast** evil spells. But not all witches are evil. In Ⓛ *The Wizard of Oz*, the Wicked Witch of the West is a scary, green-skinned [3]**villain**, while the Good Witch of the North is a kind, beautiful [4]**sorceress** who uses her powers to help Dorothy return home. And not all witches are women either—there are also male witches called [5]**warlocks**.

被問到女巫是什麼時，大部分人的形容會是醜陋的老婦穿著黑色衣服，戴著又高又尖的黑帽，可能還會拿著一把掃帚，身旁有一隻黑貓，長長的鼻子可能還長滿了疣。她也擁有魔力，會施邪惡的魔咒。但不是所有女巫都是邪惡的，在《綠野仙蹤》中，西方的惡女巫是有著綠色皮膚的可怕反派，而北方的善女巫則善良、美麗，會用魔法幫助桃樂絲回家。而且不是所有會巫術的人都是女的，也有男的，稱為男巫。

桃樂絲和西方惡女巫。
圖片來源：維基百科

桃樂絲和北方善女巫。
圖片來源：維基百科

Ancient witches 古代的女巫

The [6]**concept** of [7]**witchcraft** has existed since ancient times. In the Middle East, ancient [8]**civilizations** worshipped powerful goddesses, and the [9]**priestesses** who served them used the powers [10]**granted** by them to heal the sick and [11]**ensure** good harvests. These priestesses, known as "wise women," were valued members of their [12]**communities**. But this changed with the arrival of Christianity. Pagan gods and goddesses were now seen as demons, and the priestesses who served them became evil witches. In the Bible, all forms of magic are considered evil, and Exodus includes the [13]**verse**, "You shall not permit a witch to live."

巫術的概念自古就已存在。在古代的中東，民眾會崇拜有法力的女神，侍奉女神的女祭司利用上天賦予的力量治療病人，確保農作物豐收。這些女祭司又稱為「智女」，是社會中的重要成員。但這情況在基督教傳入後改變了。異教的男神和女神被視為惡魔，侍奉天神的女祭司也變成邪惡女巫。在聖經中，所有形式的魔法都被視為邪惡，而《出埃及記》中更有這段經文：「不可讓女巫存活。」

🔘 Language Guide

The Wizard of Oz《綠野仙蹤》

1939 年歌舞片《綠野仙蹤》是影史上最偉大的電影之一，改編自 L. Frank Baum（1856～1919）所著的兒童故事《綠野仙蹤》（*The Wonderful Wizard of Oz*）。故事講述小孤女桃樂絲（Dorothy）與稻草人（Scarecrow）、錫人（Tin Man）、膽小獅子（Cowardly Lion）同行，請求奧茲國巫師（Wizard of Oz）幫忙的故事。飾演桃樂絲的 Judy Garland 因本片一砲而紅，主題曲 Over the Rainbow 更成為家喻戶曉的名曲。

🎧 026 Vocabulary

1) **pact** [pækt] (n.) 協定，契約
2) **familiar** [fə`mɪljə] (n.)（傳說故事中）供女巫使喚的妖精
3) **failure** [`feljə] (n.)（農作物）歉收
4) **healer** [`hilə] (n.) 傳統治療者，巫醫
5) **suspected** [sə`spɛktɪd] (a.) 有嫌疑的
6) **try** [traɪ] (v.) 審判
7) **settler** [`sɛtlə] (n.) 移民，殖民者，拓荒者
8) **minister** [`mɪnɪstə] (n.) 牧師，神職人員
9) **ultimately** [`ʌltəmɪtlɪ] (adv.) 最終，最後

🎧 025 The witch hunts 獵巫

While belief in witches was common during the Middle Ages, it wasn't until the 14th century that the witch hunts began. The fear of Satan was strong at that time, and people believed that witches gained their magical powers by making [1] **pacts** with the Devil. It was also believed that witches flew through the air at night to secret meetings called "sabbats," where they had sex with demons, and even with Satan himself; that they had "[2] **familiar** spirits" in the form of animals; and that they murdered children to eat them and make magical ointments from their fat.

女巫的信仰在中世紀是常見的，但到了 14 世紀才開始出現獵巫。當時人們對撒旦的恐懼很強烈，大家都相信女巫之所以會魔法，是因為跟撒旦達成協議。也相信女巫夜晚會在空中飛行，去參加一種稱為「巫魔夜會」的祕密聚會，在聚會中和惡魔甚至撒旦交媾；相信她們會養以動物形式出現的「使魔」；相信她們會殺害並吃掉小孩，並用小孩的脂肪製作魔法藥膏。

Whenever bad things happened that people couldn't explain—like mysterious illnesses or crop ³⁾**failures**—people blamed them on witches. But how did you find the witches? The obvious targets were folk ⁴⁾**healers**, who were thought to have magical powers, or older women without families who lived by themselves. People also began to realize that if they wanted revenge against their enemies, they could accuse them of being witches. Between the years 1500 and 1660, up to 80,000 ⁵⁾**suspected** witches were ⁶⁾**tried** and 🔟 **put to death** in Europe. Most of them were women.

只要發生無法解釋的壞事,比如神祕的疾病或收成不佳,就會歸咎於女巫。但要怎麼找出女巫?明顯的目標就是民間治療師,他們被認為擁有魔力,或沒有家人的獨居老婦。大家也開始發現,若是想對敵人進行報復,只要指控他們會巫術就好。在 1500 年到 1660 年期間,歐洲有多達八萬疑似會巫術的人接受審判並被處死,大部分是女性。

The Salem witch trials 塞勒姆審巫案

Just as the witch hunts were ending in Europe in the late 1600s, English ⁷⁾**settlers** brought their fear of witches with them to America. Although a number of witch trials were held in New England, the ones that took place in Salem, Massachusetts in 1692 are the most famous. The Salem witch trials began when two ill girls—one the daughter of a local ⁸⁾**minister**—claimed to be witches and accused many of their neighbors of witchcraft. ⁹⁾**Ultimately**, around 150 people were accused and 18 were put to death.

塞勒姆審巫案當中,兩名女性正在法庭受審。
插畫家／Howard Pyle

歐洲的獵巫現象在 1600 年代末消退之際,英國移民帶著對女巫的恐懼來到美國。雖然新英格蘭舉行過不少女巫審判,但 1692 年在麻州塞勒姆的審巫案是最有名的。有兩名病重的女孩——其中一位是當地牧師的女兒——自稱是女巫,並指控許多鄰居會巫術,於是塞勒姆審巫案就此展開。最後約有 150 人被指控會巫術,有 18 人被處死。

🎙️ **Language Guide**

put sb. to death 處死
這邊的 put 是「處以…(狀態)」,put to death 就是「處死」。

A: Did the murderer get a life sentence?
兇手有被判處無期徒刑嗎?

B: No. He was <u>put to death</u>.
沒有。他被判處死刑。

🎧028 Vocabulary

1) **broomstick** [ˋbrum͵stɪk] (n.) 掃帚（柄）
2) **identify** [aɪˋdɛntə͵faɪ] (v.) 認出，識別，確定
3) **birthmark** [ˋbɝθ͵mɑrk] (n.) 胎記
4) **mole** [mol] (n.) 痣
5) **scar** [skɑr] (n.) 疤，傷痕
6) **execute** [ˋɛksɪ͵kjut] (v.) 處死

威卡教徒的聚會。

🎧027 Modern witchcraft 現代巫術

By the 20th century, belief in witchcraft had mostly disappeared in Europe and America. But then a strange thing happened. In the 1920s, a British historian named Margaret Murray presented the idea that witchcraft was actually a pagan religion that had been destroyed by the Christian Church in the European witch trials. This probably wasn't true, but that didn't stop British author Gerald Gardner from turning witchcraft into a real religion in the 1950s. Called Wicca (the Old English word for witch), the pagan religion involves worshiping a nature goddess, celebrating Halloween and the changing seasons, and practicing magic. You may think that people would hesitate to call themselves witches considering how they were treated in the past, but Wicca is more popular than ever today.

　　到了 20 世紀，歐洲和美國的巫術信仰大部分已消失。但後來發生一件奇怪的事。1920 年代，英國歷史學家瑪格麗特莫瑞提出一個概念，認為巫術其實是一種非基督教的宗教信仰，在歐洲的女巫審判中遭到基督教會毀滅，這應該不是事實，但也無法阻止英國作家傑拉德加德納在 1950 年代將巫術變成真正的宗教。這種異教信仰稱為威卡教（古英語中女巫的意思），包括崇拜自然女神，慶祝萬聖節和季節更迭，以及施魔法。想到女巫在過去所受到的待遇，你或許會覺得不太有人願意自稱女巫，但威卡教現在比以往越來越受歡迎。

1555 年，德國兩名女性在獵巫時期被施以火刑（16 世紀版畫重新上色）。

Characteristics of witches 女巫的特徵

Witches are people with magical powers, which may be used for either good or evil. They have the ability to cast spells and curse people, and to create magical potions—like love potions or sleeping potions. They can also fly on [1]**broomsticks** and often have familiar spirits, like black cats, that assist them in performing magic. Although typical witches are ugly old ladies dressed all in black, they could just as easily be beautiful young women—or even men.

女巫是擁有魔力的人，魔法可以用來做好事或壞事。她們能施魔咒和對人下詛咒，也會製作魔法藥水，比如愛情藥水或催眠藥水。她們也可以騎掃帚飛行，通常會養使魔，比如黑貓，以協助她們施魔法。雖然典型的女巫形象是全身穿黑衣服的醜陋老婦，但她們也可以是漂亮的年輕女性，或甚至男人。

Getting rid of witches 驅離女巫

During the European witch trials, witches were [2]**identified** by the Devil's mark—usually a [3]**birthmark** or unusual [4]**mole** or [5]**scar** on the suspect's body. Another method they used was to toss the suspect in deep water. If they floated they were a witch, and if they sank they were innocent. Of course, it's not much use being innocent if you end up drowning. Those who were found guilty were [6]**executed** either by hanging or burning at the stake. Their magic powers, it seems, didn't protect them from death.

在歐洲的女巫審判中，疑似女巫的人因為有惡魔的印記而被指認出，通常是身體上有胎記、不尋常的痣或疤痕。另一個指認方式是將嫌疑人扔進深水中，若能浮起來，就是女巫，若是沉入水中就是無辜的。當然，最後證明無辜也沒什麼用，因為此時可能已淹死了。被判有罪的人會處以絞刑或綁在木樁上燒死。看來魔法也無法保護他們免於被處死。

Legendary Demons and Spirits

傳說中的妖魔和幽靈

🎧 029 The Headless Horseman 無頭騎士

Most people are familiar with the headless horseman from 🔵 **Washington Irving**'s 1820 story *The Legend of Sleepy Hollow*, which has been turned into countless films and TV shows. But the idea of the headless horseman has existed for centuries in European folklore. In Ireland, legend tells of a headless demon called a Dullahan, which rides a black horse and carries a whip made from a human [1]**spine**. And the German [2]**fairy tales** collected by the Brothers Grimm include several about headless hunters on horses. These stories spread to Holland, and were later brought to America by Dutch settlers. It was in the Dutch town of Sleepy Hollow in New York that Irving heard the stories that inspired *The Legend of Sleepy Hollow*. In his story, a 🔵 **Hessian**—a German soldier who fought for the British in the [3]**Revolutionary** War—was [4]**decapitated** in battle and buried in the local [5]**cemetery**. On dark nights, he rises from his grave and rides through Sleepy Hollow looking for his head. Unable to find it, he takes the head of any living person he encounters.

大部分人都熟知華盛頓歐文在 1820 年的《沉睡谷傳奇》中的無頭騎士故事，也已被改編成無數部電影和電視劇。但無頭騎士的典故早已在歐洲民間傳說中存在好幾個世紀。在愛爾蘭的傳說中，有個無頭惡魔叫杜拉漢，騎著黑馬，拿著用人類脊椎製成的鞭子。由格林兄弟收集的德國童話中，也收錄了幾個騎馬的無頭獵人故事。這些故事傳到荷蘭，後來經由荷蘭移民傳到美國。歐文在紐約州沉睡谷的荷蘭鎮聽到這故事，成了他寫下《沉睡谷傳奇》的靈感來源。在他的故事中，有位黑森傭兵——在美國獨立戰爭中為英國打仗的德國士兵——在戰役中被斬首，並被埋在當地墓地。在黑夜時，他會從墓地中爬出來，騎著馬在沉睡谷四處尋找他的頭。他在找不到頭的情況下，只要遇到生人就會砍下對方的頭。

🎧 030 Banshees 報喪女妖

In Irish legend, a banshee is a female spirit that announces a coming death with loud [6]**wails** or [7]**shrieks**. Each family of pure Irish blood is said to have its own banshee, and its cries can only be heard by family members. Banshees are rarely seen, but when they are they may appear as a beautiful young woman in a white robe or an ugly old [8]**hag** in a gray. They usually have long [9]**flowing** hair and eyes red from crying. The word banshee comes from the Irish *bean sí*, which means "woman of the fairy [10]**mound**." Some say that banshees are fairies that live in these mounds—which are ancient [11]**burial** mounds that can be found all over Ireland. Others say they are the ghosts of women who were murdered or died in [12]**childbirth**. The [13]**myth** most likely has its origins in the ancient tradition of [14]**keening**, where women would [15]**lament** the death of a loved one with loud weeping and wailing.

　　在愛爾蘭傳說中，報喪女妖是會用響亮的哀嚎聲或尖叫聲報死訊的女精靈。據說有純正愛爾蘭血統的家庭都有各自的報喪女妖，只有自己家族的成員能聽到她的叫聲。極少有人見到報喪女妖，但見到時可能是穿著白色長袍的美麗少女，或穿著灰色斗篷的醜陋老婦。她們通常有一頭飄逸的長髮和一雙哭紅的雙眼。banshee 源自愛爾蘭語 bean sí，意思是「仙丘的女子」。有人說報喪女妖是住在仙丘裡頭的精靈，仙丘是散佈在愛爾蘭各地的墳堆。另外有些人說，報喪女妖是被殺害或分娩時過世之婦女的鬼魂。這個神話的起源很可能出自古代的哭喪傳統，當時的女子會為過世的至親大聲哀悼慟哭。

🎧 Succubi 魅魔

　　A succubus is a female demon who [16]**seduces** men in their dreams, using sex to rob them of their [17]**vital** energy. Repeated sex with a succubus can cause mental and [18]**physical** illness, and even death. Sexual demons can be found in the myths of ancient cultures all over the world, but the succubus first appears in Christian texts from the Middle Ages. Christian scholars believed that succubi—who also appeared in a male form called incubi—were [19]**agents** of the devil who tempted people to [20]**commit** sexual sins. The word succubus comes from the Latin *succubare* (to lie beneath), and incubus from *incubare* (to lie upon). Both of these demons appear to their victims as sexually attractive humans, but their true form may include sharp claws, bat-like wings and even a tail. According to the Church, it's possible to get rid of succubi and incubi by confessing one's sins and making the sign of the cross. In more serious cases, an exorcism may be required.

　　魅魔（複數 succubi）是在男人夢中引誘他們的女惡魔，透過性交奪走他們的精力。與魅魔反覆性交會導致身心受損，甚至死亡。性惡魔可在世界各地古文化的神話中看到，而魅魔源自於中世紀的基督教經文。當時的基督教學者相信魅魔——以男人形式出現則稱為男魅魔——是撒旦派來的使者，引誘人類犯下性罪行。succubus 一詞源自拉丁文 succubare（躺在下面），incubus（夢魔）源自 incubare（躺在上面）。這兩種惡魔以性感的人類形象出現在受害者面前，但他們的真實面貌可能有鋒利的爪子、蝙蝠般的翅膀，甚至有尾巴。根據教會的說法，透過告解和畫十字架可驅離魅魔和夢魔。在較嚴重的情況下，可能需要驅魔儀式。

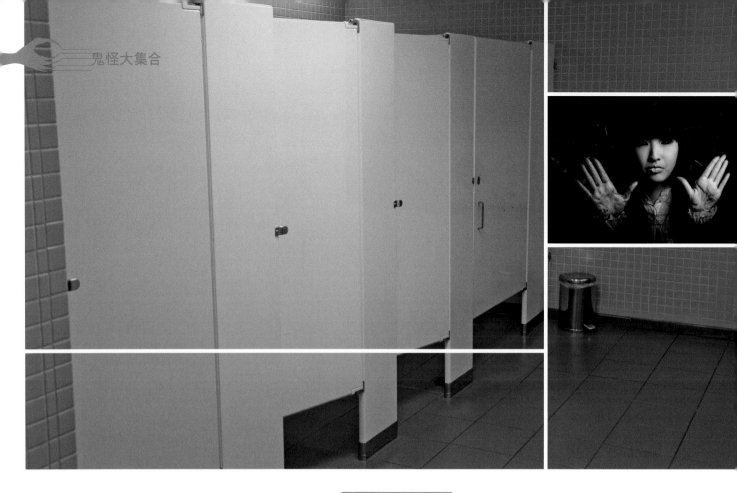

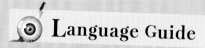 Vocabulary 〔035〕

1) **slumber** [ˋslʌmbɚ] (n./v.) 睡眠；**slumber party** 是美國兒童、青少年到朋友家過夜的派對
2) **in a row** [ɪn ə ro] (phr.) 連續
3) **frightful** [ˋfraɪtfəl] (a.) 可怕的，醜陋的
4) **apparition** [͵æpəˋrɪʃən] (n.) 亡靈，幻影
5) **Protestant** [ˋprɑtɪstənt] (n./a.) 新教徒；新教的
6) **air raid** [ɛr red] (phr.) 空襲
7) **stall** [stɔl] (n.) 小隔間
8) **bully** [ˋbʊlɪ] (v./n.) 霸凌；惡霸
9) **inhabit** [ɪnˋhæbɪt] (v.) 居住，棲息
10) **summon** [ˋsʌmən] (v.) 召喚
11) **harmless** [ˋhɑrmlɪs] (a.) 無害的
12) **version** [ˋvɝʒən] (n.) 版本

〔🔧〕 Language Guide

urban legend 都市傳奇

都市傳奇是一種現代民間傳說，由宣稱真實且看似可信的二手故事組成。都市傳奇通常會包括恐怖、道德訓示，甚至戲謔幽默等元素，而且據說是真人實事。讀者可參考本書 pp. 66~72 的「恐怖都會傳說」單元。

BTW日本著名女鬼

〔033〕 Hanako-san 廁所裡的花子

Japan is home to countless 🔵 **urban legends**, but the one about Hanako-san is one of the most popular. Also known as *toire no Hanako-san* (Hanako of the toilet), she is the spirit of a young girl who haunts restrooms at Japanese schools. Some believe that she's the ghost of a girl who was killed during an [6)]**air raid** in World War II, while others claim she committed suicide in a bathroom [7)]**stall** after being [8)]**bullied** by her classmates. Said to [9)]**inhabit** the third stall of the third-floor girls' restroom, Hanako-san is often used by schoolchildren as a test of courage. According to legend, she can be [10)]**summoned** by knocking on the stall door three times and asking, "Are you there, Hanako-san"? After a while, a small voice may reply, "Yes, I'm here." Those brave enough to enter the stall will see a pale little girl in a red skirt. While usually [11)]**harmless**, in some [12)]**versions** of the story she is known to pull students into the toilet, never to be seen again.

日本有無數的都市傳奇，但花子是其中最有名的。花子又稱廁所裡的花子，是經常在日本學校廁所裡出沒的年輕女鬼。有人相信她是第二次世界大戰時在空襲中喪生的女鬼，也有人說她是因為被同學霸凌而在廁所隔間裡自殺。據說花子住在三樓女廁的第三間隔間，經常被學生用來當試膽遊戲。根據傳說，召喚花子的方式是敲

隔間的門三次並說：「花子，妳在嗎？」等了一會兒，會有細小的聲音回答：「是，我在。」有膽進入隔間的人，會看到穿著紅裙的蒼白小女孩。在大部分故事版本中，花子通常無害，但在某些故事版本中，花子會把學生拖進馬桶後從此消失。

BTW不是喝的血腥瑪麗

🎧 034 Bloody Mary 血腥瑪麗

Popular with children—especially girls—at [1]**slumber** parties, the game of Bloody Mary isn't for the easily frightened. The game is played by entering a dark room with a lit candle, standing in front of a mirror, and saying "Bloody Mary" three times [2]**in a row**. At this point, the [3]**frightful** [4]**apparition** of Bloody Mary may appear in the mirror. She might look like a corpse or a ghost, and might even be covered in blood. If she's in a good mood, she may answer questions about the future. But if she's in a bad mood, she may scratch your face, scream at you, or even pull you into the mirror! Who is Bloody Mary? Some say she's the ghost of a witch named Mary Worth who was executed for practicing 🔵 **black magic**. Others say she's the spirit of 🔵 **Queen Mary I**, who gained the nickname Bloody Mary after burning hundreds of [5]**Protestants** at the stake. Are you brave enough to play Bloody Mary?

血腥瑪麗的遊戲相當受到睡衣派對的孩子歡迎，尤其是女孩子，但這遊戲不適合容易受驚嚇的人玩。這遊戲的玩法是拿著點火的蠟燭進入黑暗的房間，站在鏡子前，然後連續說三次「血腥瑪麗」。此時血腥瑪麗的可怕幻影可能會出現在鏡子裡。她可能看起來像屍體或鬼，甚至可能渾身是血。她心情好的話，可能會回答跟未來有關的問題。但她若心情不好，可能會抓傷你的臉、朝你大吼，甚至把你拖進鏡子中！誰是血腥瑪麗？有人說她是女巫瑪麗沃斯的鬼魂，因為施黑魔法而被處決。另外有人說，她是瑪麗女王一世的鬼魂，因為以火刑燒死數百名新教徒而得此綽號。你有膽量玩血腥瑪麗嗎？

🔵 Language Guide

black magic 黑魔法

黑魔法是指為了私欲，如報復、謀殺、控制他人身心等所施的邪惡法術。另一種說法認為黑魔法是為魔鬼服務，進行邪惡工作的人才有辦法施行的法術。出於善意的法術則稱為白魔法（white magic），像是祈雨、治病等。

Queen Mary I 瑪麗一世

瑪麗一世（Mary I，1516～1558年），是亨利八世和第一任妻子凱瑟琳王后唯一存活的孩子，儘管備受父王寵愛，享有許多英國王儲才有的禮遇，但她的父親最後還是希望能生出男性子嗣繼承王位，而再娶安寶琳（詳見「世界十大鬼域」倫敦塔補充介紹）。亨利八世自任英國國教領袖，與反對這樁婚姻的羅馬天主教廷決裂，瑪麗被貶為私生女，從此飽受虐待及死亡威脅，直到安寶琳被處死後，她的地位才漸漸恢復。虔信天主教的瑪莉於弟弟愛德華六世死後登基，展開殘酷打壓英國國教（即新教的一種），為剷除異己下令燒死約 300 名宗教異議人士，因而被稱作「血腥瑪麗」。

19世紀初版畫，作者／H.T.Ryall

血腥瑪麗雞尾酒調法

黑胡椒及鹽巴、醃漬綠橄欖
冰塊、伏特加（1½ 盎司／45 毫升）
帶葉芹菜梗、檸檬塊
番茄汁（4 盎司／120 毫升）

Trolls, Ogres and Gnomes

各種山怪和妖精

© Popova Valeriya / Shutterstock.com

芬蘭土庫市（Turku）位於奧拉河（Aura River）出海口。一座橋下有女性 troll 的雕像。

038 🎧 Vocabulary

1) **post** [post] (v./n.)（在網站上）發布資訊，發文；貼文

2) **offensive** [ə`fɛnsɪv] (a.) 冒犯人的，令人不快的

3) **comment** [`kamɛnt] (n./v.) 意見，評論；發表意見

4) **maiden** [`medən] (n.) 少女，處女

5) **expose** [ɪk`spoz] (v.) 使接觸到，使暴露於

6) **formation** [fɔr`meʃən] (n.) 形狀，結構

7) **toll** [tol] (n.) 通行費

8) **romance** [`ro, mæns] (n.) 中古世紀騎士故事，傳奇小說，浪漫愛情故事

9) **publication** [, pʌblɪ`keʃən] (n.) 出版，出版物，刊物

10) **puss** [pʊs] (n.)（俚）小貓

11) **inspiration** [, ɪnspə`reʃən] (n.) 靈感，啟發

036 🎧 Trolls 巨怪

These days, most trolls are the kind that [1)]**post** [2)]**offensive** [3)]**comments** on the Internet. But in 🅛🅖 **Scandinavian** folklore, trolls are large, ugly creatures that live in caves in the mountains. They look similar to humans, but are covered with hair or fur and have long, round noses and cup-shaped ears high on their heads. Although they are slow and stupid, trolls have great strength and are known to eat people when they catch them. They are also known to capture young [4)]**maidens** and make them their slaves. If [5)]**exposed** to sunlight, trolls turn into stone, which may be why there are so many strange rock [6)]**formations** in 🅛🅖 **Scandinavia**. In modern fairy tales, trolls are man-sized creatures that usually live under bridges. They don't eat humans, but they do make people pay a [7)]**toll** or answer a riddle if they want to cross their bridge.

現在的 troll 大部分指的是在網路上發表攻擊性言論的人（又稱「酸民」），但在北歐民間傳說中，是巨大、醜陋、住在山洞裡的怪物。他們長得像人類，但全身覆蓋毛髮，有長長渾圓的鼻子，頭頂有杯子形狀的耳朵。雖然巨怪緩慢笨拙，但力氣很大，據說抓到人類的話會把他們吃掉，還聽說他們會抓少女當奴隸。巨怪若接觸到陽光會變成石頭，也許這也是為什麼北歐會有這麼多奇形怪狀的岩石。在現代的童話故事中，巨怪的大小跟人類一樣，通常住在橋下，不吃人類，但若有人經過他們住的橋，他們會要求人類付過橋費或回答謎語。

🎧 037 Ogres 食人魔

    In European folklore, ogres are hideous giants who feed on human beings, especially babies and young children. Like trolls, ogres are strong but not very smart. The word ogre, which is of French origin, comes from the name of the **Etruscan** god Orcus, who eats human flesh. A female ogre is called an ogress. The word first appears in a 12th century French [8]**romance**, but only came into wider use after the [9]**publication** of *The Tales of Mother Goose*, by French author Charles Perrault, in the late 1600s. Many of the fairy tales in this collection, like *Sleeping Beauty* and [10]***Puss in Boots***, remain popular to this day. The ogre that appears in *Puss in Boots* was the [11]**inspiration** for the ogre star of the *Shrek* movies. Although Shrek doesn't eat people, he doesn't hesitate to use their fear of ogres to his advantage.

    在歐洲民間傳說中，食人魔是吃人的醜陋巨人，尤其喜歡吃嬰兒和小孩。食人魔就像巨怪，強壯但不怎麼聰明。ogre 一詞源自法語，來自伊特魯里亞的死神名稱 Orcus，也會吃人肉。女食人魔則稱為 ogress。這個詞首次出現在第 12 世紀法國的騎士故事中，不過在 17 世紀末法國作家夏爾佩羅的《鵝媽媽故事》出版後才廣泛使用。這本童話集中有許多故事至今仍相當受歡迎，比如《睡美人》和《穿長靴的貓》。在《穿長靴的貓》中出現的食人魔，是《史瑞克》電影系列中綠色食人魔的靈感來源。雖然史瑞克不吃人，但他也毫不猶豫地善加利用人類對食人魔的恐懼。

電影《史瑞克》的主角就是 ogre。

🔊 Language Guide

Scandinavia 斯堪地那維亞

這個詞原始的意思是指「危險的島嶼」，因為斯堪地那維亞半島附近隱藏許多危險沙洲，容易使船隻觸礁沉沒。由於歷史和政治的影響，斯堪地那維亞一詞包含的國家並不明確。地理上斯堪地那維亞半島（Scandinavian Peninsula）只包含了挪威和瑞典，歷史上 19 世紀時，半島上的國家曾有意與文化政治上有深厚淵源的丹麥組成聯盟，共同對抗普魯士，此時芬蘭屬於俄羅斯芬蘭大公國，而冰島還未從丹麥的統治下獨立，因此這一時期斯堪地那維亞只包含了挪威、瑞典、丹麥三個國家。後來這幾個國家在二戰後接觸越來越密切，今日為了避免產生誤解，常改用北歐五國稱呼。

Etruscan 伊特拉斯坎文化

西元前 12 世紀至前 1 世紀於現今義大利及科西嘉島的發展出來的伊特拉斯坎（Etruscan [ɪˈtrʌskən]）文化，是伊特魯里亞人所遺留下來，對古羅馬文明影響至深，尤其是在文化習俗及建築方面。後來被羅馬共和國（西元前 509 至前 27 年）完全同化。

The Tales of Mother Goose 《鵝媽媽故事》

The Tales of Mother Goose 是法國作家夏爾佩羅（Charles Perrault）所著兒童故事集《附道德訓示的古代故事》的副標題。這本書除了有文中提到的〈睡美人〉及〈穿長靴的貓〉，〈小紅帽〉、〈灰姑娘〉也在其中。至於大家耳熟能詳的《鵝媽媽童謠》（Mother Goose's Melody）則是被譽為兒童文學之父的英國作家約翰紐貝里（John Newbery，1713～1767）所著。

🎧 039 Gnomes 地精

Gnomes are small, [1]**dwarf**-like earth spirits that can be traced back to the folklore of the 🔠 **Renaissance**. These creatures first appear in the [2]**writings** of 🔠 **Paracelsus**, a Swiss doctor and [3]**alchemist** who lived in the 16th century. He likely [4]**derived** the name from the Latin *genomos*, meaning "earth [5]**dweller**." According to Paracelsus, they are 1-2 ft. tall, stay away from humans, and able to move through solid earth as easily as people move through air. These gnomes mostly live underground, where they protect the earth's precious metals and [6]**gems**. These days, however, gnomes are most often seen on lawns in Europe and America, and even in movies like *Gnomeo and Juliet* and *Sherlock Gnomes*. These garden gnomes can be recognized by their long white beards, tall red caps and pipes.

地精是像侏儒一樣矮小的大地精靈，可追溯至文藝復興時期的民間傳說。這種生物第一次出現在 16 世紀時瑞士醫生帕拉塞爾蘇斯的文章中，他同時也是煉金術士。名稱可能取自拉丁文 genomos，意思是「大地居住者」。根據帕拉塞爾蘇斯的描述，地精身高一到二英尺，會避開人類，能輕易鑽進堅硬的地底，就像人類在空氣中行動一樣自如。這種地精大部分住在地底，保護地底下珍貴的金屬和寶石。不過現在地精經常能在歐洲和美國的草坪上看到，甚至出現在《糯米歐與茱麗葉》和《糯爾摩斯》之類的電影。這種花園地精的特徵是有著白色的長鬍子、紅色的高帽和煙斗。

傳說中的哥布林

🎧 041 Vocabulary

1) **dwarf** [dwɔrf] (n.) 侏儒，矮子

2) **writing** [ˋraɪtɪŋ] (n.) 文學作品，著作

3) **alchemist** [ˋælkəmɪst] (n.) 煉金術士

4) **derive (from)** [dɪˋraɪv] (v.) 衍生，從…取得

5) **dweller** [ˋdwɛlɚ] (n.) 居住者

6) **gem** [dʒɛm] (n.) 寶石，珍品

7) **vs.** (prep.) 讀作 **versus** [ˋvɜsəs]（法律和運動用語）對抗，相對於…

8) **grotesque** [groˋtɛsk] (a.) 古怪的，奇形怪狀的

9) **mischievous** [ˋmɪstʃɪvəs] (a.) 調皮的，愛惡作劇的

10) **valuables** [ˋvæljəbəlz] (n.) 貴重物品

11) **invention** [ɪnˋvɛnʃən] (n.) 發明，創造

12) **specialize** [ˋspɛʃəˏlaɪz] (v.) 專門（從事或研究）

13) **machinery** [məˋʃinərɪ] (n.) 機器，器械

14) **malfunction** [mælˋfʌŋʃən] (v.) 故障，機能失常

15) **mechanical** [məˋkænɪkəl] (a.) 機械的

16) **confusion** [kənˋfjuʒən] (n.) 不確定，困惑

040 Goblins [7] vs. Gremlins 哥布林、小精靈比一比

People often confuse goblins and gremlins, but the two creatures are actually quite different. First appearing in European folklore in the Middle Ages, goblins are small, [8]**grotesque** creatures that are usually [9]**mischievous** and sometimes wicked. They often live in caves, but sometimes move into people's houses, where they like to steal [10]**valuables**, play tricks and make loud noises at night. Gremlins, on the other hand, are a modern [11]**invention**. They're mischievous like goblins, but they [12]**specialize** in causing airplanes and other [13]**machinery** to [14]**malfunction**. During WWII, British pilots often had trouble explaining frequent [15]**mechanical** problems on their planes, so they made up gremlins to blame them on. Nobody ever actually saw a gremlin, and they certainly didn't keep the **Allies** from winning the war. Speaking of blame, perhaps the [16]**confusion** about goblins and gremlins can be blamed on the 1984 film *Gremlins*, which features mischievous little monsters that look and behave much more like goblins.

大家常將哥布林和小精靈搞混，但這兩種生物其實完全不一樣。哥布林源自於歐洲中世紀的民間傳說，是一種身材小的古怪生物，通常很頑皮，有時是邪惡的。他們通常住在洞穴中，但有時會住進人類的家，偷走貴重物品、搞惡作劇，並在晚上製造噪音。小精靈反而是現代發明出來的，像哥布林一樣淘氣，但他們專門造成飛機或其他機械故障。在第二次世界大戰期間，英國飛行員經常在飛機上遇到難以解釋的機械問題，所以他們捏造出小精靈，並把問題怪到他們身上。沒人真正看過小精靈，他們確實也沒妨礙同盟國贏得戰爭。說到責怪，或許可以把搞混哥布林和小精靈的原因怪到1984年的電影《小精靈》，裡面淘氣的怪物長相和行為還真有點像哥布林。

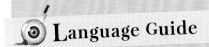

Language Guide

Renaissance 文藝復興

renaissance 一詞有「重生、更新」之意，是發生於 14 世紀中期的人文運動，由於當時的價值觀都以教會至上，甚至連畫作、雕塑、文學都多以宗教為題材，忽略「人」所扮演的角色，再加上教會貪腐奢侈，造成大眾反感，因此當代的藝文人士便開始對此進行反思，發起一場復興古典文化的運動，希望能重現古希臘羅馬時期的榮光，並且更強調「以人為本」的人文精神，以世俗生活為重心，開拓出一種新的價值思維和時代風格。

Paracelsus 帕拉塞爾蘇斯

原名菲利普斯馮霍恩海姆（Philippus von Hohenheim）的中世紀瑞士醫師帕拉塞爾蘇斯（約西元 1493 ～ 1541 年），是將煉金術與醫學化學結合的關鍵人物。他反對煉製當時流行能治百病的複方萬靈丹，主張應服用單一成分藥劑，以便追蹤療效、區別藥物與毒物。他的想法促進了專科疾病研究，藥劑學因此得到發展的理論基礎。

Allies 同盟國

文中的 Allies 是指二戰同盟國（the Allies of World War II）。alliance 是為了各種利益、目的結合的「同盟」，同盟的成員就是 ally（複數為 allies）。Allies 首字母大寫時，表示第一次世界大戰時「協約國」（Entente Powers），對抗當時德意志帝國、奧匈帝國、奧斯曼帝國、保加利亞王國組成的同盟國（Central Powers），及第二次世界大戰時的「同盟國」，對抗由德、日、義為中心的軸心國（Axis Powers）。

Goblin 哥布林

BTW

© chrisdorney / Shutterstock.com
英國一個機械工藝展覽中的作品，描繪哥布林惡搞莎士比亞畫像的情景。

Gremlin 小精靈

GREMLINS THINK IT'S FUN TO HURT YOU
USE CARE always
BACK UP OUR BATTLESKIES!

圖片來源：U.S. National Archives and Records Administration
二戰期間美國緊急事務管理局軍工生產委員會的海報。標上寫著：「小精靈覺得讓你受傷很好玩。隨時小心注意。加強我們的空中戰技！」

© NieGi / Shutterstock.com
電影《小精靈》Gremlins 當中小精靈的造型，長得很像哥布林。

Mythological Monsters

神話傳說中的怪物

法國畫家魯東（Odilon Redon，1840～1916 年）的名畫《獨眼巨人》。

義大利佛羅倫斯傭兵涼廊（Loggia dei Lanzi）的珀爾修斯手提美杜莎頭顱的雕像。

042 ▶ Cyclops 獨眼巨人

In Greek and Roman mythology, a Cyclops is a member of an ancient race of giants with a single eye in the middle of the forehead. The word Cyclops means "round-eyed" in ancient Greek. According to Homer, the Cyclops were bad-tempered [1]**cannibals** who lived in caves in a distant land, often thought to be Sicily. In Homer's *Odyssey*, the hero escapes death by blinding a Cyclops named Polyphemus. In the writings of Hesiod, the Cyclops were the sons of sky god Uranus and earth goddess Gaia, and brothers of the Titans. Skilled [2]**blacksmiths**, the Cyclops were placed in charge of making [3]**thunderbolts** for Zeus. In later stories, however, they are killed by Apollo for making the thunderbolt that Zeus used to kill his son.

在希臘和羅馬神話中，獨眼巨人屬於古代巨人族，這一族巨人在前額中央有個眼睛。Cyclops 在古希臘文中的意思是「圓眼」。根據荷馬提到，獨眼巨人是脾氣暴躁的食人族，住在遠方的洞穴中，可能是西西里島。在荷馬的《奧德賽》中，英雄刺瞎獨眼巨人波利菲莫斯的眼睛後逃過死劫。在赫西俄德寫的詩中，獨眼巨人是天神烏拉諾斯和大地女神蓋亞的兒子，是泰坦的兄弟。獨眼巨人是熟練的鐵匠，負責為宙斯製造雷電。但在後來的傳說中，獨眼巨人被阿波羅殺死，因為他們製造的雷電被宙斯用來殺死阿波羅的兒子。

043 ▶ Gorgons 蛇髮女妖

Like Cyclops, Gorgons are [4]**monstrous** creatures that appear in Greek mythology. Homer spoke of a single Gorgon, a monster who lived in the underworld, and whose hideous appearance struck [5]**terror** in the hearts of men. Hesiod later increased the number of Gorgons to three—sisters named Stheno, Euryale and Medusa. Daughters of the sea god Phorcys and his sister Ceto, the Gorgons looked like beautiful women, but with bird-like wings and snakes instead of hair. While Medusa wasn't [6]**immortal** like Stheno and Euryale, she had a special power—the ability to turn anyone who looked at her to stone. The hero Perseus was able to kill Medusa by looking only at her reflection in his [7]**shield**, and then chopping off her head when he got close enough. But even in death, her [8]**gaze** still had the power to turn people to stone.

蛇髮女妖就像獨眼巨人，是希臘神話中的可怕生物。荷馬曾提到一個蛇髮女妖，住在地底下，恐怖的外表令人心生恐懼。赫西俄德後來將蛇髮女妖的數量增至三個，也就是斯忒諾、歐律阿勒和美杜莎三姊妹。蛇髮女妖是海神福耳庫斯和其姊妹刻托的女兒，外表是美女的模樣，但有著像鳥一樣的翅膀和一頭蛇髮。與斯忒諾和歐律阿勒不一樣，美杜莎並非不朽之身，但有特殊的能力，只要看到她的人都會變成石頭。英雄珀爾修斯只看她盾牌上的美杜莎倒影，然後趁靠近她時將她的頭砍下，因此得以殺掉她。但就算死了，她的眼神仍有能力將人變成石頭。

044 Griffins 獅鷲

The griffin (sometimes spelled gryphon) is a [9]**mythical** creature with the head and wings of an eagle and the body and tail of a lion. Sometimes it has the front legs of a lion, but usually the claws of an eagle. First appearing in ancient Persia and Egypt, the griffon was considered the king of all beasts. Seen as [10]**protectors** against evil, these noble creatures—like the stone lions of ancient China—could often be found guarding palaces, tombs and temples. In Greek mythology, the sun god Apollo's [11]**chariot** was pulled by a griffin. And in [12]**medieval** Europe, because they were symbols of strength and courage, griffins often appeared on LG **coats of arms**. Even today, these creatures still serve as protectors—the griffin is the symbol of the Philadelphia Museum of Art, and [13]**bronze** griffins on its roof guard the treasures within.

獅鷲（有時拼作 gryphon）是一種神祕生物，有著老鷹的頭和翅膀，以及獅子的身體和尾巴，有時前腿像獅子，但通常爪子像老鷹。獅鷲源自於古代的波斯和埃及，被視為萬獸之王。獅鷲被當成避邪的保護獸，這種高貴的生物就像中國古代的石獅子，通常用於守護宮殿、墳墓和神殿。在希臘神話中，太陽神阿波羅的戰車就是由獅鷲拉的。在中世紀的歐洲，獅鷲象徵力量和勇氣，因此常出現在盾形紋章上。就算在今天，這種生物仍被當成保護獸──獅鷲就是費城藝術博物館的象徵符號，屋頂上的青銅獅鷲就是用來保護博物館裡的寶物。

© meunierd / Shutterstock.com

德國柏林音樂廳屋頂上的雕像，就是獅鷲拖行太陽神阿波羅的戰車。

Language Guide

Homer 荷馬

希臘神話相關著作當中，最有名的要算是將神話穿插於戰爭故事中的荷馬史詩《伊利亞德》*Iliad* 和《奧德賽》*Odyssey*。荷馬的大約生存年代在西元前 9～8 世紀，因為關於他的資料太少，也有學者認為荷馬其實是傳說人物，代表當時以傳唱英雄故事維生的盲人歌手。希臘神話最早是透過口述傳播，直到西元前 7 世紀才開始出現以文字編寫神話的作家，所以荷馬史詩一開始也是透過口述，西元前 8 世紀才文字化。

Hesiod 赫西俄德

希臘詩人赫西俄德的身份是農民，大約生存年代在西元前 750～650 年，與荷馬同期但稍晚，被認為是西洋第一位書寫詩人。他的敘事詩《神譜》（*Theogony*）主要在描述眾神起源，是研究希臘神話的重要文獻；而他所寫的田園詩《農作與時日》（*Works and Days*）有系統地紀錄了當時的農耕生產方式，對古希臘農業及經濟、天文及計時法的研究極為重要。

coat of arms 盾形紋章

中世紀騎士作戰時，會在紋章盾（escutcheon）、戰袍、外套上裝飾盾形紋章，以表示自己的身份。後來這種做法不再僅限於戰場，而成為上流社會世襲的象徵物。沿襲至今許多歐美皇室、大學及企業仍會用盾形紋章作為標誌。研究紋章設計的學問則為紋章學（heraldry）。

Hydra 九頭蛇妖海卓拉

🎧 046 Hydra 海卓拉

The Hydra of Lerna, usually known simply as the Hydra, was a [1]**serpentine** water monster in Greek and Roman mythology. Its [2]**lair** was the Lake of Lerna, which was said to be an entrance to the Underworld. As if a huge serpent wasn't scary enough, the Hydra had nine heads, one of which was immortal. According to Hesiod, the creature was the [3]**offspring** of two of Greece's most [4]**fearsome** monsters: Typhon, a giant with 100 heads, and Echidna, who was half woman and half serpent. As one of his 🎧 **Twelve** [5]**Labors**, 🎧 **Hercules** was ordered to [6]**slay** the Hydra, and it was no easy task. When he chopped off one of its heads, two grew back in its place. So he got his nephew Iolaus to help him by [7]**cauterizing** the [8]**stumps** after he cut each head off. When Hercules cut off the final head—the immortal one—he buried it under a large [9]**boulder**, thus completing his task.

勒拿九頭蛇，又稱海卓拉，是希臘和羅馬神話中的蛇形水怪。海卓拉的巢穴在勒拿湖，是傳說中通往地獄的入口。光是巨蛇還不夠可怕似的，海卓拉還有九顆頭，其中一顆是不死之頭。根據赫西俄德所言，這種生物是希臘最可怕的兩個怪物所生，分別是有一百顆頭的巨人堤豐，以及半女半蛇的厄客德娜。在海克力士的十二項英雄偉績中，海克力士獲令殺死海卓拉，但這並非簡單的任務。他砍掉其中一顆頭時，原斷頸處又長回兩顆頭，所以他請侄子伊奧勞斯幫忙，在他砍掉頭時，用火燒灼斷頸。海克力士砍掉最後一顆頭後，也就是不死的那顆，將那顆頭埋在一塊巨石下，才算完成了任務。

🎧 047 Cerberus 地獄犬

Cerberus, also known as the [10]**Hound** of [11]**Hades**, is the monstrous three-headed dog that guards the gates of the underworld. Like the Hydra, he is the offspring of Typhon and Echidna. Cerberus may be a dog, but he [12]**takes after** his parents with a serpent for a tail and snakes growing from his back. Also like Hydra, Cerberus was one of Hercules' Twelve Labors. For this labor, the hero was given the task of descending into the underworld, [13]**kidnapping** Cerberus, and bringing him back to King Eurystheus. After entering the underworld with the help of Hermes and Athena, Hercules was given permission by Hades to take Cerberus with him, but 🎧 **only if** he could

🎧 049 Vocabulary

1) **serpentine** [ˈsɝpənˌtin] (a.) 蛇般的，彎彎曲曲的，名詞為 **serpent** [ˈsɝpənt]，「大蛇」之意

2) **lair** [lɛr] (n.) 窩，巢

3) **offspring** [ˈɔfˌsprɪŋ] (n.) 後代

4) **fearsome** [ˈfɪrsəm] (a.) 令人畏懼的

5) **labor** [ˈlebɚ] (n.) 勞動，工作

6) **slay** [sle] (v.) 殺死，殺害

7) **cauterize** [ˈkɔtɚˌraɪz] (v.) 燒灼

8) **stump** [stʌmp] (n.)（樹幹等斷裂後）殘餘的部分，樹墩

9) **boulder** [ˈboldɚ] (n.) 巨石，大圓石

10) **hound** [haʊnd] (n.) 獵犬

11) **hades** [ˈhediz] (n.) 地獄，陰曹地府。首字母大寫為希臘神話中的死神黑帝斯

12) **take after** [tek ˈæftɚ] (phr.) 像，相似

13) **kidnap** [ˈkɪdˌnæp] (v.) 綁架

14) **subdue** [səbˈdu] (v.) 征服，壓制

15) **manage (to)** [ˈmænɪdʒ] (v.) 設法做到，能應付（困難）

16) **crest** [krɛst] (n.)（鳥禽的）頭冠，冠毛，（頭盔的）頂飾

17) **weasel** [ˈwizəl] (v.) 鼬，黃鼠狼

18) **venom** [ˈvɛnəm] (n.)（蛇、毒蟲的）毒液

19) **symbolize** [ˈsɪmbəˌlaɪz] (v.) 象徵

20) **crow** [kro] (v./n.)（公雞）啼叫

[14)]**subdue** the beast without using weapons. He [15)]**managed to** capture Cerberus with his bare hands and bring him to Eurystheus, who was so frightened by the sight that he promised to make this labor his last if he returned the monster to Hades, which he did.

Cerberus 地獄犬

刻耳柏洛斯，又稱地獄犬，是巨大的三頭犬，看守地獄之門。地獄犬跟海卓拉一樣，是堤豐和厄客德娜所生。刻耳柏洛斯或許是犬類，但遺傳到父母的蛇形尾巴，背部也有長蛇。跟海卓拉同樣的是，刻耳柏洛斯也是海克力士的十二項英雄偉績之一。在這項偉績中，海克力士接獲的任務是要進入冥界綁架刻耳柏洛斯，並交給歐律斯透斯國王。在荷米斯和雅典娜的協助下，海克力士進入冥界後，獲得冥王的准許，可以帶走刻耳柏洛斯，唯一條件是不用武器制服地獄犬。海克力士得以用雙手抓住刻耳柏洛斯，並交給歐律斯透斯，歐律斯透斯一看到地獄犬就嚇得保證，只要海克力士將地獄犬送回冥界，這就是他的最後一項任務，於是海克力士將地獄犬送回去。

048 Basilisk 巴西利斯克

The basilisk, a serpent-like creature capable of destroying other creatures—and even plants—with its stare or breath, first appeared in Greek and Roman legends. The word basilisk comes from the Greek *basilískos*, or "little king," a name that refers to the crown-shaped [16)]**crest** on the creature's head. Only the [17)]**weasel**, which was said to have [18)]**venom** deadly to the basilisk, was safe from its powers. In medieval myths, it was often used to [19)]**symbolize** the devil. The basilisk was believed to come from an egg laid by a cock and hatched by a serpent, which is why it has the head and wings of a cock and the tail of a serpent. In some legends, cocks, strangely enough, were also said to be enemies of the basilisk—if the creature heard a cock [20)]**crow**, it would shortly die. For this reason, travelers in regions where basilisks were thought to live would carry cocks with them for protection.

巴西利斯克是一種蛇形生物，只要以眼神或呼氣就能摧毀其他生物，甚至植物，第一次出現時是在希臘和羅馬傳說。basilisk 一詞源自希臘文 basilískos，意指「小王」，是形容這種生物頭上的王冠狀頂飾。據說黃鼠狼的毒液能致巴西利斯克於死，所以只有黃鼠狼能對巴西利斯克的致命能力免疫。在中世紀傳說中，巴西利斯克通常象徵惡魔。巴西利斯克被認為是由公雞所生的蛋並由蛇所孵化而出，所以有公雞的頭和翅膀，以及蛇尾巴。奇怪的是，在某些傳說中，公雞也是巴西利斯克的敵人，如果巴西利斯克聽到公雞叫聲，很快就會死亡。因此旅人若身在巴西利斯克出沒的地區，會隨身攜帶公雞以自保。

Basilisk
巴西利斯克

© jack1986 / Shutterstock.com

🎧 051 Vocabulary

1) **prosperity** [prɑˋspɛrəti] (n.) 繁榮
2) **serpent** [ˋsɝpənt] (n.) 大蛇，毒蛇
3) **deadly** [ˋdɛdli] (a.) 致命的，致死的
4) **saint** [sent] (n.) 聖人，聖徒
5) **reptile** [ˋrɛptaɪl] (n.) 爬蟲類
6) **barbed** [bɑrbd] (a.) 有尖刺的。**barb** [bɑrb]是名詞「尖刺，倒鉤」
7) **fantasy** [ˋfæntəsi] (a./n.) 奇幻（作品）
8) **lizard** [ˋlɪzəd] (n.) 蜥蜴

西方的惡龍

🎧 050 Dragons 龍

While Chinese dragons have always represented [1]**prosperity** and good luck, even becoming a symbol of the Emperor, Western dragons are a different story. The earliest of these, which appeared in the ancient Middle East, took the form of giant [2]**serpents**. And because the snakes that lived there were large and [3]**deadly**, dragons became a symbol of evil. It's no wonder that the Devil appeared to Adam and Eve in the form of a serpent. The word dragon comes from the ancient Greek *drakon*, which was used to describe any large snake.

中國的龍一直代表著繁榮和好運，甚至成為皇帝的象徵，西方的龍則截然不同。西方最早的龍是以巨蛇的形象出現在古代的中東。由於那裡的蛇巨大且致命，因此龍象徵邪惡。也難怪出現在亞當和夏娃面前的撒旦是以蛇的形象出現。dragon這個詞是源自古希臘文drakon，原本是用來形容大蛇。

東方的祥龍

In the Middle Ages, Christians saw dragons as symbols of sin and pagan religion, and made them the enemies of knights and [4]**saints**, as in the legend of  *Saint George and the Dragon*. By this time, dragons no longer looked like snakes. Instead, they were giant fire-breathing [5]**reptiles** with sharp claws, bat-like wings and [6]**barbed** tails. Today, dragons can be found in popular [7]**fantasy** fiction like *The Lord of the Rings*, the Harry Potter series and *Game of Thrones*. But not all dragons are fictional. Komodo dragons, which live on the Indonesian island of Komodo, are giant [8]**lizards** that can reach 10 feet in length and weigh over 300 pounds!

在中世紀時，基督徒將龍視為原罪和異教的象徵，是騎士和聖徒的敵人，如在故事《聖喬治和龍》中所見。此時龍不再是蛇的形象，而是會噴火的巨大爬行類動物，有鋒利的爪子、蝙蝠般的翅膀和帶刺的尾巴。現今的龍會在受歡迎的奇幻作品中看到，例如《魔戒》、《哈利波特》系列和《權力遊戲》。但不是所有龍都是虛構的，在印尼科莫多島的科摩多龍，是身長可達十英尺、體重超過三百磅的巨蜥！

Komodo dragons
真實存在的科摩多龍

Language Guide

Saint George and the Dragon
《聖喬治和龍》

聖喬治和龍的故事簡單來説，就是村民深受食人惡龍荼毒，某日一位公主即將被送去獻祭時，聖喬治出現，表示只要村民改信基督教，他就出手相救。於是村民放棄異教信仰，聖喬治以十字架護體，殺了惡龍。這類「邪不勝正」的故事原型早在基督教之前就有，後來被基督教信仰採用，屠龍者也就與十字軍東征騎士、基督教聖徒的形象結合。

Monsters That Could Be Real

可能真的存在的怪物

052 Loch Ness Monster 尼斯湖水怪

The Loch Ness Monster, also known by the nickname Nessie, is a [1]**legendary** dinosaur-like creature said to inhabit Loch Ness in the Scottish [2]**Highlands**. Sightings of a monster there date back to ancient times, but the modern legend of the Loch Ness Monster began in 1933, when a couple saw an [3]**enormous** creature—which they compared to a dragon—cross their car's path and enter the water. In 1934, an English doctor took the most famous picture of the monster, which showed its head and neck sticking out of the water. The *Daily Mail* printed the photograph, causing an international [4]**sensation**. Some believed that the creature was a plesiosaur, a dinosaur that disappeared over a million years ago. Over the years, many scientists have attempted to locate the creature with scientific instruments, but none have been successful. [5]**Despite** the lack of evidence, the Loch Ness Monster is still as popular as ever, and is a major source of tourist dollars in Scotland.

名聞遐邇的尼斯湖水怪長得像恐龍，又稱尼西，據說住在蘇格蘭高地的尼斯湖裡。自古以來就有看到尼斯湖水怪的傳聞，但現代關於尼斯湖水怪的傳說是從 1933 年開始，當時有對夫妻看到一個巨大怪物橫越他們前方路面進入湖中，他們將那個怪物比作龍。1934 年，有位英國醫生拍下最著名的水怪照片，顯示出水怪的頭和脖子浮出水面。《每日郵報》刊登了那張照片，在國際間造成轟動。有些人認為這個生物是蛇頸龍，一種在一百多萬年前消失的恐龍。多年來，許多科學家想用科學儀器找出水怪，但都沒有成功。儘管缺乏證據證實，但尼斯湖水怪受歡迎的程度依舊不減，也是蘇格蘭重要的觀光財源。

053 [6]Abominable Snowman 雪人

In the folklore of Nepal, the Abominable Snowman is a mysterious ape-like beast said to live among the snowy peaks of the Himalayas. Also called the Yeti—"rock bear" in the Tibetan language of the LG **Sherpas**—they are described as large, [7]**muscular** creatures with white fur that walk on two legs like men. According to locals, they carry large stones as weapons and communicate with each other by whistling. They're also said to have large, wide feet that act like snowshoes, helping them move through the snow without sinking. While actual sightings of the creature are rare, many "Yeti [8]**footprints**" have been found. Some claim that

Illustration of a Yeti by Philippe Semeria

these footprints—which can be up to 13 in. long and 9 in. wide—prove that the Abominable Snowman exists, but others say that they are prints left by large bears.

在尼泊爾的民間傳說中，雪人是長得像人猿的神祕野獸，住在白雪皚皚的喜馬拉雅山峰。雪人又稱雪怪，在雪爾帕人的西藏語中是「石熊」的意思，被形容成巨大健壯的生物，全身覆蓋白色毛皮，像人類一樣用雙腳走路。據當地人說，他們隨身攜帶大石頭當武器，用吹口哨的方式互相溝通。還聽說他們寬大的雙腳就像雪鞋，可以讓他們在雪地上行走，不會下沉。鮮少有人真正看過雪人，多數是看到「雪怪的腳印」。有人聲稱這些腳印——最長可達13 英吋，最寬 9 英吋——證實雪人是存在的，但也有人說，那是大熊的腳印。

Bigfoot 大腳怪

Like the Abominable Snowman, Bigfoot is a large, hairy ape-like creature said to inhabit remote [9]**wilderness** areas. While Bigfoot sightings have been made all over North America, the highest [10]**concentration** has been in the Pacific Northwest. Indian legends about these hairy giants go back centuries—the creature's other name, Sasquatch, is a Salish word meaning "wild man"—but the first modern discovery of a Bigfoot footprint was made by British [11]**explorer** 🄻 **David Thompson** in 1811. Hundreds of similar footprints have been found since then, and people have even taken photographs and videos, although none of this [12]**evidence** has [13]**convinced** scientists of Bigfoot's existence. The creature is usually described as a tall (6-12 ft.) ape covered with dark brown hair that walks upright and has extremely large feet—some of the footprints discovered have been up to 24 in. long and 8 in. wide.

大腳怪就像雪人，是巨大、毛茸茸、像人猿的生物，據說住在偏僻的荒野地區。北美各地都有人看到大腳怪，但最常看到的地區是在太平洋西北地區。這種毛茸茸的大腳怪在印地安傳說中可追溯至幾百年前，這種生物的另一個名稱 Sasquatch 是賽利希語，意思是「野人」。但現代首次看到的大腳怪腳印，是英國探險家大衛湯普森在 1811 年發現的。自那時候起就有幾百個類似腳印陸續被發現，甚至有人拍下照片和影片，不過這些證據都不足以說服科學家有大腳怪的存在。這種生物通常被形容為高大（6 到 12 英尺）的人猿，全身覆蓋深褐色毛髮，會直立行走，有巨大的雙腳，被發現的腳印中有些長達 24 英吋，寬 8 英吋。

圖片來源：維基百科，攝影／Alexander Migl

🎧 Vocabulary

1) **legendary** [ˈlɛdʒənˌdɛri] (a.) 傳奇的，著名的
2) **highland** [ˈhaɪlənd] (n.) 高地
3) **enormous** [ɪˈnɔrməs] (a.) 巨大的
4) **sensation** [sɛnˈseʃən] (n.) 轟動（的人事物）
5) **despite** [dɪˈspaɪt] (prep.) 儘管
6) **abominable** [əˈbɑmənəbəl] (a.) 討厭的
7) **muscular** [ˈmʌskjələ] (a.) 肌肉發達的
8) **footprint** [ˈfʊtˌprɪnt] (n.) 腳印，足跡
9) **wilderness** [ˈwɪldənɪs] (n.) 荒地，荒野
10) **concentration** [ˌkɑnsənˈtreʃən] (n.) 集中，密度，濃度
11) **explorer** [ɪkˈsplorə] (n.) 探險家。動詞為 **explore** [ɪkˈsplor] 探險
12) **evidence** [ˈɛvədəns] (n.) 證據，物證
13) **convince** [kənˈvɪns] (v.) 說服，使人信服

056 Kitsune 狐妖

Kitsune means "fox" in Japanese, but the kitsune of Japanese *yōkai* folklore are no ordinary foxes. Like the Chinese *hulijing* they are based on, kitsune are [1]**intelligent** fox spirits that have the ability to shapeshift into human form. These creatures live very long lives, and the older they become, the greater their magical powers and wisdom (and number of tails—they can grow up to nine). Some kitsune are servants of *Inari*, the god of rice, and are worshipped at [2]**Shinto** [3]**shrines** for their ability to protect people and places from evil. Others are more mischievous, and use their powers to punish people for bad behavior or possess them and drive them crazy. While kitsune can take any human form, they most often appear as beautiful young women to seduce men and feed on their vital energy. But sometimes they fall in love with the men and make [4]**loyal** wives, although their marriages usually end when the husband discovers their true nature.

Kitsune 在日語中是「狐狸」的意思，但日本民間傳說中的妖怪狐狸不是一般的狐狸。日本的狐妖源自中國的狐狸精，一樣也是聰明的狐狸妖精，能變身成人類。這種生物的壽命很長，活得越久法力越高強，也越有智慧（而且尾巴也越長越多，最多可以長到九條）。有些狐妖是穀物之神稻荷神的使者，因保護人民和居所免於禍害而位列神社，接受膜拜。有些狐妖則較淘氣，會用法力懲罰為非作歹的人，或附在人身上，把人逼瘋。狐妖能化身成各種人的模樣，而最常變身成美少女引誘男人，吸取他們的精力。但狐妖有時會愛上男人，成為他們忠誠的妻子，然而當丈夫發現她們的真面目時，婚姻通常會以結束收場。

日本稻荷神社前的狐狸雕像。

057 Vocabulary

1) **intelligent** [ɪnˋtɛlədʒənt] (a.) 聰明的

2) **Shinto** [ˋʃɪnto] (n.) 日本神道教

3) **shrine** [ʃraɪn] (n.) 神殿，神壇

4) **loyal** [ˋlɔɪəl] (a.) 忠誠的，忠心的

日本能劇當中的狐妖面具。

PARANORMAL
NEWS

恐怖哦～～靈．異．新．聞

058 *Xiong zhai* 凶宅

（台灣學生佩琪與美國學生湯姆做語言交換，美國學生要讀中文報紙，兩個人在瀏覽報紙上的文章。）

Pei-chi : Hey, Tom. I brought a paper. What section do you want to read?

Tom : The crime section, of course. That's where all the [1]**juicy** stories are— murders, suicides….

Pei-chi : Ha-ha. That reminds me of a story that was in the news lately. A group of friends rented a house, and after they moved in bad things started happening to them, like traffic accidents and strange illnesses. Then the faucets started turning on by themselves, and every night the smell of baking cake filled the air. When they started asking around, a neighbor told them that the house's previous owner committed suicide there by burning [2]**charcoal**. They were so [3]**freaked out** that they broke their [4]**lease** and moved out.

Tom : So they thought the house was haunted by the suicide victim?

Pei-chi : Yeah. In Taiwan, we call a house where a murder or suicide took place a "*xiong zhai*."

Tom : So it doesn't count if somebody dies of natural causes.

Pei-chi : Right. In Taiwan it's a big [5]**taboo** to buy a *xiong zhai*. People believe it can cause bad health and bring bad luck. When someone sells a house where there was a murder or suicide, they're required to [6]**disclose** that to the buyer. There's even a *xiong zhai* [7]**website** where you can look up addresses to see if anything bad happened there. Do you have taboos like that in America?

Tom : I don't think it's *that* big of a deal, but nobody wants to live in a house where some [8]**grisly** murder took place. As far as I know, some states have [6]**disclosure** laws, but most don't.

Pei-chi : Oh, there was another [9]**weird** story in the news recently. A worker fell off a roof into an alley between two houses, and it was too narrow for

059 Vocabulary

1) **juicy** [ˈdʒusi] (a.) 精彩的，有料的，有趣的

2) **charcoal** [ˈtʃɑrˌkol] (n.) 木炭

3) **freak out** [frik aʊt] (phr.)（使人）緊張害怕，崩潰

4) **lease** [lis] (n.) 租約

5) **taboo** [təˈbu] (n.) 禁忌

6) **disclose** [dɪsˈkloz] (v.) 公開，揭露。名詞為 **disclosure** [dɪsˈkloʒɚ]，**disclosure law** 是指依法強制公開事實（如政治人物財產、交易房屋狀況、訴訟資料）

7) **website** [ˈwɛbˌsaɪt] (n.)（電腦）網站

8) **grisly** [ˈɡrɪzli] (a.) 可怕的，陰森的

9) **weird** [wɪrd] (a.) 奇怪的，詭異的

10) **ambulance** [ˈæmbjələns] (n.) 救護車

11) **paramedic** [ˌpærəˈmɛdɪk] (n.) 救護人員

12) **creepy** [ˈkripi] (a.) 令人毛骨悚然的，恐怖的

the [10]**ambulance** to drive into.
The [11]**paramedics** asked the owner of one of the houses if he could open his back door so they could carry the injured man out, but he refused. He was afraid that if the guy died in his house it would affect his property value!

Tom : Wow, I guess people really take this stuff seriously.

Pei-chi : Well, not everybody's a believer. Some people even invest in *xiong zhai*, and I hear  **the money is good**.

Tom : Are you considering an investment?

Pei-chi : Apartments here are so expensive that I couldn't even afford a *xiong zhai*. How about you? Would *you* live in a *xiong zhai*?

Tom : I don't know. All these [12]**creepy** stories are giving me **the heebie-jeebies**. How about showing me that website so I can see if my apartment is a *xiong zhai*?

嗨，湯姆，我帶報紙來了。你想讀哪一版？

湯姆 當然是社會版。精彩的新聞都在這裡——謀殺、自殺……

佩琪 哈哈。這讓我想到最近的一則新聞。有幾個朋友合租了一棟房子。住進去之後，每個人都開始碰到倒楣的事，像是出車禍、生怪病，然後水龍頭開始自己打開，而且每天晚上都飄出烤蛋糕的味道。他們向鄰居打聽，一個鄰居透露之前的屋主在這棟房子燒炭自殺，嚇得他們趕緊退租搬家。

湯姆：所以他們認為是自殺者在屋裡作祟？

佩琪：是的。在台灣，我們稱曾發生謀殺或自殺的房屋為「凶宅」。

湯姆：所以如果有人自然死亡並不算？

佩琪：對。在台灣非常忌諱買到凶宅，大家相信這對健康和運勢非常不利。出售曾發生謀殺或自殺的房屋時，賣方必須告知買主。這裡甚至有「凶宅網」供人查詢地址，看那裡是否曾經出事。在美國，你們有這樣的忌諱嗎？

湯姆：我不認為這在美國是嚴重的問題，但沒人想住在發生過可怕凶殺案的住宅。據我所知，有些州有揭露法，但大部分沒有。

佩琪：對了，最近還有一則很詭異的新聞。有工人從屋頂跌落兩棟房屋中間的窄巷，救護車開不進去。救護人員請一戶人家打開後門，讓他們將傷患抬出去，那位屋主拒絕。因為他怕傷患死在他家裡，會影響他的房價！

湯姆：哇，看來有人真的把這種事看得很嚴重。

佩琪：不過也有人不信邪。甚至有人專門投資凶宅，聽說利潤很不錯。

湯姆：妳也考慮投資嗎？

佩琪：房子實在太貴了，我連凶宅都買不起。那你呢？如果是凶宅，你敢住嗎？

湯姆：我不知道。這些恐怖的新聞令我坐立難安。給我看看那個網站如何，看我的公寓是不是凶宅？

1)Paranormal photographs
靈異照片

Pei-chi : Hey, look. There's a ghost story in the international section too!

Tom : Well, it says the source is the *Daily Mail*. It's a British 2)**tabloid** that 3)**specializes** in 4)**sensational** stories. What's it about?

Pei-chi : It's about a paranormal photograph. This woman took a picture of family and friends at a picnic, and when she was looking at the photo later, she noticed a 5)**spooky** hand in the background that didn't belong to anybody in the group. When she saw it, she **got goose bumps** all over. What's even creepier is that the guy in the photo the hand is pointing at died later in an accident. See, there's a gray hand behind that guy in the photo.

Tom : The color *is* strange, but it could be the hand of the woman next to him. It could also be the light or the angle that makes it look unnatural.

Pei-chi : I guess. The article also says she showed the photo to a paranormal expert—probably a 6)**psychic**—who said the hand belonged to a woman who died years ago, and that she knew the man in the photo who died in the accident.

Tom : Well, it sounds spooky, but there's no way of proving if it's true or not.

Pei-chi : **I suppose.** I saw an article online yesterday that had a bunch of paranormal photos from Thailand. Let me find it on my phone. Here, check out these photos—some of them are really creepy.

Tom : Yeah, they're pretty 7)**eerie**, but pictures like this are easy to 8)**photoshop**. The media, or whoever posted the photos online, could have faked the photos for 9)**clicks**.

Pei-chi : You don't think *all* the photos are fake, do you?

🎧 Vocabulary

1) **paranormal** [ˌpærəˋnɔrməl] (a.) 超自然的

2) **tabloid** [ˋtæblɔɪd] (n.) 小報，八卦報

3) **specialize** [ˋspɛʃəˌlaɪz] (v.) 專門從事，專攻

4) **sensational** [sɛnˋseʃənəl] (a.) 聳動的，轟動 社會的

5) **spooky** [ˋspuki] (a.)（口）令人毛骨悚然的， 幽靈般的

6) **psychic** [ˋsaɪkɪk] (n.) 靈媒，通靈的人

7) **eerie** [ˋɪri] (a.) 怪異的，可怕的

8) **photoshop** [ˋfotoˌʃɑp] (v.) 數位影像處理

9) **click** [klɪk] (n./v.) 點閱（率）；點擊滑鼠

10) **explanation** [ˌɛkspləˋneʃən] (n.) 說明，解釋

11) **exposure** [ɪkˋspoʒɚ] (n.)（底片的）曝光， 曝露

12) **apparition** [ˌæpəˋrɪʃən] (n.) 亡靈，幻影

13) **selfie** [ˋsɛlfi] (n.) 自拍照（尤指用智慧型手機 拍攝上傳社群網站的照片）

Tom : Well, there may be other [10]explanations for some of the "ghosts." A long [11]exposure can create a ghostlike image. And on a cold day, the mist from your breath—or fog on the camera lens—can look like an [12]apparition.

Pei-chi : Even so, after looking at all these photos, I'm gonna think twice about taking [13]selfies. If I saw a strange face or a hand behind me in a selfie I took, I'd totally freak out.

佩琪：嘿，你看，國際新聞版也有靈異新聞耶！

湯姆：呃，上面寫來源是《每日郵報》，這家英國小報專門報導聳動新聞。是在講什麼？

佩琪：是關於一張靈異照片。這位女士出外野餐時幫親友拍照，後來發現照片上背後多出一隻詭異的手，那隻手不屬於同行的任何人。她一看到那隻手就嚇到起雞皮疙瘩。更可怕的是之後不久，被那隻手指著的這個男人就意外死亡了。你看，照片裡這個男人背後有一隻灰灰的手。

湯姆：手的顏色是很怪，但有可能是他旁邊這個女人的手。看起來不自然可能是光線或角度的關係。

佩琪：或許吧。新聞上還說，這位女士有拿照片去給超自然專家鑑定——應該是找靈媒吧——說那是一個多年前死亡的女人的手，這個女人跟照片中後來意外身亡的男人認識。

湯姆：嗯，聽起來很詭異，但沒辦法證實這個故事的真實性。

佩琪：也對啦。我昨天在網路上還看到好多泰國的靈異照片。我拿手機找找看。來，你看這些照片——有些還滿可怕的。

湯姆：是啊，真的很怪異，但這種照片很容易電腦合成製作。媒體或是在網路上 po 照片的人，可能會造假衝點閱率。

佩琪：你不會覺得這些照片全都是假的，對吧？

湯姆：這裡面的一些「鬼」可以有其他解釋。長時間曝光過會造成類似鬼影的影像。冷天拍照時，呼吸產生的霧氣——或是相機鏡頭上的霧——看起來很像鬼。

佩琪：即便如此，看過這些照片之後，我以後自拍之前要多想想了。要是看見自拍照背後多出一張臉還是一隻手，我一定會嚇死。

英國《每日郵報》是專門報導聳動新聞的小報。2017 年 6 月 12 日頭版頭條為「獨家公開 黛安娜私密錄影帶」。

Language Guide

get goose bumps 起雞皮疙瘩

也可以拼做 goosebumps。人在感覺冷或感到害怕、興奮、肉麻時會起雞皮疙瘩。「讓人起雞皮疙瘩」則說 give sb. goose bumps。

A: How's the water?
水裡舒服嗎？

B: Cold! Look—I've got goose bumps all over my arms.
好冷！你看——我兩條手臂都是雞皮疙瘩。

I suppose (so). 或許吧。

這句話是用來表示模稜兩可的贊同，當別人作出提議或表達意見，你沒意見或是不想多說什麼的時候，就可以用這句話帶過。

A: Is it OK if I borrow your car tonight?
我今天晚上可以跟你借車嗎？

B: I suppose. Just have it back before eleven.
可以吧。但十一點前要歸還。

062 *Gui da qiang* 鬼打牆

Tom : You're from Kaohsiung, right? Here's an article about your hometown. How about using it for today's lesson?

Pei-chi : OK. Let's see—it's about a [1]**fatal** accident in the Cross-harbor Tunnel. The Cross-harbor Tunnel is famous for paranormal activity, and this article is about the *gui da qiang* [2]**phenomenon**.

Tom : What does *gui da qiang* mean?

Pei-chi : The [3]**literal** [4]**translation** is "ghost hits wall." It describes a situation where you keep going in circles and can't seem to escape a place. The article says a group of friends was riding through the tunnel at night and when they reached the other end they noticed somebody was missing. The tunnel is only a little over a kilometer long, but they waited at the entrance for over an hour and he never [5]**showed up**. When one of them rode back into the tunnel and brought him out, he **looked like he'd seen a ghost**.

Tom : Did his [6]**scooter** [7]**break down** in the tunnel?

Pei-chi : No. He said he saw his friends stop up ahead in the tunnel and so he stopped too. After a while, he asked them when they wanted to get going, but they didn't answer. He started to feel like something wasn't right, so he got back on his scooter and started riding. That's when he ran into his friend and they rode out together.

Tom : What if he hadn't started riding? Would his friend have been able to find him?

Pei-chi : Who knows? Maybe he would have been carried away by ghosts. In the article it says that locals all know never to stop inside the tunnel, because if you have a weak [8]**constitution** you may be taken away by ghosts.

063 Vocabulary

1) **fatal** [ˋfetəl] (a.) 致命的

2) **phenomenon** [fəˋnɑmə͵nɑn] (n.) 現象，複數：**phenomena** [fɪˋnɑmə͵nə]

3) **literal** [ˋlɪtərəl] (a.) 照字面的，原義的

4) **translation** [trænsˋleʃən] (n.) 翻譯，譯文

5) **show up** [ʃo ʌp] (phr.) 出現，出席

6) **scooter** [ˋskutɚ] (n.) （車輪小的）機車，速克達

7) **break down** [brek daʊn] (phr.) 故障，拋錨

8) **constitution** [͵kɑnstɪˋtuʃən] (n.) 體質，體格

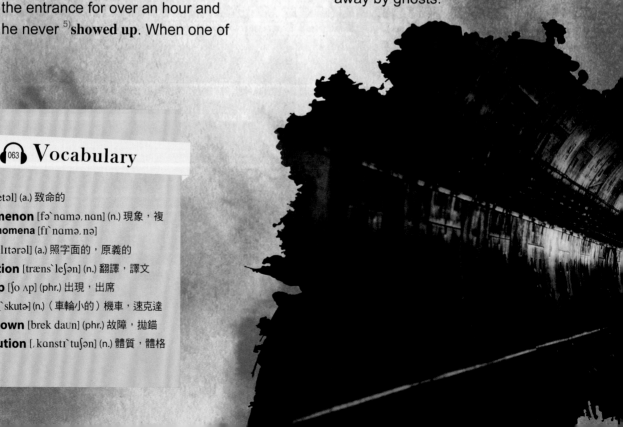

Tom : Does that mean you would die?

Pei-chi : Well, usually *gui da qiang* means that you keep going in circles until 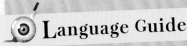 **the break of dawn**. If you get taken to some remote place, we have another saying for that. And if you get taken by ghosts and die, there's another saying for that too. We have a *lot* of stories about ghosts, ha-ha.

Tom : Well, that's OK—as long as they're not true. They're not true…right?

湯姆：妳是高雄人對吧？這裡有一篇妳家鄉的新聞，我們今天用這上課如何？

佩琪：好呀。我看看——這是在講過港隧道發生死亡車禍。過港隧道靈異事件頻傳很有名，這篇報導有提到「鬼打牆」的現象。

湯姆：什麼是「鬼打牆」？

佩琪：字面直譯為「鬼打牆」，是指一直在原地繞圈走不出來的狀況。報導上說：一群年輕人騎機車夜遊通過這個隧道發現有人不見了。這條隧道只有一公里多，但這群人在隧道口等了一個多小時，那個人還是沒出現。有人騎車回隧道裡找，才把神色驚慌的同伴帶出來。

湯姆：那個人的機車是在隧道裡拋錨嗎？

佩琪：不是。他說他看到前面的朋友在隧道裡停車，他也跟著停下來。過了一會兒，他問那些人何時才要繼續走，但那些人都沒回應。他發覺不對勁，於是坐上機車騎走，才遇到他的朋友，一起出來。

湯姆：如果他沒繼續騎呢？他的同伴也能找得到他嗎？

佩琪：誰知道呢，說不定就被鬼帶走了。報導上說：當地人都知道在這個隧道裡絕對不可以停車，因為體質較弱的人，可能會被鬼帶走。

湯姆：被鬼帶走是指死亡嗎？

佩琪：呃，一般說「鬼打牆」就只是在原地兜圈子一直到天亮。如果是被帶到偏僻的地方，我們有另一種說法。如果是被鬼帶走而死亡，我們還有另一種說法…跟鬼有關的傳說講不完的，哈哈。

湯姆：嗯，無所謂——只要不是真的就好。都不是真的…對吧？

Language Guide

look like (as if/as though) one has seen a ghost 神色驚慌

當我們看到一個人一臉恐懼、驚慌失措，會問他「你是看到鬼喔？」You look like you've seen a ghost! 就是這句話的英文版。

A: What's wrong? <u>You look like you've seen a ghost!</u>
怎麼了嗎？你一副看到鬼的樣子！

B: I almost got hit by a car crossing the street.
我過馬路時差點被車撞。

the break of dawn 破曉

也可以說 the crack of dawn，是指天空一剛開始亮的時候。

A: Are you getting up early for your trip tomorrow?
你們明天要早起出遊嗎？

B: Yeah. We're leaving at <u>the crack of dawn</u>.
是啊。我們天一亮就要上路。

064 *Moo-sin-a* 魔神仔

Pei-chi : Weren't you asking me about what happens when somebody's taken away by ghosts?

Tom : Yeah, when we were reading the article about that tunnel in Kaohsiung. Why?

Pei-chi : I saw an article online today about someone being taken away by ghosts!

Tom : Really? Let's read it!

Pei-chi : Here it is. It says that an old farmer from Hsinchu disappeared while he was picking bamboo shoots in the mountains. On the advice of locals, his family went and prayed at a nearby earth god temple and then bought some 1)**firecrackers** and went into the mountains with a 2)**rescue** team. They searched for hours with no luck, but as soon as they set off the firecrackers, they found the old farmer in a spot they'd already searched a dozen times.

Tom : Wow, that's really weird.

Pei-chi : The reporter asked a folklore expert about it, and he said that according to legend, when people get lost in the mountains under strange circumstances, it may be because of an encounter with a female spirit called a *moo-sin-a*. When that happens, the family needs to gather a group of strong men and bang 3)**gongs** or set off firecrackers while they search for the missing person. Little boys are even told that if they get lost in the mountains they should pull down their pants and 4)**pee** on the ground. The idea is to break the spell by using their "yang energy" to 5)**overcome** the "yin energy" of the *moo-sin-a*.

Tom : So if girls get lost in the mountains, the peeing trick won't work?

Pei-chi : Probably not. Have you seen *The* 6)*Tag-Along*? It was a big 7)**box office** 8)**hit**.

Tom : No. I never watch horror movies.

065 Vocabulary

1) **firecracker** [ˈfaɪrˌkrækɚ] (n.) 鞭炮

2) **rescue** [ˈrɛskju] (n./v.) 營救，解圍

3) **gong** [gɔŋ] (n.) 鑼

4) **pee** [pi] (v./n.) 小便

5) **overcome** [ˌovɚˈkʌm] (v.) 克服，戰勝

6) **tag along** [tæg əˈlɔŋ] (phr.) 跟著某人

7) **box office** [bɑks ˈɔfɪs] (n.) 票房（收入）

8) **hit** [hɪt] (n.) 成功、受歡迎的事物

9) **disoriented** [dɪsˈɔriəntɪd] (a.) 失去方向感的，失去判斷力的

10) **gross** [gros] (a.) 令人噁心的，令人討厭的

11) **senile** [ˈsinaɪl] (a.) 老糊塗的，老邁的

12) **delirious** [dɪˈlɪriəs] (a.) 神經錯亂的

Pei-chi : Ha-ha. The movie is actually based on a true story. Years ago, a family went hiking in the mountains near Taichung. When they looked at the video they filmed during the hike, there was a little girl in red following them. But they were positive that she wasn't there at the time, and nobody who lived in the area knew who she was. Some people believe that she was a *moo-sin-a*.

Tom : Did anybody in the family disappear?

Pei-chi : Not that I know of. Ooh, there's a link here to a story about an old woman in Hualien who was taken away by a ghost. Let me take a look. It says she has trouble getting around, but they found her after she'd been missing for four days in a mountainous area that's really hard to get to. When they found her, she was weak and [9]**disoriented** and…eww, [10]**gross**! She had dirt and bugs in her mouth, but she said the person who brought her there had given her chicken and rice!

Tom : Wow, that *is* gross. But she could just be [11]**senile**, or maybe she was [12]**delirious** with hunger.

佩琪：你之前不是問我被鬼帶走會怎樣嗎？

湯姆：對啊，我們是讀到高雄那條隧道的新聞。怎樣了嗎？

佩琪：今天網路上剛好有人被鬼帶走的新聞喔！

湯姆：真的嗎？我們來讀這篇！

佩琪：在這裡：一位新竹的老農上山採竹筍失蹤。老農夫的家人聽從當地人的建議，去附近的土地公廟拜拜，然後買鞭炮跟救難隊上山。他們找了好久都沒消息，但一放鞭炮，就在已經來回找過十幾次的地方發現老農夫。

湯姆：這也太詭異了。

佩琪：記者就這件事去請教民俗專家，專家表示根據傳說，如果有人在山區莫名其妙迷路，就可能是碰到女性精靈「魔神仔（*moo-sin-a*）」，這種時候，親友要找一群壯漢，一路敲鑼或放鞭炮去找。人們還會教小男孩在山裡迷路要馬上脫褲子尿尿，用「陽氣」壓制山中女鬼的「陰氣」，以求破除魔障。

湯姆：如果是女生在山裡迷路，尿尿這招就沒效了？

佩琪：應該沒用。你有看過《紅衣小女孩》這部電影嗎？這部片很賣座。

湯姆：沒。我從來不看恐怖片。

佩琪：哈哈。這部電影是根據一個真實事件所拍攝而成的。很多年前，一家人去台中近郊山區健行。他們看健行時拍攝的錄影帶時，看到一個紅衣小女孩跟著他們。但他們確定當時那裡沒有那個人，當地居民也沒人認識她。有人認為她就是「魔神仔」。

湯姆：那一家人有人失蹤嗎？

佩琪：據我所知沒有。喔，旁邊這條連結是老太太在花蓮被鬼牽走的新聞，我看一下。報導說她行動不便，但失蹤四天之後竟然在很難抵達的山區裡找到她。她被發現的時候，身體虛弱、有點恍惚…噁！她嘴裡有泥土和昆蟲，說是帶她過去的人請她吃雞肉和飯！

湯姆：哇，還真噁心。但她可能是老糊塗了，也可能是餓到發昏了吧。

圖片來源：網路圖片

《紅衣小女孩》由程偉豪導演，於2015年上映。這部劇情靈感得自台灣都市傳説「紅衣小女孩」的驚悚電影，曾入圍2015年韓國富川奇幻影展創投項目、2015年金馬國際影展閉幕片及第53屆金馬獎四項提名。本片為《紅衣小女孩》三部曲的第一部。

圖片來源：網路圖片翻攝自 YouTube
台灣著名的靈異影片「紅衣小女孩」，錄影帶中可以清晰看到一個不知名的紅衣女孩跟在登山隊伍最後面。

066 Giving away rice dumplings
送肉粽

Pei-chi : Hey, I brought you a rice dumpling. Eat it while it's hot.

Tom : Wow, thanks! I love rice dumplings. But the Dragon Boat Festival was months ago. How come you brought me a rice dumpling?

Pei-chi : Because the news I brought for you to read today is about rice dumplings.

Tom : 🎧 **I'm so hungry I could eat a horse**, ha-ha. Can I eat while we read?

Pei-chi : Sure. It says here that there's a place in Changhua where they're going to "give away rice dumplings" tonight at ten.

Tom : So a lot of people will show up, right?

Pei-chi : Ha-ha, no—just the opposite. "Giving away rice dumplings" is a tradition in Changhua. When someone commits suicide by [1]**hanging**, the locals have a [2]**Taoist** priest perform a [3]**ritual**, and then take the rope used in the hanging to the seaside and burn it to keep the spirit of the suicide victim from "catching a replacement." In the folk religion, it's believed that if [4]**malevolent** spirits can find someone near where they died to take their place as a ghost, they can be reborn into a new life.

Tom : So why does the news report announce the [5]**location** where they're "giving away rice dumplings"?

Pei-chi : It's to remind people who live nearby to keep their doors and windows shut tight and not try to catch a [6]**glimpse** of the ritual. Otherwise, they may be "caught as a replacement."

Tom : And people driving by can also take a different [7]**route**?

Pei-chi : Yes. But "catching a replacement" doesn't just apply to suicides. There are stories about it happening in places where people often die in accidents, like roads where there are lots of fatal crashes or places where people often drown.

067 Vocabulary

1) **hanging** [ˋhæŋɪŋ] (n.) 吊死，絞刑
2) **Taoist** [ˋtauɪst] (a./n.) 道教的；道教徒。
   Taoist priest 即「道士」
3) **ritual** [ˋrɪtʃuəl] (n.) 儀式
4) **malevolent** [məˋlɛvələnt] (a.) 有惡意的，有害的
5) **location** [loˋkeʃən] (n.) 地點，位置，所在地
6) **glimpse** [glɪmps] (n.) 一瞥
7) **route** [raʊt / rut] (n.) 路徑，路線
8) **generation** [ˌdʒɛnəˋreʃən] (n.) 代，世代

Tom : So you're saying people get taken away by ghosts and die?

Pei-chi : Yeah. That's why the older [8]generation always tells us not to take trips to the beach or the mountains, or go out at night, during Ghost Month. 'Cause if we do, we may be "caught as a replacement" and die.

Tom : So why is that ritual called "giving away rice dumplings" anyway?

Pei-chi : Well, you finished your dumpling, so I guess I can tell you. You know how they wrap rice dumplings in string and hang them up? What does that remind you of?

Tom : Oh, I get it now. Good thing you waited to tell me, ha-ha. I just [10] **lost my appetite.**

佩琪：嗨，我帶了一個粽子給你，趁熱吃。

湯姆：哇，謝謝！我好喜歡吃粽子。但端午節過好久了，妳為什麼要買粽子給我？

佩琪：因為我今天要帶你讀的新聞，跟粽子有關。

湯姆：我快餓死了，哈哈。我可以邊吃邊讀嗎？

佩琪：好啊。這裡說：彰化今天晚上十點有一個地方要「送肉粽」。

湯姆：應該會很多人去吧？

佩琪：哈哈，正好相反！「送肉粽」是彰化的習俗。如果有人上吊自殺，當地人會請道士作法，再將上吊用的繩子送到海邊燒掉，以免自殺者的鬼魂「抓交替」——在民間信仰中，相信懷著怨恨的鬼魂要在死亡地點附近抓人來代替他當鬼，他才能去投胎。

湯姆：那為什麼要在新聞上公布「送肉粽」的地點呢？

佩琪：是要提醒住附近的人緊閉門窗，不要好奇偷看儀式。否則可能會被「抓交替」囉。

湯姆：而且開車經過的人也好繞道而行？

佩琪：沒錯。不過抓交替並不只限於自殺。多次發生意外造成死亡的地點，像是一再發生死亡車禍的路段、經常有人溺斃的水域，都會有抓交替的傳說。

湯姆：所以這就是被鬼帶走會死掉的情況？

佩琪：沒錯。所以每到農曆七月，老一輩都會叮嚀我們不要到海邊、山裡玩，也不要在夜裡出門。因為如果這麼做，可能會被捉交替而死亡。

湯姆：但為什麼那個儀式要叫做「送肉粽」呢？

佩琪：呃…你粽子已經吞下去了吧？我應該可以跟你說了。你也知道包粽子會用繩子把粽子吊起來吧？這讓你聯想到什麼嗎？

湯姆：喔，我懂了。還好妳等到現在才告訴我，哈哈。我的食慾全消了。

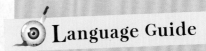

068 Ghost marriage 冥婚

Tom : Hey, look. There's a red envelope on the ground. It looks pretty thick.

Pei-chi : If you see a red envelope on the ground, *never* pick it up!

Tom : Why not?

Pei-chi : In Taiwan, when some women die before they 🎧 **tie the knot**, their family may try to find them a [1)]**groom** anyway. They put a slip of paper with their daughter's date of birth and death in a red envelope along with things like ghost money and [2)]**locks** of her hair, and then leave it on the sidewalk. Then if a "lucky groom" picks it up, he has to marry the dead daughter.

Tom : But who would agree to that!?!

Pei-chi : They say you don't have a choice because she'll follow you whether you agree or not. And sometimes the girl's family will offer a generous [3)]**dowry**, which may be hard to [4)]**turn down**.

Tom : But why do they try to marry their daughter off if she's already dead?

Pei-chi : According to tradition, sons are supposed to [5)]**inherit** everything. It isn't acceptable for unmarried daughters to stay in the family even if they're dead. And so her parents try their best to marry her off, so another family can [6)]**worship** her. I get mad just thinking about it—it's so [7)]**sexist**!

Tom : Yeah, really. I'm having trouble 🎧 **wrapping my head around it**.

Pei-chi : 🎧 **Tell me about it.** But there are also situations where guys willingly accept a ghost marriage. Like sometimes when a guy's [8)]**fiancée** dies, he'll decide to marry her anyway.

Tom : That's actually kind of romantic—in a creepy sort of way. Does the law recognize ghost marriages?

Pei-chi : No, it's just a folk tradition. If a man enters a ghost marriage, he can still get married in real life later on. I remember reading about a guy who cheated on his girlfriend. She ended

069 Vocabulary

1) **groom** [ɡrum] (n.) 新郎
2) **lock** [lɑk] (n.) 一綹頭髮
3) **dowry** [ˋdaʊrɪ] (n.) 嫁妝
4) **turn down** [tɜn daʊn] (phr.) 拒絕
5) **inherit** [ɪnˋhɛrɪt] (v.) 繼承，遺傳
6) **worship** [ˋwɜʃɪp] (v.) 拜神，做禮拜
7) **sexist** [ˋsɛksɪst] (a./n.) 性別歧視的；性別歧視者
8) **fiancée** [ˌfiɑnˋse] (n.) 未婚妻，**fiancé** 即「未婚夫」，兩字發音相同
9) **much less** [mʌtʃ lɛs] (conj.) 更別說，更何況

up committing suicide, and to **make amends**, the guy told her family he'd be willing to marry her in a ghost marriage.

Tom : I guess he thought it was the responsible thing to do, ha-ha.

Pei-chi : Yeah, right. If I were her, I wouldn't forgive him for cheating, [9)]**much less** marry him!

對話中所討論「幫未婚女性死者找歸宿」，只是冥婚的情況之一。有些時候若論及婚嫁的男女雙雙過世，家屬也可能協議為他們舉辦冥婚。還有為未婚男性死者找「鬼新娘」的冥婚形式，一些窮困地區甚至會販賣女屍供應這類冥婚市場。

湯姆：嘿，妳看地上有個紅包。看起來蠻厚的耶。

佩琪：如果在地上看到紅包，千萬不可以撿喔！

湯姆：是會怎樣？

佩琪：在台灣，有些家庭會為沒有出嫁就過世的女兒找新郎。他們會在紅包裡放寫有女兒生辰、忌日的紙，以及冥紙、女兒的頭髮等等東西，然後放在路邊。如果有哪個「有緣人」撿到紅包，就要他跟死去的女兒冥婚。

湯姆：哪有人會答應這種事？！

佩琪：據說不同意也不行，因為不論答應與否，那個女鬼都會跟著你。而且有些時候女方會附贈豐厚的嫁妝，讓人難以拒絕。

湯姆：但為什麼女兒死了還要想辦法把她嫁出去？

佩琪：根據傳統習俗，一切都要由男丁繼承。沒有出嫁的女兒留在家裡是不能接受的，即使是死了也不行。所以她的雙親會想盡辦法把她嫁到別家去接受祭拜。想到這種事就讓我生氣──根本是性別歧視！

湯姆：對啊。對我而言真是匪夷所思。

佩琪：就是說啊。但也有男生自願冥婚的狀況。好比有時未婚妻過世，男生還是決定把她娶回家。

湯姆：那其實蠻浪漫的──但有點讓人發毛。法律認定冥婚嗎？

佩琪：不，這只是民間習俗。冥婚的男人以後還是可以結婚。我還看過一則新聞是男生劈腿，女生因此自殺，那個男生為了賠罪，向女方家人表示願意冥婚。

湯姆：我猜他以為這麼做就是在負責任，哈哈。

佩琪：真是夠了。我要是那女生才不會原諒他劈腿，更別說還要嫁給他！

Language Guide

tie the knot 結婚

tie the knot 字面上是「打個結」的意思，由於西方傳統婚禮上有打結的儀式，象徵新郎新娘的結合，因此這個片語就有「結婚」之意。

A: **Sheryl and Bill finally tied the knot.**
雪若兒和比爾終於結婚了。

B: **It's about time. They've been dating for five years!**
也是時候了。他們在一起五年啦！

wrap one's head around 理解

這個片語經常以否定句表示一件事難以理解，讓人想不通。

A: **Did you hear about Anthony Bourdain committing suicide?**
你聽說安東尼波登自殺了嗎？

B: **Yeah. I just can't wrap my head around it. He had so much to live for.**
聽說了。我真想不通。他的人生那麼有意義。

Tell me about it. 我也這樣覺得。

這句話是在同意別人的看法，表示自己有過相同的經驗，可以了解對方的感受。

A: **The professor's lecture today was so boring.**
教授今天的課有夠無聊。

B: **Tell me about it. I almost fell asleep.**
就是說啊。我差點睡著了。

make amends 賠罪，和解

amend 這個動詞是「修正，改過」，名詞固定加 s。這個片語用來表示為錯誤做出彌補。

A: **I'm so sorry I forgot your birthday. How can I make amends?**
真抱歉我忘了你的生日。我要怎麼彌補？

B: **How about a trip to Hawaii?**
帶我去夏威夷玩如何？

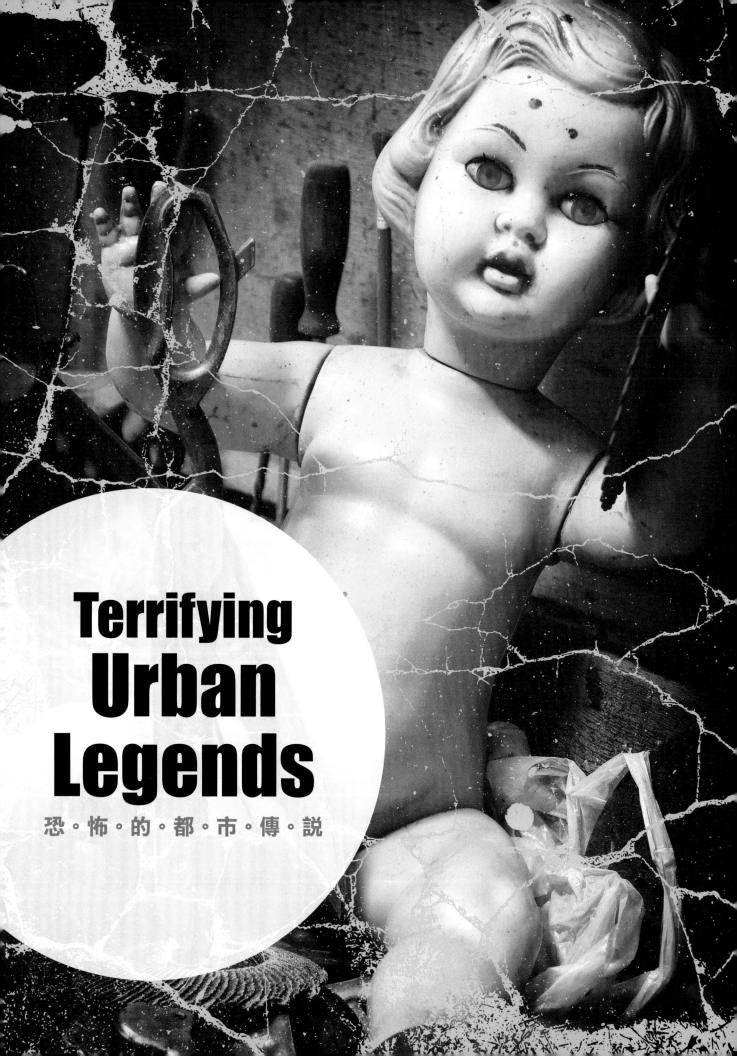

Terrifying Urban Legends

恐。怖。的。都。市。傳。説

The Hook Man
鉤子人

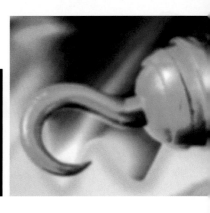

Late one night, a teenage boy drove his date to **lovers' lane** for a **make out** [1]**session**. He turned on the radio, put his arm around the girl, and began kissing her. Minutes later, the mood was broken when the music suddenly stopped and an [2]**announcer**'s voice came on, warning that a murderer had just escaped from the insane [3]**asylum**, which was located a half-mile from where they were parked. The announcer [4]**urged** anyone who saw a man wearing a steel [5]**hook** in place of his missing right hand to immediately report his [6]**whereabouts** to the police.

某個深夜，有個青少年開車載女友到情侶巷親熱。他打開收音機，手臂環抱著女孩，開始吻她。過了幾分鐘，音樂突然停了，破壞了氣氛，接著傳來播報員的聲音，警告有殺人犯逃離瘋人院，就距離他們停車處半英里。播報員敦促若看到有人斷掉的右手是用鋼鐵鉤代替，要立刻向警方報告他的行蹤。

The girl got frightened and asked to be taken home. The boy wasn't afraid, however, so he locked the doors, [7]**assured** his date they would be safe, and attempted to kiss her again. But she became [8]**frantic** and pushed him away, insisting that they leave. Upset about being rejected, the boy turned on the engine and [9]**peeled out** of the parking space. When they arrived at the girl's house, she got out of the car, and as she reached to close the door, she began screaming **at the top of her lungs**. The boy ran to her side to see what was wrong and there, hanging from the door handle, was a bloody hook!

女孩嚇壞了，要求男孩載他回家。但男孩不害怕，他鎖上車門，跟女友保證他們很安全，然後想繼續吻女孩。但女孩開始恐慌，推開男孩，堅持要離開。因被拒絕而惱羞成怒的男孩發動引擎，駛離停車處。他們抵達女孩的家門，她下車後要關車門時，突然大聲尖叫。男孩跑到她的車門那邊看是出了什麼問題，結果發現有個血淋淋的鉤子掛在門把上。

Vocabulary

1) **session** [ˋsɛʃən] (n.) 一段（用來進行特定活動的）時間
2) **announcer** [əˋnaʊnsə] (n.) 新聞播報員，主持人
3) **asylum** [əˋsaɪləm] (n.) 精神病院；此為舊式用法，精神病院現在大多稱為 **mental hospital**
4) **urge** [ɝdʒ] (v.) 力勸，催促
5) **hook** [hʊk] (n./v.) 鉤子，釣魚鉤；鉤住
6) **whereabouts** [ˋwɛrəˏbaʊts] (n.) 下落，行蹤
7) **assure** [əˋʃʊr] (v.) 確定，向…保證
8) **frantic** [ˋfræntɪk] (a.) 激動的，恐慌的
9) **peel out** [pil aʊt] (phr.) 迅速離開、汽車緊急加速駛離

Language Guide

lovers' lane 情侶巷
開車的情侶會將車子開到遠離塵囂、夜景很好的浪漫地點，或是僻靜無人的地點（如大型停車場）幽會，這種地方就是 lovers' lane。

make out 親熱
make out 這個片語的用法很廣，在文中是指情侶間的親密動作，一般包含親親、抱抱。

A: Why did your parents ground you?
你爸媽為什麼罰你禁足？

B: My dad caught me <u>making out</u> with a boy.
我老爸抓到我跟男生親熱。

at the top of one's lungs 大喊大叫
也可以說 at the top of one's voice，形容用非常大的聲音狂叫。

A: Why is your voice so hoarse?
你的聲音怎麼這麼沙啞？

B: I was screaming <u>at the top of my lungs</u> every time our team scored.
我們校隊每次進球時我都為他們大聲歡呼。

Man's Best Friend

人類最好的朋友

🎧 **Vocabulary** [074]

1) **faucet** [ˈfɔsɪt] (n.) 水龍頭

2) **sliding** [ˈslaɪdɪŋ] (a.) 滑動的

3) **blind** [blaɪnd] (n.)（常用複數）百葉窗，窗簾

4) **terrified** [ˈtɛrə.faɪd] (a.) 恐懼的，非常害怕的

5) **puzzled** [ˈpʌzəld] (a.) 困惑的，搞糊塗的，茫然的

[072] Once there was an old lady who lived alone with her dog. One day, she heard on the radio that a crazy murderer had escaped from prison and that everyone should lock all their doors and windows. So she locked every door and window in the house except for a small one upstairs to let some air in. She figured a murderer would never be able to get in through that one small window.

從前有個獨居老婦養了一隻狗。有一天，她聽廣播得知有個瘋狂的殺人犯逃離監獄，大家被告知要鎖好門窗。於是她鎖上屋子裡的每道門窗，只留樓上一道小窗讓空氣流通。她認為殺人犯不可能從那麼小的窗戶進來。

That night, the old lady went to bed with her dog lying by her on the floor as usual. She knew everything was OK because when she reached down, the dog licked her hand. A little later, a dripping sound woke her up. She reached down, and the dog licked her hand again. She got up and went downstairs to check the kitchen [1]**faucet**, but it wasn't dripping, so she went back to bed.

那晚，老婦像往常一樣上床，讓狗睡在身旁的地板上。她知道一切都沒問題，因為她將手往下伸時，狗舔了舔她的手。過了一會兒，有滴水的聲音吵醒她。她將手往下伸，狗又舔了她的手。她起身到樓下查看廚房的水龍頭，但沒在滴水，於是她回到床上。

But early in the morning, the dripping sound woke her up again. Thinking it must be coming from the bathroom, she went to check, and there was her dog, hanging dead in the shower, dripping blood into the tub. Written on the mirror were the words: "Humans can lick too." And behind her in the mirror, she saw the murderer!

但半夜時，她又被滴水聲音吵醒。她心想一定是浴室傳來的聲音，於是她去檢查，發現她的狗吊死在淋浴間，血滴到浴缸裡。鏡子上寫著幾個字：「人也會舔。」在鏡中的她身後，她看到了殺人犯！

The Killer in the Window
窗戶裡的殺手

073 A young woman was home alone watching TV on a cold winter night. The TV set was in front of a ²⁾**sliding** glass door, and the ³⁾**blinds** were open. Suddenly, she saw a creepy old man staring at her through the glass! She screamed, then grabbed the phone next to the couch and pulled a blanket over her head so the man couldn't see her while she called the police. She was so ⁴⁾**terrified** that she stayed under the blanket until the police arrived at her house.

在某個寒冷的冬夜，一位年輕女子獨自在家中看電視。電視是放在玻璃拉門前，百葉窗是拉開的。突然她看到有個可怕的老人透過玻璃門盯著她看！她驚聲尖叫，然後抓起沙發旁的電話，拉過一條毛毯蓋住她的頭，不讓那男人看到她在打電話報警。她因為過於害怕而一直躲在毛毯下，直到警察抵達她家。

It had snowed during the day, so the police decided to look for footprints. But there were no footprints at all in the snow outside the sliding door. ⁵⁾**Puzzled**, the police went back inside the house, and that's when they saw a trail of wet footprints on the floor leading to the couch where the girl was still sitting. The policemen looked at each other in silence for a moment. "Miss, you're very lucky," one of them finally said to her. "Why?" she asked. "Because the man wasn't outside the sliding door," he said. "He was in here, standing right behind the couch! What you saw in the window was his reflection."

那天下過雪，因此警察決定出去查看腳印。但玻璃拉門外的雪地都沒有腳印。大惑不解的警察回到屋內，這時他們看到一串濕濕的腳印通往女孩仍坐著的沙發。警察默默地對望了一下 。其中一名警察終於對她說：「小姐，妳很幸運。」她問：「為什麼？」。他說：「因為那男人不是在玻璃門外，他在屋內，就站在沙發後面！妳在窗戶看到的是他的倒影。」

The Missing Bride
失蹤的新娘

Vocabulary

1) **backyard** [ˌbækˋjɑrd] (n.) 後院
2) **hide-and-seek** [ˌhaɪdənˋsik] (n.) 捉迷藏
3) **groom** [ɡrum] (n.) 新郎
4) **attic** [ˋætɪk] (n.) 閣樓
5) **slam** [slæm] (v.)（使）猛撞，猛然關上
6) **briefcase** [ˋbrifˌkes] (n.) 公事包
7) **attendant** [əˋtɛndənt] (n.) 服務員
8) **rental** [ˋrɛntəl] (a./n.) 出租的；租賃車
9) **rear** [rɪr] (a.) 後面的
10) **mechanic** [məˋkænɪk] (n.) 修理工，技師
10) **driveway** [ˋdraɪˌwe] (n.) 私家車道
12) **identification** [aɪˌdɛntəfɪˋkeʃən] (n.) 身分證明
13) **butcher** [ˋbʊtʃɚ] (n.) 屠夫，肉販
14) **duct tape** [dʌkt tep] (n.)（布面）強力膠帶
15) **length** [lɛŋθ] (n.)（長條形的物品）截，段

[075] A young couple was about to get married, and the bride decided she wanted to hold their wedding in the [1]**backyard** of the large country house where she grew up. After the ceremony, they decided to play some games, and someone suggested [2]**hide-and-seek**. The [3]**groom** was "it," and after half an hour, he'd found everybody except for the bride. He wasn't worried though. He figured she must have gotten tired and gone inside to rest. When the party was over and all the guests had gone home, the groom and the bride's parents carefully searched the yard and house again, but couldn't find her anywhere. The next day, they went to the police and filed a missing person report, but the bride was never found.

　　一對年輕情侶即將結婚，新娘決定在她長大的鄉間別墅後院舉行婚禮。婚禮過後，他們決定玩些遊戲，有人提議玩捉迷藏。新郎當「鬼」，過了半小時後，他找到除了新娘之外的所有人。但他不太擔心，他認為新娘一定是太累，進屋去休息了。派對結束，所有賓客都回家後，新郎和新娘的父母再次仔細搜尋了後院和屋子，但都找不到新娘。隔天，他們向警方報告失蹤人口案件，但一直都沒找到新娘。

When the bride's mother died a few years later, her father climbed up to the [4]**attic** to go through his late wife's things. He found an old chest with a lock on it, and after a long search he finally located the key. Opening the lid, he was terrified to see his daughter's decaying body in the chest! Apparently, she'd climbed into the chest during the game of hide-and-seek, and the lid had [5]**slammed** shut, trapping her inside.

　　幾年後新娘的母親過世，她父親到閣樓上整理妻子的遺物。他發現一個上鎖的舊箱子，找了好一陣子，終於找到鑰匙。打開蓋子後，他驚恐地發現箱子裡是女兒腐爛的屍體！看來她是在玩捉迷藏時爬進這箱子裡，結果蓋子關上時自動上鎖，將她困在裡面。

The Knife in the ⁶⁾Briefcase
公事包中的刀子

⸨076⸩ One summer day, a woman stopped at a gas station to fill her tank. As the ⁷⁾**attendant** pumped gas, the woman told him she was in a hurry to pick up her daughter, who had just finished an art class in town. Just then, a well-dressed man walked over to her car and explained that his ⁸⁾**rental** car had broken down and he needed a ride into town for an important appointment. She said she'd be happy to give him a ride, so he opened the ⁹⁾**rear** door and started to get in. Then he said, "Oh, right. I'd better tell the ¹⁰⁾**mechanic** I'll be back later to pick up the rental. I'll be right back."

　　某個夏日，有個女子在加油站停車加油。服務員在加油時，那女子跟他說她急著去市區接剛上完美術課的女兒。此時一名穿著體面的男子走向她的車，說明他租來的車拋錨了，他想搭便車進城赴重要約會。女子說她樂意載他一程，於是他打開後門準備上車。然後他說：「喔，對了，我最好跟修車師傅說一聲，晚點會回來開那輛租賃車。我馬上回來。」

As the woman was waiting, she looked at her watch and realized she was late to pick up her daughter. So she drove off, leaving the man at the gas station. She forgot all about him until she pulled into the ¹¹⁾**driveway** with her daughter and saw that he'd left his briefcase in the back seat. She opened the briefcase to look for some form of ¹²⁾**identification** so she could get in touch with the man and return it. But inside she found nothing but a ¹³⁾**butcher** knife, a roll of ¹⁴⁾**duct tape** and several ¹⁵⁾**lengths** of rope!

　　那女子在等他時看到手錶，發現自己接女兒要遲到了。於是她把車開走，把那男子留在加油站。她完全忘了他，直到她載著女兒回家把車停在車道上時，才看到他留在後座的公事包。她打開公事包，想找找是否有身分證之類的東西，好聯絡那男子還給他。但她在公事包裡只發現一把屠刀、一卷強力膠帶和幾根繩子！

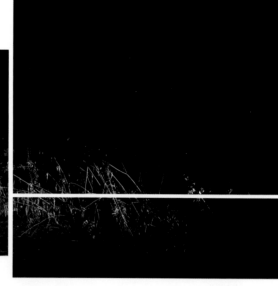

消失的搭便車旅人

The Vanishing ¹⁾Hitchhiker

🎧 **Vocabulary** 079

1) **hitchhiker** [ˈhɪtʃ͵haɪkə] (n.) 搭便車的人；動詞為 **hitchhike** [ˈhɪtʃ͵haɪk]
2) **honeymoon** [ˈhʌnɪ͵mun] (n.) 蜜月，蜜月旅行
3) **porch** [portʃ] (n.) 門廊
4) **hit-and-run** [͵hɪtənˋrʌn] (a.) 肇事逃逸的

🎧 078 A young couple was driving up the coast to spend their ²⁾**honeymoon** at a seaside hotel. They spotted a young woman in a white dress standing by the road with her thumb up, and as it was getting dark, they decided to give her a lift. "Can we give you a ride?" asked the man. "Yes, thank you," replied the young woman. "I have to get home. My parents will be worried sick." The man then asked her where she lived. "About ten miles up the road there's a gas station, and it's the white house across from it," she said before falling asleep in the back seat.

　　一對年輕夫婦正沿著海岸開車，要到濱海旅館度蜜月。他們看到路旁站著一名年輕女子，身穿白洋裝，豎起大拇指，此時天色已漸漸暗了，他們決定載她一程。那男子問道：「我們能載妳一程嗎？」那年輕女子回答：「好，謝謝你。我要回家，我父母會很擔心。」於是那男子問她住在哪裡。「這條路往前約十英里有座加油站，對面有間白色屋子。」說完她就在後座睡著了。

　　When they arrived at the white house a few minutes later, the man turned around to wake the woman up, but she was gone! A light came on and an elderly couple stepped out onto the ³⁾**porch**. "Can we help you?" the old man asked. When the young couple explained about the vanishing hitchhiker, the old man sighed and said "That was our daughter, and you're not the first to pick her up. She passed away seven years ago, killed by a ⁴⁾**hit-and-run** driver on the highway. They never caught whoever did it. I guess her spirit won't rest until they do."

　　幾分鐘後他們抵達那棟白色屋子，男子回頭要叫醒女子，但她消失了！有盞燈亮了，一對老夫妻出來走到門廊上，那位老先生問：「有事嗎？」這對年輕夫婦解釋有個搭便車旅人消失的事，老先生嘆口氣說：「那是我們的女兒，你們並不是第一個載到她的。她七年前過世了，在公路上被肇事逃逸的駕駛人撞死。他們從沒抓到肇事者。我猜沒抓到肇事者前，她的靈魂是不會安息的。」

The World's
Most Haunted
Places

世 ○ 界 ○ 十 ○ 大 ○ 鬼 ○ 域

Language Guide

William the Conqueror 征服者威廉

威廉一世（William I）是1066到1087年間的英國統治者。他對英國發動入侵之前，是諾曼第公國（現今法國北部）的領導者，宣稱他的遠親英王懺悔者愛德華（Edward the Confessor）因膝下無子後繼無人，曾許諾將王位傳給他；又在一次海難中營救另一位英王繼承人選哈羅德時，誆騙他立下白骨誓約（在聖經中夾藏聖人遺骨，在當時被視為不得毀約），答應要支持威廉繼任英王。懺悔者愛德華逝世後，哈羅德毀約即位為哈羅德二世，威廉在教皇的支持下，率領法蘭克大軍橫渡英吉利海峽入侵英國，滅了盎格魯薩克遜王朝，建立諾曼第王朝。

Anne Boleyn 安寶琳

圖片來源／維基百科

亨利八世（Henry VIII）的第二任皇后（在位期間1533至1536年），伊莉莎白一世（Elizabeth I）的生母。她在成為皇后之前，是第一任皇后凱薩琳的女侍官（maid of honor）。安寶琳被斬首之後，身首異處的屍體被草草埋葬於倫敦塔，即便在他女兒統治英國的時代，也未獲平反，直到維多利亞女王（Queen Victoria）時期才被正式埋葬。

🎧 080 The Tower of London

Built nearly 1,000 years ago by 🔊 **William the** [1]**Conqueror**, the Tower of London isn't just one of the city's top tourist [2]**attractions**, but also one of the most haunted. Why? As the historic castle [3]**served as** a prison for centuries, many people—including members of the royal family—were tortured, [4]**executed** and murdered here. Famous ghosts at the tower include 🔊 **Anne Boleyn**, who was [5]**beheaded** for [6]**adultery** on Tower Green in 1536 by order of her husband, Henry VIII. She can often be seen wandering the Green with her head under her arm. Be sure to check out the Bloody Tower, where two young 🔊 **princes, Edward V and Richard**, were murdered by the Duke of Gloucester. If you're lucky, you may hear the princes' screams echoing through the tower.

英國倫敦塔

近一千年前由征服者威廉興建的倫敦塔，不但是倫敦數一數二的旅遊景點，也是最著名的鬧鬼地點之一。為什麼？這座城堡歷史悠久，有幾百年是被當成監獄，包括皇室成員等許多人曾在此遭受酷刑、處決和殺害。倫敦塔出現的知名鬼魂中，包括安寶琳，她在1536年因通姦罪在倫敦塔綠地被丈夫亨利八世下令斬首。常有人看到她在綠地遊蕩，懷中還抱著自己的頭顱。一定要去看一看血腥塔，愛德華五世和理查這兩位年輕的王子就是在此遭到格洛斯特公爵殺害。你若幸運的話，可能會聽到王子的尖叫聲在塔內迴盪。

倫敦塔綠地的行刑台，安寶琳於1536年5月19日在此被處決。

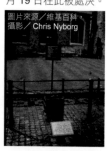

圖片來源／維基百科，攝影／Chris Nyborg

© Victoria Ditkovsky / Shutterstock.com
班夫溫泉酒店華麗的大廳。

🎧 (081) Banff Springs Hotel

    Located in the beautiful Canadian Rockies, Banff Springs Hotel was built in the 19th century as a [7]**luxury** hotel for train travelers. The hotel has [8]**hosted** many famous guests, including Marilyn Monroe and Queen Elizabeth. Some guests, however, checked in but never checked out. Most famous is the [9]**Phantom** Bride, who came here for her wedding [10]**banquet** in the 1920s. While walking down a [11]**staircase**, she tripped and fell to her death. Since then, hotel staff and guests have reported seeing her walking on the same stairs or dancing alone in the [12]**ballroom**. Another ghost is Sam the [13]**Bellman**, who died in 1976. Many guests have been helped by this friendly ghost, who always disappears before they can tip him. And then there's Room 873, where a man murdered his family. Guests in the room are often awakened by screaming, only to see bloody handprints on the mirror!

加拿大班夫溫泉酒店

    班夫溫泉酒店是 19 世紀為火車旅客興建的奢華酒店，位在美麗的加拿大洛磯山脈。這家飯店接待過多名知名賓客，包括瑪麗蓮夢露和伊莉莎白女王。不過有些旅客入住後再也沒有出來。最有名的是鬼新娘，她在 1920 年代到這裡舉辦婚宴。在下樓梯時失足跌落而死。自那時候起，就有旅館員工和旅客表示看到她走在同一道樓梯上，或在舞廳獨自跳舞。還有一個鬼是行李員山姆，他在 1976 年死亡。許多旅客都被這位友善的鬼服務過，但他總是在客人掏出小費前就消失。還有 873 號房間，有個男子曾在這裡殺害他的家人。此後這房間的旅客常被尖叫聲驚醒，然後看到鏡子上有血手印！

🎧 (082) Vocabulary

1) **conqueror** [ˈkɑŋkərə] (n.) 征服者

2) **attraction** [əˈtrækʃən] (n.) 景點，具吸引力的特色

3) **serve as** [sɝv æs] (phr.) 當作⋯使用

4) **execute** [ˈɛksɪˌkjut] (v.) 處死、處決

5) **behead** [bɪˈhɛd] (v.) 砍頭，斬首

6) **adultery** [əˈdʌltəri] (n.) 通姦

7) **luxury** [ˈlʌkʃəri] (a./n.) 豪華的，奢侈的；奢侈（品）

8) **host** [host] (v./n.) （以主人身分）招待，主辦，主持；主人

9) **phantom** [ˈfæntəm] (n.) 幽靈

10) **banquet** [ˈbæŋkwɪt] (n.) 宴會

11) **staircase** [ˈstɛrˌkes] (n.) 樓梯

12) **ballroom** [ˈbɔlˌrum] (n.) 開舞會用的大廳

13) **bellman** [ˈbɛlmən] (n.) 旅館服務員，即 bellhop [ˈbɛlˌhɑp]

© Andreas H / Shutterstock.com
拉汪賽烏的走廊有無頭幽靈遊蕩的傳聞。

© Hristo Vitanov Avramov / Shutterstock.com
印尼傳說中的食人女鬼龐蒂雅娜。

🎧 Vocabulary

1) **occupy** [ˈɑkjəˌpaɪ] (v.) 佔領，佔據
2) **captive** [ˈkæptɪv] (n.) 俘虜，囚徒
3) **retake** [riˈtek] (v.) 重新取得，奪回
4) **abandon** [əˈbændən] (v.) 丟棄，遺棄
5) **roam** [rom] (v.) 漫遊，流浪
6) **corridor** [ˈkɔrɪdə] (n.) 走廊，迴廊
7) **canal** [kəˈnæl] (n.) 運河
8) **outskirts** [ˈaʊtˌskɝts] (n.) 郊區，市郊
9) **appease** [əˈpiz] (v.) 撫慰，平息
10) **apparently** [əˈpærəntli] (adv.)
似乎，看樣子

🎧 Lawang Sewu

Lawang Sewu—which means "thousand doors" in Indonesian—was built in 1919 in Semarang on the island of Java as the headquarters of the 🅛🅖 **Dutch East Indies** Railway Company. When Japanese forces [1]**occupied** Indonesia in WWII, the basement was turned into a prison where many [2]**captives** died horrible deaths. And when the Dutch [3]**retook** Semarang in 1945, a number of soldiers died at Lawang Sewu. The building was [4]**abandoned** for many years, but since it opened to tourism in 2011, there have been many ghostly sightings. Visitors have seen headless spirits [5]**roaming** the [6]**corridors**, as well as the ghost of a Dutch woman who committed suicide there. Lawang Sewu is also said to be haunted by a *pontianak*—an evil female ghost who kills people and eats their organs.

印尼拉汪賽烏

拉汪賽烏是印尼語「千門」的意思，1919 年在爪哇島的三寶瓏興建時是作為荷蘭東印度鐵路公司的總部。第二次世界大戰時印尼被日軍佔領，拉汪賽烏的地下室被當成監獄，許多戰俘在此慘死。荷蘭人在 1945 年奪回三寶瓏時，許多士兵在拉汪賽烏戰死。這棟大樓被棄置多年，但在 2011 年開放觀光後，就出現許多鬧鬼傳聞。遊客曾看到無頭幽靈在走廊上遊蕩，還有在那裡自殺的荷蘭女鬼。拉汪賽烏據說也有「龐蒂雅娜」出沒，那是一種會殺人並吃掉受害人器官的邪惡女鬼。

🎧⁰⁸⁴ Isla de las Muñecas

Among the ⁷⁾**canals** of 🔊 **Xochimilco**, a neighborhood on the ⁸⁾**outskirts** of Mexico City, lies one of the world's creepiest islands Isla de las Muñecas, or Island of Dolls. Many years ago, the island's owner, Don Julián, found a dead girl and her doll floating near the shore. He buried the girl on the island, and hung her doll in a tree as a sign of respect. When Don Julián heard strange crying sounds at night, he began hanging more dolls on the island to ⁹⁾**appease** the girl's spirit. But ¹⁰⁾**apparently** it didn't work. Fifty years later, the man's body was found floating in exactly the same spot where he found the girl. The island has since become a tourist attraction, and visitors say the dolls' eyes follow them as they move. Some even say they can hear the dolls whispering, especially at night.

墨西哥玩偶島

墨西哥市郊區的索奇米爾科運河上，座落著全世界最恐怖的小島之一——玩偶島。多年前島主唐胡利安發現河岸附近漂著一名死去的女孩，還有她的玩偶。他將女孩埋在島上，並把她的玩偶吊在一棵樹上以示尊重。唐胡利安在晚上聽到奇怪的哭聲後，他吊了更多玩偶以安撫女孩的鬼魂。但這辦法似乎沒用。50 年後，他的屍體就在他發現女孩的同一個地點漂浮著。這座島後來成了旅遊景點，遊客還說那些玩偶的眼睛會跟著他們移動。有些甚至說可以聽到玩偶在竊竊私語，尤其是在晚上的時候。

Language Guide

Eastern State Penitentiary
東州監獄

位於美國賓州費城，1971年停用，哥德式城堡造型建築極具特色，1966年獲選進入美國國家史跡名錄（National Register of Historic Places），1994年開放成為觀光景點。

Al Capone 艾爾卡彭

一次世界大戰後，美國於1920年正式立法實行禁酒令（Prohibition），儘管立意良好，實際上卻提供了犯罪組織獲利機會，許多大小犯罪組織因從事私酒業，獲得非常可觀的利潤，其中最著名的就是芝加哥黑幫老大艾爾卡彭，他的犯罪帝國就是靠非法販酒建立起來的。

© Anton_Ivanov / Shutterstock.com

舊金山杜莎夫人蠟像館的艾爾卡彭像，描繪他在監獄中的生活情境。

艾爾卡彭在東州監獄的牢房。

086 Eastern State [1]Penitentiary

Considered one of the most haunted locations in the world, Eastern State Penitentiary first opened its doors in 1829. The prison was designed to hold 253 prisoners, each living in [2]**solitary** [3]**confinement** for their entire [4]**sentence**. It was believed at the time that solitary confinement could help [5]**reform** prisoners, but in reality it drove many of them [6]**insane**. Even Al Capone, the prison's most famous [7]**inmate**, claimed his cell was haunted by the ghost of a man he'd killed. Although [8]**executions** weren't carried out there, there were [9]**numerous** murders and suicides over the years. No wonder the place is haunted. In [10]**Cellblock** 4, people have reported visions of ghostly faces; in Cellblock 6, [11]**shadowy** figures have been seen moving along the walls; and in Cellblock 12, evil [12]**cackling** is often heard.

美國東州監獄

東州監獄是世上鬧鬼最嚴重的地點之一，在 1829 年首次啟用。監獄設計來容納 253 名囚犯，服刑期間均為單獨監禁。當時人們認為單獨監禁有助於教化囚犯，但實際上許多囚犯因此發瘋。就算是這所監獄最有名的囚犯艾爾卡彭，也聲稱他的牢房出現被他殺害者的鬼魂。雖然那裡並不執行死刑，但多年來發生過許多起凶殺和自殺，也難怪那地方會鬧鬼。曾有人表示在四號獄區看到鬼臉；有人在六號獄區看到牆上出現黑影在移動；在 12 號獄區則常傳出邪惡的咯咯笑聲。

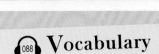

圖面來源：維基百科，攝影／Chris 73

🎧087 Poveglia Island

The island of Poveglia, which lies between Venice and Lido in the Venetian [13]**Lagoon**, was first settled in the 5th century by people [14]**fleeing** [15]**barbarian** attacks in Northern Italy. The island was eventually abandoned, but when the plague struck in the Middle Ages, plague victims were sent there to die. The dead, and even those too sick to [16]**protest**, were placed in large piles at the island's center and burned. A mental hospital was built on the island in the late 1800s, and it's said that a doctor performed cruel experiments on the patients there. The doctor later went crazy himself and jumped from the hospital's bell tower. The island was again abandoned in the 20th century, and is now closed to visitors. But fishermen who come too close report hearing the [17]**moans** of all the souls who died there. Some even hear the bell tower ringing, even though the bell was removed decades ago.

義大利波維利亞島

威尼斯潟湖中的波維利亞島位於威尼斯和利多之間，第五世紀義大利北部受蠻族攻擊，開始有人逃難到此定居。這座小島後來被棄置，但在中世紀爆發瘟疫時，瘟疫病患便被送來這裡自生自滅。死者和那些病入膏肓無力抵抗的人被堆到小島中央火化。1800 年代末期，島上興建了一間精神病院，據說有個醫生在那裡對病患進行殘忍的實驗。那位醫生後來自己也發瘋，從醫院的鐘樓跳下。小島在 20 世紀再度被棄置，現已封島拒絕訪客。但有漁民表示靠近小島時會聽到在那裡死亡的鬼魂悲鳴，有些人甚至聽到鐘樓的鐘聲響起，雖然那口鐘早在幾十年前就被移走了。

🎧088 Vocabulary

1) **penitentiary** [ˌpɛnəˈtɛnʃəri] (n.) 監獄
2) **solitary** [ˈsɑləˌtɛri] (a.) 單獨的
3) **confinement** [kənˈfaɪnmənt] (n.) 監禁，限制
4) **sentence** [ˈsɛntəns] (n./v.) 刑罰，刑期；判決
5) **reform** [rɪˈfɔrm] (n./v.) 改過，自新
6) **insane** [ɪnˈsen] (a.) （患）精神病的，精神病患者的
7) **inmate** [ˈɪnˌmet] (n.) （監獄、精神病院）收容的犯人、病人
8) **execution** [ˌɛksɪˈkjuʃən] (n.) 死刑
9) **numerous** [ˈnumərəs] (a.) 為數眾多的
10) **cellblock** [ˈsɛlˌblɑk] (n.) 監獄分區
11) **shadowy** [ˈʃædəwi] (a.) 模糊的，幽靈般的
12) **cackle** [ˈkækəl] (v./n.) 咯咯笑
13) **lagoon** [ləˈgun] (n.) 潟湖
14) **flee** [fli] (v.) 逃離，逃亡
15) **barbarian** [bɑrˈbɛriən] (n.) 野蠻人，異族人
16) **protest** [prəˈtɛst；ˈprotɛst] (v./n.) 抗議，反對
17) **moan** [mon] (v.) 哀歎，悲鳴，呻吟

攝影／Angelo Meneghini

Language Guide

Edinburgh Castle 愛丁堡城堡

愛丁堡城堡座落於愛丁堡市的城堡岩（Castle Rock）頂上，是愛丁堡市內的一道天際線，在市中心各角落都可看到。城堡目前由蘇格蘭文物局管理，仍有軍隊駐紮在內，是蘇格蘭最受歡迎的旅遊景點之一。城堡內有軍事博物館，陳列蘇格蘭、英國及歐洲的軍事歷史文物。

鬼城愛丁堡找鬼之旅

愛丁堡最為人推薦的找鬼之旅，就在皇家大道（Royal Mile）上的瑪麗金街（Mary King's Close）。這裡原為16世紀貧民區的地下街，當時住戶多一扇窗就得多付錢，窮人集居在這陰暗、骯髒的地方，黑死病引爆便一發不可收拾，於是政府下令封死入口，卻因此造成6百多人餓死和病死，因此這裡傳說鬧鬼。現在會有身穿16、17世紀服飾的人帶遊客探索民宅，體驗當時的恐怖。

© Scott Heaney / Shutterstock.com

皇家大道上的聖吉爾斯大教堂（St. Giles Cathedral）。

🎧089 Edinburgh Castle

With a history dating back to the 12th century, Edinburgh Castle sits on a hill [1]overlooking Scotland's capital, said to be one of the world's most haunted cities. The castle served as a royal [2]residence for hundreds of years before being [3]converted into a military [4]barracks in the 1600s. Over the centuries, the castle has [5]witnessed countless battles, executions and murders, which may explain why there are so many ghosts there. Visitors to the castle have reported seeing a phantom [6]piper, a headless drummer, and even the ghost of a dog wandering the grounds. When a paranormal [7]investigation was carried out at the castle in 2001, the scientists [8]involved were surprised by the results. Over 200 visitors were led through the castle in groups, and nearly half of them reported paranormal experiences!

英國愛丁堡城堡

歷史可追溯至12世紀的愛丁堡城堡，座落在俯瞰蘇格蘭首府的山坡上，愛丁堡據說是世上鬧鬼最嚴重的的城市之一。這座城堡做為皇家住所好幾百年，才在1600年代改為軍營。這千百年來，城堡見證過無數場戰役、處決和謀殺，也就不難解釋為何有這麼多鬼。參觀城堡的遊客曾表示看到風笛手幽靈、無頭鼓手，甚至有狗的鬼魂到處徘徊。2001年，城堡進行一項超自然研究調查時，參與的科學家對研究結果均感到驚訝。超過200名遊客分組由科學家帶領逛城堡，幾近半數遊客表示有超自然感應！

© flickr.com/photos/sinay/

🎧091 Vocabulary

1) **overlook** [ˌovɚˋluk] (v.) 眺望，俯瞰
2) **residence** [ˋrɛsədəns] (n.) 住所，居住地
3) **convert** [kənˋvɜt] (v.) 改變形態、用途
4) **barracks** [ˋbærəks] (n.) 軍營（恒用複數型）
5) **witness** [ˋwɪtnəs] (v./n.) 目擊，見證；目擊者
6) **piper** [ˋpaɪpɚ] (n.) 吹笛者，風笛手
7) **investigation** [ɪnˌvɛstəˋgeʃən] (n.) 研究，調查
8) **involve** [ɪnˋvɑlv] (v.) 涉入，致力
9) **construct** [kənˋstrʌkt] (v.) 建造
10) **brutal** [ˋbrutəl] (a.) 殘忍的，粗暴的
11) **resort** [rɪˋzɔrt] (n.) 度假村
12) **fall through** [fɔl θru] (phr.) 失敗，不能實現
13) **apparition** [ˌæpəˋrɪʃən] (n.) 亡靈，幻影

🎧090 Old Changi Hospital

[9]**Constructed** by the British as the Royal Air Force Hospital in 1935, the hospital was turned into a prison camp when the Japanese occupied Singapore during WWII. It was also used as a base by the Kempeitai, the Japanese Army's [10]**brutal** military police, who are said to have tortured and murdered many prisoners there. The hospital was returned to the British after the war, and later became a Singapore military hospital and finally a public hospital before closing its doors in 1997. A company bought the site in 2006 to turn it into a luxury [11]**resort**, but the plan soon [12]**fell through**. Some say it's because the old hospital is haunted. The building has been abandoned ever since, and those brave enough to visit have reported hearing loud screaming and seeing strange "shadow people." Others claim to have seen the [13]**apparitions** of bloody soldiers walking the halls.

新加坡舊樟宜醫院

這家醫院是英國在 1935 年興建的皇家空軍醫院，日本在第二次世界大戰佔據新加坡時，把醫院當戰俘營使用，也被日本殘酷的憲兵隊（日文發音 Kempeitai）當作總部，據說他們在這裡虐待和殺害許多囚犯。戰後醫院回到英國人手上，後來成了新加坡軍醫院，最後變成公立醫院，並在 1997 年關閉。有家公司在 2006 年買下這塊地，要將醫院改建成豪華度假村，但這項建案後來落空。有人說是因為舊醫院鬧鬼。此後這棟建築一直被棄置，有勇氣踏入醫院的人說會聽到巨大尖叫聲，看到奇怪的「人影」。另有人聲稱看到血淋淋的士兵亡靈在走廊裡徘徊。

© flickr.com/photos/beggs/

© A G Baxter / Shutterstock.com

© Sergey Goryachev / Shutterstock.com

🎧092 The Queen Mary

Aside from a short [1]**stint** as a troop transport ship during World War II, the RMS Queen Mary served as a luxury ocean [2]**liner** from 1936 to 1967. During that time, the ship was the site of at least one murder, a sailor being [3]**crushed** to death in the engine room, and children drowning in the pool. In 1967, the California city of Long Beach bought the Queen Mary and turned it into a floating luxury hotel. The rooms aren't cheap, but the ghosts of the deceased passengers get to stay for free. On the guided ghost tours offered [4]**year-round**, you may just see one of the over 100 ghosts said to haunt the ship. You can even spend the night in Cabin B340, where a staff member was murdered years ago. Some guests have reported having their covers pulled off and waking to see a dark figure standing by the bed!

英國瑪麗皇后號

皇家郵輪瑪麗皇后號（RMS 為 Royal Mail Ship 的縮寫）除了在第二次世界大戰期間短暫用來當部隊運輸船外，自 1936 年到 1967 年是豪華的遠洋客輪。這段時間裡，這艘船至少發生過一次凶殺案，還曾有一名水手在機艙中被壓死，另外有小孩在游泳池裡溺斃。1967 年，加州長堤市買下瑪麗皇后號並改造成水上豪華旅館。住宿費不便宜，但已故的乘客鬼魂可以免費入住。全年都有幽靈導覽服務，據說船上有一百多個幽靈出沒，你或許能在幽靈導覽中看到一個。你甚至可以在 B340 號艙房留宿一晚，多年前這裡有員工遭殺害。有些旅客曾說他們的被子被掀開，醒來時看到床邊站著一個黑影！

🎧094 Vocabulary

1) **stint** [stɪnt] (n.) 從事某項工作（或活動）的時間

2) **liner** [ˋlaɪnə] (n.) 有固定航班的郵輪、飛機。**ocean liner** 即「遠洋客輪」

3) **crush** [krʌʃ] (v.) 擠壓，壓扁，壓壞

4) **year-round** [ˋjɪrˋraʊd] (a.) 整年的

5) **rifle** [ˋraɪfəl] (n.) 步槍，來福槍

6) **tragedy** [ˋtrædʒədi] (n.) 悲劇，慘事，災難

7) **tuberculosis** [tʊˏbɝkjəˋlosɪs] (n.) 結核病

8) **widow** [ˋwɪdo] (n.) 寡婦

9) **grief** [grif] (n.) 悲傷，悲痛

10) **head** [hɛd] (v.) （朝特定方向）前往

11) **mansion** [ˋmænʃən] (n.) 豪宅

🎧 ⁰⁹³ Winchester Mystery House

When Sarah Pardee married William Winchester—owner of the Winchester ⁵⁾**Rifle** Company—in 1862, she had no idea her life would 🔊 **be marked by** ⁶⁾**tragedy**. Her only child died of a mysterious illness, and her husband died of ⁷⁾**tuberculosis** in 1881, leaving Sarah a ⁸⁾**widow** at the age of 41. In her ⁹⁾**grief**, she sought a medium to communicate with her dead husband. Through the medium, William told her that they'd been cursed by the spirits of all the people killed by Winchester rifles, and that to appease them, she must use their fortune to ¹⁰⁾**head** West and build them a house. So she moved to San Jose, California and hired a team of carpenters who worked night and day building a 🔊 **Victorian** ¹¹⁾**mansion**. When they 🔊 **hung up their** hammers 38 years later, at Sarah's death, the mansion had 160 rooms, 10,000 windows and 47 staircases—some leading nowhere. The house has been a tourist attraction since 1923, and many visitors report ghostly encounters on the third floor, where the servants lived. And if you smell roses—Sarah's favorite flower—that means her spirit is nearby.

© CREATISTA / Shutterstock.com

溫徹斯特神祕屋的一道怪門。

美國溫徹斯特神祕屋

　　莎拉帕狄在 1862 年嫁給溫徹斯特步槍公司的老闆威廉溫徹斯特時，沒料到自己的人生將充滿悲劇。她唯一的孩子死於神祕疾病，丈夫在 1881 年死於肺結核，讓她 41 歲時就成了寡婦。她在悲痛之下找靈媒與亡夫溝通。威廉透過靈媒告訴她，他們都被死在溫徹斯特步槍下的亡魂所詛咒，為了安撫這些亡魂，她必須用他們的財產到西部為亡魂建造一棟房子。於是她搬到加州聖荷西，聘請一群木匠日以繼夜地建造一棟維多利亞式豪宅。豪宅在 38 年後莎拉過世時終於完工，有 160 個房間、一萬扇窗戶和 47 道樓梯，而且有些樓梯是死路。這棟住宅自 1923 年成了觀光景點，許多遊客表示在三樓遇到靈異事件，那裡曾是僕人居住的地方。你若聞到莎拉最愛的玫瑰花香，那就表示莎拉的靈魂在附近。

圖片來源：flickr.com/photos/sfmine79/

🎧 Vocabulary

1) **descendent** [dɪˋsɛndənt] (n.) 子孫，後代
2) **(be) associated (with)** [əˋsoʃɪˌetɪd] (phr.) 有關聯
3) **construction** [kənˋstrʌkʃən] (n.) 建造，建築（物），動詞 **construct** [kənˋstrʌkt]
4) **bizarre** [bɪˋzɑr] (a.) 怪異的
5) **maze** [mez] (n.) 迷宮
6) **interior** [ɪnˋtɪrɪə] (n.) 內部

🐌 Language Guide

Baroque architecture 巴洛克式建築

文藝復興之後，17世紀的義大利開始出現巴洛克式裝飾風格的建築，其特點在於有豐富的情緒、華麗的裝飾和雕刻，以及強烈的色彩，追求自由奔放，室內色彩以紅、黃為主，大量飾以金箔、寶石和青銅材料，極盡奢華和繁瑣。法國凡爾賽宮（Palace of Versailles）即為當中代表性的建築之一。

BTW台灣最著名鬼屋
劉家古宅民雄鬼屋

🎧 095 This **LG** **Baroque-style** brick mansion in the town of Minxiong in Chiayi County was built in 1929 by a rich businessman named Liu Rong-yu for his family to live in. It was eventually abandoned after his [1]**descendents** all moved away, and because there's a graveyard nearby, there are many ghost stories [2]**associated with** the mansion.

這棟巴洛克式紅磚樓房位於台灣嘉義民雄，是富商劉溶裕於 1929 年為其家族興建。後因子孫陸續遷居住而荒廢，加上附近有墳場，關於古宅的各種靈異傳說因此產生。

BTW台灣最怪鬼屋
龍潭怪怪屋葉山樓

This strange building has been under [3]**construction** for 40 years and still isn't finished. Although many people call it the Longtan Haunted House, it isn't known to be haunted. The structure was designed and built by a man named Ye Fa-bao, who has been adding floors and making additions since the 1970s. With its [4]**bizarre** shape and [5]**maze**-like [6]**interior**, no wonder it's called a ghost house.

這棟古怪的房子蓋了四十年還沒蓋完，儘管許多人稱其為「龍潭鬼屋」，但這裡並沒有鬧鬼。這棟樓是由葉發苞先生自行設計興建，從 1970 年代開始不斷加高、擴建。這棟樓造型詭異，內部宛如迷宮，難怪會被稱為鬼屋。

圖片來源：TWOCHSE~commonswiki

Ghostly Encounters

好毛哦～～撞 。 鬼 。 經 。 驗

🎧⁰⁹⁹ Vocabulary

1) **fingertip** [ˈfɪŋɡəˌtɪp] (n.) 指尖
2) **pointer** [ˈpɔɪntə] (n.) 指針，指示物
3) **sleepover** [ˈslipˌovə] (n.)
   （美國）小孩到朋友家玩耍過夜的聚會
4) **flicker** [ˈflɪkə] (v.) 閃爍，顫動
5) **technically** [ˈtɛknɪklɪ] (adv.) 嚴格說來
6) **charge** [tʃɑrdʒ] (v./n.) 向前衝；衝鋒
7) **growl** [ɡraʊl] (v.) 嗥叫

🎧⁰⁹⁷ Ouija board 通靈板

Ashley : I have a scary story about a 🅛🅖 **Ouija board**.

Ben : What's that?

Ashley : It's a board with letters on it that you can use to communicate with spirits. Everybody sits around it and puts their ¹⁾**fingertips** on a ²⁾**pointer**, and when you ask questions, spirits answer by spelling out words.

Ben : Oh. We have a game like that called *die xian*. So what's your story?

Ashley : When my aunt was a teenager, she was having a ³⁾**sleepover** with friends, and they decided to play with a Ouija board. They asked if anybody was there, and the answer was "Yes." Then they asked the spirit to give them a sign, and all of the sudden the lights in the room started ⁴⁾**flickering**! When my aunt asked who the spirit was, it said it was her friend Ed, who had been missing for a week. She asked where he was, and he said he was in a lake—but then stopped communicating with them. A month later, a car was pulled out of a nearby lake, and Ed's body was found inside.

艾希莉：我有個恐怖的故事，是關於通靈板。

班　恩：那是什麼？

艾希莉：那是一塊板子，上面有字母，可以跟鬼魂溝通。大家圍坐在板子旁，把手指放在乩板上，問問題時，鬼魂會拼字回答問題。

班　恩：噢，我們有類似的遊戲，叫「碟仙」。那妳的故事是什麼？

艾希莉：我阿姨十幾歲時到朋友家過夜，他們決定一起玩通靈板。他們問說是不是有鬼在場，鬼回答說「有」。然後他們請鬼魂顯靈，突然房間的燈全部開始閃爍！我阿姨問鬼魂是誰，它回答說是她的朋友艾德，而他當時已經失蹤一星期。她問它身在哪裡，它說它在一座湖裡，然後對話就終止了。一個月後，一輛車被人從附近一座湖中拖出，而艾德的屍體就在車子裡。

098 Water ghost 水鬼

Liam : I didn't use to believe in ghosts, but then I had an encounter of my own.

Emma : Ooh, creepy! You saw a ghost?

Liam : Well, [5)]**technically** my dog saw it. I took Rusty hiking one day, and it was a weekday, so there was no one around. He usually just [6)]**charges** ahead on the trail, but **LG** **for some reason** he stopped in the middle and wouldn't move. I literally had to drag him along, and he was [7)]**growling** the whole way.

Emma : So he must have seen something—or sensed it.

Liam : Yeah. I ended up getting mud on my shoes, so I went to the stream next to the trail to wash it off. Rusty suddenly started barking like crazy and I slipped and fell into the water. The water was really shallow, but for some reason I couldn't climb out. I felt like there were hands on my ankles pulling me down!

Emma : You must have run into a water ghost.

Liam : Luckily somebody walking by saw me and pulled me out.

里安：我以前都不相信有鬼，但後來我自己有一次碰到了。

艾瑪：好毛喔！你看到鬼啦？

里安：嚴格說起來是我的狗看到。有一次我帶羅斯提去爬山。那天不是假日，所以附近都沒人。平常牠在山路上都會一直往前衝，但那天很奇怪，牠走到一半就不肯動。我真的是硬拖著牠走，而牠一路上一直低吼。

艾瑪：那牠一定是看到什麼——或感應到了。

里安：是啊。後來因為鞋上沾了泥巴，我就到路旁的小溪洗鞋。羅斯提忽然狂吠起來，我滑了一跤跌進水裡。那裡的水很淺，但奇怪的是我怎麼都爬不出來，我感覺到有手在拉我的腳踝要拖我下去！

艾瑪：你一定是碰到水鬼了。

里安：幸好有人經過看到把我拉起來。

Language Guide

Ouija board 通靈板

西方人會聚在一起玩通靈板（Ouija board [ˋwidʒə bord]）來和鬼神溝通，詢問有關未來的問題。Ouija 為法語 oui 與德語 ja 的組合，這兩個字相當於英語的 yes，通靈板上有字母 A 到 Z，以及數字 0 到 9，靈魂可用上面的字來回答問題，對未來做出預測，有點類似中國人玩的「碟仙」。

for some reason 不知為何

也可以説 for some reason or other。當你不知道要怎麼解釋一件事時，就可以用這句話表達。

A: You haven't been sleeping well lately?
你最近都沒睡好嗎？

B: No. **For some reason** I keep waking up in the middle of the night.
沒。不知為何我半夜都會醒過來。

102 ## Vocabulary

1) **suffer** [ˋsʌfɚ] (v.) 遭受，受苦
2) **anxious** [ˋæŋkʃəs] (a.) 焦慮的，擔心的
3) **funeral** [ˋfjunərəl] (n.) 葬禮
4) **boarding school** [ˋbordɪŋ skul] (n.) 寄宿學校
5) **bloodshot** [ˋblʌd͵ʃɑt] (a.) 有血絲的
6) **exorcist** [ˋɛksəsɪst] (n.)（以禱告或符咒）驅邪除魔的法師

The *Shoujing* ritual
收驚

100

Aaron : My uncle is a Taoist priest, and sometimes people who've had paranormal experiences come to him for the *shoujing* ritual.

Sarah : What's that?

Aaron : Taoists believe that people have more than one soul, and that when you [1]**suffer** a big shock, some of them can leave the body. So priests perform the *shoujing* ritual to bring the souls back into your body.

Sarah : Having your soul leave your body sounds pretty serious.

Aaron : Most people just come for the *shoujing* ritual because they're feeling [2]**anxious**, but I've seen more serious cases. When this one guy arrived, he was **white as a sheet** and sweating all over. And he had this look in his eyes like he wanted to kill someone.

Sarah : Did your uncle say what was wrong with him?

Aaron : Yeah. He said the guy got possessed by a ghost when he was walking by a place where a [3]**funeral** was being held. It took a lot of effort for my uncle to save him.

亞倫：我的伯父是道士，碰到靈異事件時，許多人會去找他「收驚」。

莎拉：那是什麼？

亞倫：道教相信人不只有一個魂魄，受到巨大驚嚇時，一些魂魄可能飛出體外，要請道士收驚把魂魄收回來。

莎拉：魂飛魄散聽起來很嚴重。

亞倫：雖然大部分來收驚的人都只是因為心神不寧，但我看過情況很糟的。有個人送來的時候皮膚蒼白、渾身冒汗。他盯著人看的表情，像是要殺人的樣子。

莎拉：你伯父有說他為什麼會這樣嗎？

有啊。說是這個人經過辦喪事的地方被鬼附身。我伯父費了很大功夫才把那個人救回來。

🎧 101 Possession 中邪

Mark : Speaking of possession, I had a teacher who saw a possessed girl once.

Eva : Whoa! Was this at your school?

Mark : No. My teacher used to teach at a ⁴⁾**boarding school**, which is where it happened. They were having movie night one night, and one of the students left to go to the bathroom. She was gone for a really long time, so my teacher went to check on her. When he got there, she was sitting in the corner 🅛🅖 **foaming at the mouth**. Her eyes were ⁵⁾**bloodshot**, and she was speaking in a deep voice.

Eva : What was she saying?

Mark : It was some strange language that my teacher couldn't understand. She 🅛🅖 **snapped out of it** after a couple minutes, and when my teacher took her back to her room, he saw the words "I love Satan" **carved** on the side of her bed.

Eva : Did they call in an ⁶⁾**exorcist** or something?

Mark : No. She left the school right after that.

📀 Language Guide

white as a sheet 面色慘白

也可以說 white as a ghost，是在形容一個人看起來面色慘白。

A: Why did you ask if I've seen a ghost?
你幹嘛問我是不是看到鬼？

B: Because you're white as a sheet!
因為你一臉慘白啊！

foam at the mouth 口吐白沫

對話中的 foam at the mouth 就是字面上「口吐白沫」的意思，大都用在生病、身體不適的情況。這個說法有另一個使用情況，是用來形容一個人極為生氣，「氣到口吐白沫」。

A: Look—that dog is foaming at the mouth.
你看——那條狗口吐白沫耶。

B: We'd better stay away from it. It may have rabies.
我們最好離牠遠一點。牠說不定有狂犬病。

snap out of it 回神過來，忽然恢復

snap 有「啪一聲」、「猛然間」的意思。在對話中，snap out of it 表示忽然就從不好的情況當中恢復過來，用來表示心情、精神回復。

A: What did your teacher say when he caught you daydreaming in class?
你上課發呆被老師抓到時，他有說什麼嗎？

B: He told me to snap out of it and pay attention.
他叫我打起精神，專心聽講。

馬克：說到附身，我有個老師見過一個女孩被附身。

愛娃：哇！是在你學校發生的嗎？

馬克：不是，我的老師以前在寄宿學校教書，這件事是在那裡發生的。有一晚他們舉辦電影之夜，有個學生離開去上廁所。她去了很久，於是我的老師出去看看她。等他找到她時，她坐在角落口吐白沫，雙眼充滿血絲，用很低沉的聲音說話。

愛娃：她在說什麼？

馬克：是一種很奇怪的語言，我的老師聽不懂。幾分鐘後她突然回神過來，我的老師帶她回到她的房間時，看到她的床邊刻著「我愛撒旦」這幾個字。

愛娃：他們有找人來驅魔之類的嗎？

馬克：沒有，那件事後她就離開學校了。

103 *Gui ya chuang* 鬼壓床

Chloe : The last time I went to Thailand, I had a *gui ya chuang* experience.

Jacob : A *what* experience?

Chloe : It means there's a ghost pressing on your bed. Me and a friend [1)]**booked** a room in Bangkok online, but when we got to the [2)]**guesthouse** it was really creepy. It had this steep, dark staircase, and walking up the stairs 🅛🅖 **sent a chill up my spine**.

Jacob : Hmm, that doesn't sound good.

Chloe : No. And when I opened the door to our room I saw a dark shadow next to the [3)]**wardrobe**. But when I turned on the light, there was nothing there. My friend went to take a shower, and I got in bed and fell asleep. Suddenly, I felt something heavy pressing on my chest, and I couldn't move. I couldn't even open my eyes. I tried to scream, but no sound came out. I was completely [4)]**terrified**. After a while, my friend walked out of the bathroom and called my name, and I finally snapped out of it.

Jacob : Hmm, it sounds like a case of 🅛🅖 **sleep** [5)]**paralysis** to me.

Chloe : Maybe. In any case, whenever I go traveling now, I bring a protection [6)]**amulet** with me. And when I enter my hotel room, I always knock first. Then I go into the bathroom and turn on the faucet and [7)]**flush** the toilet….

Jacob : Ha-ha. Looks like your experience has made you pretty [8)]**superstitious**.

克蘿伊：上次去泰國時，我被「鬼壓床」。

雅　各：被什麼？

克蘿伊：意思是被鬼壓在床上。我跟一個朋友上網訂了一間曼谷的小旅館，但我們一到那間旅館就覺得很可怕。樓梯間很陡、很暗，我一邊爬樓梯一邊就覺得背脊發涼。

雅　各：嗯，聽起來不妙。

克蘿伊：是不妙。一打開房門，我就看到衣櫃旁有一個黑影。但開燈之後卻什麼也沒有。我的朋友先去洗澡，我躺在床上就睡著了。忽然間，我發現有很重的東西壓在胸口，我完全動不了，連眼睛都睜不開，我很想尖叫卻叫不出聲來。我非常害怕。過了一會兒，我朋友走出浴室叫了我一聲，我才掙脫那種感覺。

雅　各：呃…聽起來是「睡眠癱瘓」。

克蘿伊：或許吧。反正，後來我到任何地方旅行都帶著護身符，進旅館房間前一定先敲門，然後進廁所開水龍頭放一下水，再沖一下馬桶…

雅　各：呵呵，看來那次經驗讓妳變得有夠迷信。

🎧 105 Vocabulary

1) **book** [bʊk] (v.) 預訂，預約

2) **guesthouse** [ˋgɛst͵haʊs] (n.) 民宿，小旅館

3) **wardrobe** [ˋwɔrd͵rob] (n.) 大衣櫃

4) **terrified** [ˋtɛrə͵faɪd] (a.) 嚇壞的，恐懼的

5) **paralysis** [pəˋræləsɪs] (n.) 癱瘓，麻痺

6) **amulet** [ˋæmjəlɪt] (n.) 護身符，避邪物品

7) **flush** [flʌʃ] (v.) 沖水

8) **superstitious** [͵supɚˋstɪʃəs] (a.) 迷信的

9) **cord** [kɔrd] (n.) 細繩

10) **poke** [pok] (v.) 伸出，伸進，戳

Out-of-body experience
靈魂出竅

Ruby : It seems like strange things happen most often when you're lying in bed. I once had an OBE.

Jack : What does that 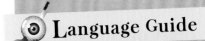 **stand for**?

Ruby : Out-of-body experience. It sometimes happens when people almost die on the operating table, but it usually happens when you're falling asleep.

Jack : Then how do you know it's not just a dream?

Ruby : Well, I'm sure mine wasn't a dream. I was lying in bed one night, and I heard a buzzing in my ears. Then I felt myself floating up in the air until I almost reached the ceiling. When I turned over, I saw my body lying on the bed below me. The weirdest part is that there was a shiny silver 9)**cord** connecting me with my body on the bed. Then I heard a knock on the door, and I floated over, 10)**poked** my head through the wall, and saw my mom standing there. After I returned to my body, I fell asleep. And when I asked my mom the next morning if she'd knocked on my door, she said "Yes."

露比：好像怪事經常都發生在躺在床上的時候。我曾有過 OBE。

傑克：那是什麼意思？

露比：靈魂出竅。在手術台上瀕死之際的人有時候會發生這種事，但通常是發生在正要入睡時。

傑克：那妳怎麼知道那不是作夢？

露比：我確定我當時不是在作夢。有天晚上我躺在床上，聽到耳邊傳來嗡嗡聲。然後我感覺身體飄浮在空中，直到幾乎碰到天花板。我翻過身來看到我的身體躺在下方的床上。最奇怪的是，有一條閃亮的銀線連接著我和我在床上的身體。接著我聽到敲門聲，我飄過去，頭穿過牆壁，看到我媽媽站在門外。等我回到身體後，就睡著了。隔天早上我問我媽媽是不是有敲我的門，她說「有」。

Language Guide

send chills up one's spine
讓人背脊發涼

對話中用這個片語表示緊張害怕、背脊發涼的感覺。但這句話也可以用在極度興奮、欣快，讓人「骨頭都酥了」的情況。

A: Did you hear a strange moaning sound coming from outside last night?
你作晚有聽到外面傳來奇怪的呻吟聲嗎？

B: Yes. It totally sent chills up my spine!
有啊。讓我一整個背脊發涼！

sleep paralysis 睡眠癱瘓

俗稱「鬼壓床」的睡眠癱瘓相關記載古今中外皆有。資料顯示有超過半數的人都有這種經驗，即在半睡半醒之際感到身體無法動彈、眼睛張不開、無法發出聲音，部分人會隨之發作恐慌症，因而呼吸困難，甚至產生幻覺幻聽。科學家一般認為睡眠癱瘓是由生活壓力造成，只要保持身心健康、生活規律，就能避免經常發作。

stand for 代表

stand for 這個片語有很多意思，可以表示「接受，忍受」：

The teacher said he wouldn't stand for students talking in class.
老師說他不會容忍學生在上課時說話。

也表示「支持」：

Our party stands for freedom and justice.
本黨支持自由及正義。

在本篇對話中，則是「代表」的意思。

A: What does CIA stand for?
CIA 代表什麼意思？

B: Central Intelligence Agency.
中央情報局。

🎧108 Vocabulary

1) **poltergeist** [ˋpoltəˌgaɪst] 亂丟東西惡作劇的鬼
2) **smash** [smæʃ] (v.) 砸，碎裂
3) **ground** [graʊnd] (v.) 禁足，（讓飛機、飛行員）停飛
4) **ornament** [ˋɔrnəmənt] (n.) 裝飾品
5) **freaky** [ˋfrikɪ] (a.) 怪異的，可怕的
6) **forbid** [fɚˋbɪd] (v.) 禁止，不許
7) **overhear** [ˌovɚˋhɪr] (v.) 無意中聽到或偷聽到（別人的談話）
8) **place setting** [ples ˋsɛtɪŋ] (phr.)（餐桌上擺設給一個人用的）餐具
9) **occult** [əˋkʌlt] (a./n.) 魔術（的），超自然能力、儀式等（的）
10) **neat freak** [nit frik] (n.)（口）有潔癖的人
11) **drawback** [ˋdrɔˌbæk] (n.) 缺點，不利條件
12) **immoral** [ɪˋmɔrəl] (a.) 不道德的，邪惡的

🎧106 1) Poltergeist 家裡鬧鬼

Megan : When I was in the sixth grade, a friend of mine had a poltergeist in her house.

Leo : Like in the movie 🄛 *Poltergeist*? That was *really* scary.

Megan : Not quite, but it was still scary. She was sitting at the kitchen table one morning, and her stepfather's coffee mug suddenly slid across the table and ²⁾**smashed** on the floor. She didn't 🄛 **get along with** her stepfather, so her mom thought she did it, and ³⁾**grounded** her for a week. But the next day, everybody was upstairs and there was a loud crash in the kitchen. When they ran down to see what happened, there were broken plates all over the floor.

Leo : Whoa. There's no way they could blame her for that.

Megan : Yeah. And then at Christmas, the tree suddenly started shaking and ⁴⁾**ornaments** were flying off the tree! Everybody saw it.

Leo : That's pretty ⁵⁾**freaky**. What did they do?

Megan : They started buying plastic dishes, ha-ha. Actually, about six months later, the poltergeist activity just stopped and never happened again.

梅根：我六年級時，有個朋友家裡鬧鬼。

李歐：像電影《鬼哭神號》那樣？那真的很可怕。

梅根：不完全是，但還是很可怕。有天早上她坐在廚房的桌子旁，她繼父的咖啡杯突然滑越桌子，掉在地上摔碎了。她跟繼父處得不好，所以她媽媽以為是她摔的，罰她禁足一星期。但隔天，所有人都在樓上，但廚房傳來一聲巨響。他們跑下樓去看時，地板上都是破掉的盤子。

李歐：哇，這件事他們就不能怪她了。

梅根：對呀。接著是在耶誕節，耶誕樹突然開始搖晃，裝飾品都從樹上飛下來！大家都看到了。

　　　好詭異！那他們怎麼辦？

梅根：他們開始買塑膠盤子，哈哈。其實，半年後，鬧鬼的情況就停了，從未再發生過。

Raising a little ghost
養小鬼

Eric : When I was a little kid, my parents took me to visit a friend of theirs. Her house was really big and really clean. She lived alone and didn't have kids, but the house was full of toys and they all looked new.

Mia : You must've been pretty excited.

Eric : **LG** **The thing is**, my parents [6]**forbid** me from even touching the toys. And while we were eating dinner, my parents had these strange expressions on their faces. As soon as we left, I [7]**overheard** my parents talking about the extra [8]**place setting** at the table. It wasn't until I saw a paranormal show years later that I realized my parents' friend was "raising a little ghost."

Mia : What does that mean?

Eric : It's a kind of [9]**occult** practice where you adopt the spirit of a baby or young child. Some people believe that they're powerful spirits who can bring you fame or fortune if you worship them. It's said that little ghosts are [10]**neat freaks**, and my parents' friend had the cleanest house I've ever seen.

Mia : Are there any [11]**drawbacks** to raising a little ghost?

Eric : If you ask the little ghost to do [12]**immoral** things, or if you perform the rituals wrong and it turns into an evil spirit, you can end up bringing bad luck on yourself.

艾瑞克：小時候有一次，我爸媽帶我去拜訪他們的朋友。那個阿姨的房子好大好乾淨。她獨居沒有小孩，可是家裡有好多玩具，而且好像都很新。

蜜雅： 你一定樂壞了。

艾瑞克：問題來了，我爸媽嚴格禁止我去碰玩具。而且吃晚飯時，我爸媽的表情也很怪。一離開那裡，就聽到我爸媽在討論餐桌上多放一副碗筷的事。直到幾年後看電視靈異節目，我才知道那個阿姨在「養小鬼」。

蜜雅： 那是什麼意思？

艾瑞克：一種收養嬰孩靈魂的法術。有些人相信小鬼法力高強，祭拜祂們能夠成名或發財。傳說小鬼很愛乾淨，我爸媽那位朋友的家真的是我所見過最乾淨的。

蜜雅： 養小鬼有壞處嗎？

艾瑞克：如果派小鬼去做不正當的事，或是作法不當，把小鬼養成惡鬼，最終會為自己帶來厄運。

Language Guide

Poltergeist 電影《鬼哭神號》

本片及第二集《陰風怒吼》(*Poltergeist II: The Other Side*)、第三集《腥風血雨》(*Poltergeist III*)為導演史蒂芬史匹柏作品，是有名的受詛咒鬼片。故事敘述一家人搬進一間陰森的房子，經歷許多恐怖事件。而本片演員銀幕下的故事也一樣嚇人：飾演姊姊的女星在第一集上映後被謀殺；第二集有兩位演員病逝；而貫穿演出三集的童星撐不到第三集上映，12 歲就因克隆氏症去世。

get along (with sb.) (跟人)合得來

get along 有多意思，對話中是「相處愉快」，經常與 with 運用。

A: Do you get along with your brothers and sisters?
你跟兄弟姐妹處得來嗎？

B: Not really. We're always fighting.
不算是。我們老是在爭吵。

The thing is... 問題是⋯

後面接藉口或是解釋，為口語用法；也可以用以強調後接的事物。

A: Can you pick me up after work tonight?
今晚下班可以來接我嗎？

B: The thing is, my car's in the shop.
問題是，我的車子送修。

109) 1) Infant spirit 嬰靈

Nicole : A friend of mine was having a 2)**string** of bad luck, so she went to see a 3)**fortuneteller**. The fortuneteller told her she was being followed by an "infant spirit."

Kenny : Is that the same as a little ghost?

Nicole : Not exactly. When you "raise a little ghost," it's usually the spirit of a baby or small child who died an 4)**accidental** death. An "infant spirit" is the ghost of a baby who was 5)**aborted**. The fortuneteller told my friend that the spirit of her aborted baby was an innocent victim, and that it was following her because it couldn't be 6)**reincarnated**. He said the spirit **had a grudge against** her, and it was causing her bad luck. So my friend spent a lot of money having rituals performed to release the baby's spirit from 7)**purgatory**.

Kenny : So did her string of bad luck end?

Nicole : Yes, but not because of the rituals. She realized later that blaming her bad luck on the "infant spirit" was even worse than getting an 5)**abortion** in the first place. So she started being more responsible and facing her problems **head on**, and now things are going much better for her.

Kenny : Wow, that's a pretty 8)**inspiring** story!

妮可： 我有一個朋友諸事不順跑去算命。算命的人說是有「嬰靈」跟著她。

肯尼： 這也是小鬼？

妮可： 不算是。「養小鬼」是養意外死亡嬰幼兒的靈魂，「嬰靈」是墮胎未能出世胎兒的靈魂。那個算命仙跟我朋友說她那個沒出世寶寶的靈魂是無辜受害，而且因為無法投胎就一直跟著她。他說那個嬰靈怨恨它的母親，才為她帶來災禍。我朋友花了好多錢幫嬰靈辦超度法會。

肯尼： 她諸事不順的問題解決了嗎？

妮可： 解決了，但不是因為辦法會。她後來想通了：把生活不順的錯推給嬰靈，比當初墮胎還糟糕。所以她開始負起責任，積極面對問題，現在她過得很好。

肯尼： 哇，真是個勵志的故事！

111) Vocabulary

1) **infant** [ˋɪnfənt] (n./a.) 嬰兒（的）

2) **string** [strɪŋ] (n.) 一串，一系列

3) **fortuneteller** [ˋfɔrtʃən‚tɛlə] (n.) 算命師

4) **accidental** [‚æksəˋdɛntəl] (a.) 意外的，偶然的

5) **abort** [əˋbɔrt] (v.) 墮胎，流產。名詞為 **abortion** [əˋbɔrʃən]

6) **reincarnate** [‚riɪnˋkɑr‚net] (v.)（使）轉世。名詞為 **reincarnation** [‚riɪn‚kɑrˋneʃən]

7) **purgatory** [ˋpɝɡə‚tori] (n.) 煉獄

8) **inspiring** [ɪnˋspaɪrɪŋ] (a.) 激勵人心的，有啟發性的

9) **imaginary** [ɪˋmædʒə‚nɛri] (a.) 幻想的，虛構的

9) Imaginary friends
幻想出來的朋友

Sophia : I've never seen a ghost before, but my boyfriend has.

Noah : Really? When did it happen?

Sophia : When he was a little kid. He must've been about four or five. When he looked in the mirror, he'd see a man there. But he wasn't scared of him, and they would sit there having conversations. When his parents found out, they asked who the man was. My boyfriend didn't know his name, but he described what he looked like, what his hobbies were, and even what he did **for a living**.

Noah : Well, it's pretty normal for kids to have imaginary friends, right?

Sophia : That's what his parents thought. But then they found out from a neighbor that one of the house's former owners had committed suicide there. When they asked for more details, the neighbor's description perfectly matched the man my boyfriend saw in the mirror!

蘇菲亞：我從沒見過鬼，但我男友看過。

真的？什麼時候看到的？

蘇菲亞：他小時候，應該是四、五歲左右。他在照鏡子時，看到裡面有個男人，但他不怕他，他們會坐下聊天。等他父母發現時，就問他那人是誰。我男友不知道他的名字，但形容了他的長相、興趣，甚至工作。

小孩子有幻想出來的朋友很正常，對吧？

蘇菲亞：他父母也這麼認為。但之後他們從鄰居口中得知，其中一位前屋主曾在那房子裡自殺。他們進一步詢問細節時，鄰居的描述跟我男友在鏡子裡看到的男人一模一樣！

Language Guide

have a grudge (against sb.)（對某人）心懷怨恨

也可以説 bear a grudge、hold a grudge。grudge [grʌdʒ] 是「怨恨，嫉妒」，這個片語表示無法忘記過去的不愉快，對某人記恨在心，懷有餘恨。

A: Why did our teacher give you such a low grade?
老師怎麼給你打那麼低的分數啊？

B: I think he has a grudge against me.
我覺得他跟我有仇。

head on 正面迎擊

表示直接面對衝突、困難。

A: What do you think we should do?
你覺得我們該怎麼辦？

B: I think we should tackle this challenge head on.
我覺得我們應該面對這個挑戰。

for a living 賺錢維生

用在形容賺夠多的錢、足以維持生活的工作。

A: What does your father do for a living?
你父親以什麼維生？

B: I'm not sure. I think it has something to do with finance.
我不確定。好像跟金融有關係吧。

🎧112 Haitian zombie
海地喪屍

Gary : Well, my dad actually saw someone who came back from the dead.

Carol : You mean like a zombie?

Gary : Yes, but not like the kind you see in *The Walking Dead*. This was a Haitian zombie.

Carol : What's the difference?

Gary : Haitian zombies don't eat human flesh. They're brought back from the dead by [1] **witch doctors** to serve as their slaves.

Carol : And your dad actually saw one?

Gary : Yep. He was in Haiti as an 🅛🅖 **aid worker**, and one day he saw a man walking slowly down the street with a blank expression on his face. He asked a Haitian [2] **co-worker** about him, and she said the guy was a zombie!

Carol : How did she know?

Gary : The guy died in a traffic accident, and she went to his funeral and saw him get buried. Then, a few weeks later, someone saw him working in a [3] **sugarcane** field—that was owned by a local witch doctor!

🎧114 Vocabulary

1) **witch doctor** [wɪtʃ `dɑktɚ] 巫師，巫醫
2) **co-worker** [`ko͵wɔkɚ] (n.) 同事
3) **sugarcane** [`ʃugɚ͵ken] (n.) 甘蔗
4) **blindfold** [`blaɪnd͵fold] (n./v.) 遮眼布巾；矇住眼睛
5) **chant** [tʃænt] (v.) 吟誦
6) **hypnosis** [hɪp`nosɪs] (n.) 催眠

蓋瑞：嗯，我爸爸其實看過有人死而復生。

凱若：是說像喪屍那樣嗎？

蓋瑞：對，但不是像《陰屍路》裡看到的那種。是海地喪屍。

凱若：有什麼不同？

蓋瑞：海地喪屍不吃人肉。他們是被巫醫帶回人間，當他們的奴隸。

凱若：你爸爸真的看過？

蓋瑞：對。他當時在海地參與人道救援，有一天他看到有個男人在街上緩慢行走，面無表情。他問海地的同事那人怎麼了，她說那是喪屍！

凱若：她怎麼知道？

蓋瑞：因為那人已死於一場車禍，她有參加他的葬禮，親眼看到他被埋葬。然後啊，幾星期後，有人看到他在甘蔗田工作，而那座田是當地某個巫醫的！

Guan luo yin
觀落陰

Liz : Uh, this may sound a little crazy, but I actually went to the underworld to visit my father. In Chinese, it's called *guan luo yin*.

Matt : What!?

Liz : Ha. I should've 🄻🄶 **kept my mouth shut.**

Matt : No, sorry. Please continue.

Liz : A couple years ago, my dad suddenly passed away, and I was having trouble 🄻🄶 **getting over it.** My cousin said that if I went to see a Taoist priest, he could help me talk to my dad. I thought, "Why not?" So one night, my cousin took me to a Taoist temple, and there was a group of people there waiting for the *guan luo yin* ceremony. We all had to wear ⁴⁾**blindfolds** and sit on chairs in our bare feet. The priest started ⁵⁾**chanting**, and then guided us through the journey. I could actually feel myself traveling to the underworld, and then I saw my dad! The experience felt totally real. I really wanted to hug my dad and cry, but the priest said that would 🄻🄶 **break the spell.** So I just talked to him quietly and he told me he was doing well. After the ceremony, I felt like I was finally over my dad's death, and my life started returning to normal.

Matt : I gotta say, it sounds like ⁶⁾**hypnosis** to me. But it sounds like a valuable experience 🄻🄶 **all the same.**

莉茲：呃…可能聽起來有點瘋狂，但我其實到陰間找過我爸爸。中文叫做「觀落陰」。

麥特：啥米！？

莉茲：哈。我真不該說出來。

麥特：不會啦，抱歉，請繼續說。

莉茲：幾年前，我爸爸忽然過世，我一直走不出來。一個表姐問我要不要去見一位法師，讓我跟爸爸說說話。我覺得「有何不可？」於是有一天晚上，表姐帶我去一間道教的寺廟，裡面也有其他人等著要觀落陰。我們的眼睛都被綁上一塊布遮住，打赤腳坐在椅子上。道士開始唸咒，引導我們上路。我真的感覺到自己正前往陰間，接著我看到我爸爸了！這次的經驗感覺非常真實。我當時真想抱著爸爸痛哭，但道士有叮嚀那樣會破功。於是我靜靜的跟爸爸說話，他告訴我說他一切都好。法事結束後，我覺得終於能放下父親過世的傷痛，恢復正常生活。

麥特：我必須說，這聽起來很像催眠。但不論如何，這聽起來是很珍貴的經驗。

humanitarian aid 人道救援

對話中的 aid worker 是「人道救援工作者」，humanitarian aid 是指基於人道主義關懷而提出的協助，包括物資、運輸、人力等等，以拯救生命、紓解困境。人道救援可由政府及非政府組織如無國界醫生（Doctors Without Borders，簡稱 MSF，法文 Médecins Sans Frontières 的縮寫）、國際人道主義組織如紅十字會與紅新月會國際聯合會（International Federation of Red Cross and Red Crescent Societies，簡稱 IFRC）、國際救援宗教組織如世界展望會（World Vision International）提供。

keep one's mouth shut
閉嘴不講，保密

字面直譯是「把嘴閉上」，引申為保密。

A: Why shouldn't I tell my secret to Rebecca?
為什麼我不該跟蕾貝卡說我的秘密？

B: Because she just can't keep her mouth shut.
因為她沒辦法保守秘密。

get over it 淡忘（某事）

get over 是指「淡忘，熬過」，over 有「重新開始」的意思，通常是要人忘記傷痛、不好的記憶，所以 get over it 就是要人忘記過去，放眼未來，重新來過，趕快從傷痛中走出來。

A: I tried to apologize to Lisa for forgetting her birthday, but she won't even talk to me.
我試著為忘記麗莎生日的事向她道歉，但她甚至一句話也不和我說。

B: Don't worry. She'll get over it.
別擔心。她會忘的。

break the spell 破除魔咒，破功

字面上是讓一個毀掉魔法、讓符咒失效。當一切進行的很順利，卻跑出個豬隊友來毀了一切時，也可以說 break the spell 表示「破功。」

A: Did the frog turn back into a prince?
青蛙後來有變回王子嗎？

B: Yes. A kiss from a princess broke the spell.
有。公主的吻把魔咒解除了。

all the same 依然，仍舊

用法和意思跟 nevertheless、still 一樣，也可以說 just the same。

A: It rained every day on your trip to Hawaii?
你去夏威夷旅行時每天都下雨？

B: Yeah. But we had a good time all the same.
對啊。但我們還是玩得很開心。

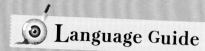 **Vocabulary**

1) **interact** [͵ɪntɚˋækt] (v.) 互動，互相影響

Language Guide

to death 形容最高程度

中文會說「高興死了」、「傷心死了」、「氣死了」，英文也一樣用 ...to death 來形容「到達極限」，比如用 work sb./oneself to death 表示過勞，意思是「把（別人／自己）操到死」。

A: Sarah is *so* irresponsible. It's driving me crazy.
莎拉超不負責任。快把我搞瘋了。

B: Yeah. I'm sick to death of hearing her excuses.
對啊。我聽膩她的藉口了。

Yin yang eyes
陰陽眼

Claire : Ever since I was a kid, I've been sensitive to the paranormal. In Taiwan, it's called having "yin yang eyes." My mom says that when I was a baby I'd always look out the window with a smile on my face, and when I was a little kid I'd talk to people who weren't there when I was playing in the living room. It scared my mom **to death**.

Dylan : Do you still see ghosts now?

Claire : Yeah, all the time. But it isn't scary. It's like seeing strangers when you walk down the street. They don't really 1)**interact** with you.

Dylan : Wait…have you seen any here?

Claire : Yes.

Dylan : Oh my god! Really? Where?

Claire : I saw one at the top of the stairs when I came in, but it's gone now.

克萊兒：我從小就有靈異體質。在台灣，這叫有「陰陽眼」。我媽媽說我還是嬰兒時，就老是看著窗戶外面笑。還有我小時候自己在客廳玩，會跟不存在的人講話。我媽都快嚇死了。

狄　倫：那妳現在還看得到鬼嗎？

克萊兒：有啊，一直都看得到。但沒什麼好怕的。感覺就像路上看見陌生人。他們不太會跟人互動。

狄　倫：等等…那妳在這裡有看到嗎？

克萊兒：有喔。

狄　倫：天啊！真的嗎！在哪？

克萊兒：我剛進來時，看到樓梯最上頭有一個，但後來走了。

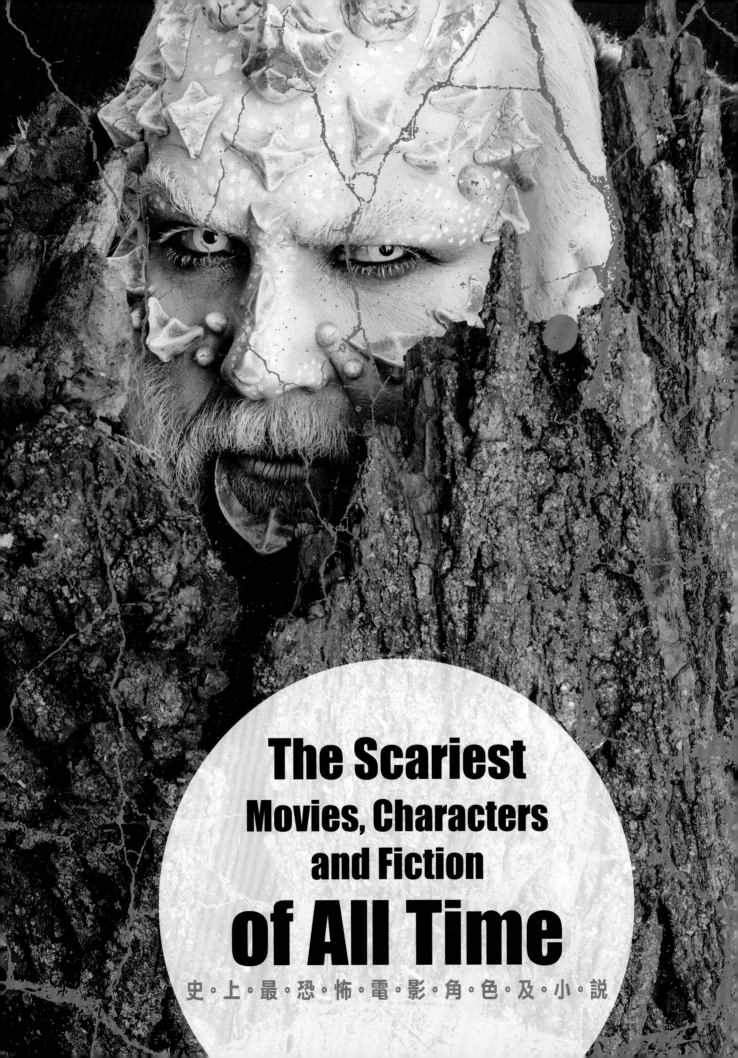

The Scariest
Movies, Characters
and Fiction
of All Time

史·上·最·恐·怖·電·影·角·色·及·小·説

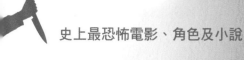

奧斯卡得獎恐怖經典

大法師
The Exorcist

©flickr.com/photos/
horrormoviecoverarchive/

🎧118 Vocabulary

1) **previously** [ˋpriviəsli] (adv.) 先前，事先；形容詞為 **previous** [ˋpriviəs]

2) **adapt** [əˋdæpt] (v.) 改編，改寫

3) **real-life** [ˋriəl͵laɪf] (a.) 真實的，真人實事的

4) **demonic** [diˋmɑnɪk] (a.) 惡魔的，有魔力的

5) **critical** [ˋkrɪtɪkəl] (a.) 評論的，批評的；名詞 **critic** [ˋkrɪtɪk] 即「評論家，批評家」

6) **box office** [bɑks ˋɔfɪs] (n.) 票房（收入）

7) **nominate** [ˋnɑmə͵net] (v.) 提名

8) **screenplay** [ˋskrin͵ple] (n.) 電影劇本

9) **babysit** [ˋbebi͵sɪt] (v.) 幫人暫時照顧小孩

10) **assume** [əˋsum] (v.) 以為，認為

11) **sinister** [ˋsɪnɪstɚ] (a.) 邪惡的，不祥的

12) **series** [ˋsɪriz] (n.) 系列，連續

13) **recite** [rɪˋsaɪt] (v.) 朗誦，背誦，詳述

14) **vomit** [ˋvɑmɪt] (n./v.) 嘔吐物；嘔吐

© Andrea Raffin / Shutterstock.com

威廉弗萊德金 2017 年為他執導的紀錄片
《神父阿摩特與惡魔》*The Devil And Father Amorth* 參加威尼斯影展。

🎧117 Directed by William Friedkin, who had [1]**previously** won Best Director and Best Picture Oscars for *The French Connection*, *The Exorcist* is regarded as one of the greatest horror films of all time. The film was [2]**adapted** by William Peter Blatty from his 1971 novel of the same name, which was inspired by a [3]**real-life** story—the 1949 exorcism of Roland Doe, a 14-year-old boy said to be a victim of [4]**demonic** possession. In *The Exorcist*, the victim becomes a girl named Regan, the 12-year-old daughter of a famous actress, and the evil spirit is Pazuzu, a powerful demon from ancient LG **Mesopotamia**. When the film LG **hit theaters** in 1973, it was a huge [5]**critical** and [6]**box office** success. At the 1974 Academy Awards, *The Exorcist* was [7]**nominated** for 10 Oscars, including Best Picture—making it the first horror film to receive this honor. In the end, however, it only won Best Sound and Best [8]**Screenplay**.

《大法師》是公認有史以來最出色的恐怖電影之一，導演威廉弗萊德金曾以《霹靂神探》獲得奧斯卡最佳導演獎和最佳影片獎。這部電影是由威廉彼得布拉蒂改編自其 1971 年出版的同名小說，這本小說的靈感源自真實故事，是發生在 1949 年的羅蘭多伊驅魔事件，14 歲的男孩羅蘭多伊據說被惡魔附身。在《大法師》中，受害者則改為知名女演員的 12 歲女兒蕾根，附身的惡靈帕祖祖是來自古美索不達米亞的強大惡魔。電影在 1973 年上映時深獲好評，也創下票房佳績。電影在 1974 年獲得十項奧斯卡獎提名，包括最佳影片獎，也是第一部榮獲提名的恐怖片。不過最後只獲得最佳音效和最佳劇本獎。

As the story begins, actress Chris MacNeil has just finished filming a movie directed by her friend Burke. After playing with a Ouija board and contacting a spirit she calls Captain Howdy, her daughter Regan begins acting strange—swearing, making weird noises, and even peeing on the floor at a party. Chris seeks medical help for her daughter, but the doctors all think her problems are psychological. And then something terrible happens. Chris returns home one evening to learn that Burke, who had been [9]**babysitting** Regan, has fallen out of a window and died. While his death is [10]**assumed** to be an accident, some suspect something more [11]**sinister**.

故事一開始，女演員克莉絲麥可尼爾剛拍完一部電影，她的朋友柏克是導演。在她玩通靈板跟鬼魂郝迪隊長溝通過後，她的女兒蕾根突然舉止怪異——咒罵、發出怪聲音，甚至在派對上隨地小便。克莉絲帶女兒去看醫生，但醫生都認為這是精神疾病。之後發生了恐怖的事。克莉絲有天晚上回家，發現那天照顧蕾根的柏克墜落窗外死亡。大家認為他的死是意外，但也有人懷疑此事有蹊蹺。

After another [12]**series** of medical tests all come up normal, one doctor suggests an exorcism, and a young priest named Father Karras is brought in to examine Regan. On hearing her speaking backwards and seeing the words "help me" scratched on her stomach, he determines that she's possessed and brings in a more experienced priest, Father Merrin, to help him perform an exorcism. The scene that follows is one of the scariest—and grossest—ever filmed. As Merrin [13]**recites** a prayer, Regan sprays him with green [14]**vomit**, floats above her bed and then turns her head in a full circle. By the time the exorcism is over and Regan is cured, both priests are dead.

蕾根又進行一連串醫療檢驗，結果都正常，有位醫生建議進行驅魔儀式，於是找來年輕的卡拉斯神父為蕾根做檢查。他在聽到她說話順序前後顛倒，並看到她的肚子上有「救我」字樣的抓痕後，他確認她被附身，並找來更有經驗的神父墨林協助他進行驅魔儀式。接下來這場戲是史上最恐怖、也最噁心的。在墨林禱告時，蕾根朝他身上吐出綠色的嘔吐物，飄浮在床上方，然後她的頭旋轉 360 度。驅魔儀式結束時，蕾根恢復正常，但兩位神父都死了。

拍攝卡拉斯神父跌落摔死場景的階梯。

被附身的蕾根（《大法師》拍片用木偶）。

Language Guide

Mesopotamia 美索不達米亞
美索不達米亞位置約當於現今的伊拉克，是古希臘對兩河流域（幼發拉底河及底格里斯河）的稱呼。發展於此的美索不達米亞文明（西元前 4000 至西元前 2000 年間）是人類最古老的文明。蘇美的楔形文字、亞述的巴尼拔圖書館、古巴比倫的《漢摩拉比法典》、新巴比倫的空中花園，都是屬於此時期。

hit theaters 上映
hit 在這裡不是「打」或「撞擊」，而是口語「到達某處」的意思，「抵達戲院」也就是上映了。

A: When is the new *Mission: Impossible* movie gonna <u>hit theaters</u>?
最新的《不可能的任務》電影什麼時候會上映？

B: I think it's coming out in July.
好像七月會上映。

惡靈帕祖祖雕像
（法國羅浮宮館藏）

119 電影好口怕 1
為什麼愛看恐怖片

Jimmy: I'm stuffed. Let's clear the table.

Sarah: OK. How about watching a movie after we do the dishes?

Jimmy: Sounds good. What do you want to watch?

Sarah: Well, there's this movie my sister recommended.

Jimmy: But your sister's taste in movies sucks.

Sarah: You'll like this one—it stars Bruce Willis.

Jimmy: An action movie? I thought you hated action movies.

Sarah: This one's a supernatural horror flick. It's called *The Sixth Sense*.

Jimmy: There's no way I'm watching a horror flick. Why do you like horror so much?

Sarah: They have a lot of imagination. And I get jumpy watching them, but I feel really relaxed when they're over.

Jimmy: I guess I don't enjoy being scared half to death or grossed out by blood and gore.

Sarah: Well, *The Sixth Sense* isn't a slasher flick. It was even nominated for a Best Picture Oscar.

Jimmy: OK, I guess I can give it a chance.

吉米：我飽了。我們把餐桌收一收吧。

莎拉：好啊。我們洗好碗之後來看一部電影吧？

吉米：好啊。妳想看哪部？

莎拉：我姊姊介紹我一部片。

吉米：但你姊的電影品味太差了。

莎拉：這部你一定愛。布魯斯威利主演。

吉米：動作片？我以為妳討厭動作片。

莎拉：這是一部靈異恐怖片。叫《靈異第六感》。

吉米：打死我也不看恐怖片。妳為什麼那麼喜歡恐怖片？

莎拉：恐怖片很有想像力。我看的時候雖然緊張，看完卻又覺得特別放鬆。

吉米：被嚇個半死，或是被血淋淋弄得超想吐，我大概無福消受。

莎拉：《靈異第六感》不是血腥恐怖片。這部片甚至入圍奧斯卡最佳影片呢。

吉米：好吧，我可以給它一次機會。

恐怖驚悚片筆記

獲得奧斯卡青睞的恐怖片（horror film）很多，驚悚片（thriller）更多。以下是曾經入圍最佳影片的恐怖驚悚片：

《大法師》*The Exorcist* (1973) 得獎

《大白鯊》*Jaws* (1975)

《沈默的羔羊》*The Silence of the Lambs* (1991) 得獎

《靈異第六感》*The Sixth Sense* (1999)

《黑天鵝》*Black Swan* (2010)

《逃出絕命鎮》*Get Out* (2017)

© 網路圖片

The Silence of the Lambs

沉默的羔羊

The Silence of the Lambs, which was adapted from the 1986 Thomas Harris novel of the same name, is the only horror film to ever win a Best Picture Oscar. Directed by Jonathan Demme, who was best known for his 1980s [1]**comedies**, the film stars Jodie Foster as young FBI [2]**agent** Clarice Starling and Anthony Hopkins as Dr. Hannibal Lecter, a brilliant [3]**psychiatrist** and serial killer who likes to eat his victims. On its release in 1991, *The Silence of the Lambs* was praised by audiences and critics alike. It was a top-[4]**grossing** film that year, and won the LG "**Big Five**" at the Oscars: Best Picture, Best Director, Best Actor (Hopkins), Best Actress (Foster) and Best Screenplay—one of only three films in history to do so.

《沉默的羔羊》是根據湯瑪斯哈里斯 1986 年的同名小說改編，是唯一獲得奧斯卡最佳影片獎的恐怖片。這部電影的導演強納森德米因 1980 年代執導喜劇而聞名，茱蒂佛斯特飾演年輕的聯邦調查局探員克麗絲史達琳，安東尼霍普金斯飾演的漢尼拔萊克特醫生是聰明的精神病醫師和連環殺手，會吃掉他殺害的人。《沉默的羔羊》於 1991 年上映時，受到觀眾和評論家一致好評，是那一年的票房之冠，並獲得奧斯卡五大獎項：最佳影片、最佳導演、最佳男主角（霍普金斯）、最佳女主角（佛斯特）和最佳劇本，而史上只有三部電影同時獲得這五項大獎。

Language Guide

Big Five Oscars 囊括奧斯卡五大獎

同時在奧斯卡獲得五大獎項：最佳影片、最佳導演、最佳男主角、最佳女主角和最佳劇本（原創或改編都算）的電影為：

《一夜風流》
It Happened One Night (1934)

《飛越杜鵑窩》
One Flew Over the Cuckoo's Nest (1975)

《沉默的羔羊》
The Silence of the Lambs (1991)

© Tinseltown / Shutterstock.com

導演強納森德米（1944 ～ 2017）。湯姆漢克斯初次獲得奧斯卡最佳男主角獎的《費城》*Philadelphia* 也是由他執導。

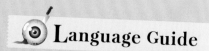 Vocabulary

1) **nickname** [ˋnɪkˏnem] (v.) 給⋯起綽號

2) **profile** [ˋprofaɪl] (n./v.)（人物）簡介，進行犯罪心理分析。犯罪心理分析專家（profiler）會協助刑事人員分析未知嫌犯的背景、特徵及犯案模式，或推斷未來可能被害者

3) **transfer** [ˋtrænsfɚ] (v.) 轉送，調動

4) **senator** [ˋsɛnətɚ] (n.) 參議員

5) **goggles** [ˋgɑglz] (n.) 護目鏡，蛙鏡

6) **cock** [kɑk] (v.)（槍）上膛

Language Guide

Buffalo Bill 水牛比爾

原名William Frederick Cody的水牛比爾（1846～1917）是南北戰爭軍人，經營過農場、到西部拓荒、當過驛馬快遞（Pony Express）騎士（西部開拓時期的騎馬快遞員）、獵過美洲野牛（American bison，也稱為buffalo），還表演馬戲雜耍，是美國西部開拓時期的最具傳奇色彩的人物。他與堪薩斯太平洋鐵路公司簽約供應肉品給工人的18個月期間（1867～1868），號稱殺了4282頭buffalo，他的綽號即因此而來（Bill 是William的小名）。

© Anton_Ivanov / Shutterstock.com

安東尼霍普金斯飾演的漢尼拔。

The Silence of the Lambs is a story about not one serial killer, but two. In the search for a serial killer [1]**nicknamed** Buffalo Bill, who skins the corpses of his female victims, the FBI sends Agent Starling to a Baltimore mental hospital to interview Hannibal Lecter, hoping he can help them create a [2]**profile** of the killer. Lecter hates Dr. Chilton, the hospital director, and agrees to help if they promise to [3]**transfer** him to another prison. Under pressure after Buffalo Bill kidnaps a [4]**senator**'s daughter, the FBI agrees to his demand. But Lector still makes Starling tell him personal details about her life in exchange for clues.

《沉默的羔羊》敘述不只一位，而是兩位連環殺手的故事。綽號野牛比爾的連環殺手會將女受害人屍體的皮剝下來，為了搜查他的下落，聯邦調查局派探員史達琳到巴爾的摩一家精神病院訪問漢尼拔萊克特，希望他能協助建立凶手的資料。由於萊克特討厭醫院的院長奇頓醫生，因此要求他們若能保證將他轉到另一間監獄，他就同意協助。在野牛比爾綁架一位參議員的女兒後，聯邦調查局在壓力下同意他的要求。但萊克特仍要求史達琳將她個人的生活細節告訴他，以交換線索。

When Starling visits Lecter at his cell in Memphis, where he's been transferred, he provides her with clues that lead her to a town in Ohio where Buffalo Bill's first victim lived. Later that evening, Lecter escapes by killing his guard and putting on his uniform—and his face! Meanwhile, Starling finds Buffalo Bill's house, and when she chases him into the basement, she finds the senator's daughter alive in the bottom of a well. But then the killer turns off the lights and pursues Starling with night-vision [5]**goggles**. Luckily, she hears him [6]**cocking** his gun and shoots him before he shoots her. Back at FBI headquarters, Starling gets a call from Lecter, who's at an airport in the Bahamas. After promising not to hunt her, he says he has to go because he's "having a friend for dinner," and then hangs up and follows Dr. Chilton into the crowd.

萊克特被轉移到曼非斯後，史達琳到他的牢房探視，然後根據他提供的線索來到野牛比爾第一位受害人曾居住的俄亥俄州小鎮。後來那晚萊克特殺害獄警，並換上他的制服——還有他的臉，藉此逃跑！此時史達琳找到野牛比爾的住處，她追著他到地下室時，發現參議員的女兒還活著，在一處井底。但殺手隨後關燈，用夜視鏡追殺史達琳。幸好她聽到他槍上膛的聲音，趁他開槍前先槍殺他。回到聯邦調查局總部後，史達琳接到萊克特的電話，他人在巴哈馬的機場。他保證不傷害她，並說他要走了，因為他要「找一個朋友吃晚餐」（雙關語，也表示「吃一個朋友當晚餐」），然後掛斷電話，尾隨著奇頓醫生走進人群中。

🎧 124 電影好口怕 2
不敢看恐怖片的理由

Julia: Hey, I'm back!

Elliot: We were just about to start a movie. Want to join us?

Julia: Sure. What are you watching?

Elliot: *Shutter*. It's a Thai horror flick.

Julia: Ooh, I think I'll pass. The last time I saw a horror movie I got so freaked out I couldn't sleep for days.

Elliot: What a scaredy-cat. What movie was it?

Julia: *Ju-on: The Grudge*.

Elliot: I saw the American remake. It wasn't scary at all. Well...I guess the ghost with no jaw was *kind of* scary.

Julia: Aaah, that's enough—don't remind me of that scene! I'll be afraid to go to the bathroom! OK, have fun you guys. I'm gonna stay at my friend's house tonight. Bye!

茱莉亞：嘿，我回來了！

艾略特：我們正要開始看電影。要一起來看嗎？

茱莉亞：好啊。你們要看哪部？

艾略特：《鬼影》，一部泰國恐怖片。

茱莉亞：喔，那我免了。我上次看恐怖片時，嚇得好幾天都睡不著覺。

艾略特：膽子也太小了。妳是看了哪部？

茱莉亞：《咒怨》。

艾略特：啊，我有看過重拍的美國版。根本一點都不可怕。呃…那個沒下巴的鬼是有點可怕啦。

茱莉亞：啊，不要再講了，不要讓我再想起那個畫面！我會不敢上廁所！好啦，你們好好看，我今天晚上去住朋友家。掰了！

恐怖驚悚片筆記

爛番茄（Rotten Tomatoes）選出影史一百部最佳恐怖片，以下是前 25 名當中，2000 年後推出的片單：

No. 1 《逃出絕命鎮》 *Get Out* (2017)　　　　　　番茄新鮮度 99%

No. 3 《噤界》 *A Quiet Place* (2018)　　　　　　番茄新鮮度 95%

No. 11 《鬼敲門》 *The Babadook* (2014)　　　　　番茄新鮮度 98%

No. 15 《靈病》 *It Follows* (2015)　　　　　　　番茄新鮮度 97%

No. 18 《血色入侵》 *Let the Right One In* (2008)　番茄新鮮度 98%

No. 24 《女巫》 *The Witch* (2016)　　　　　　　番茄新鮮度 91%

（註：新鮮度百分比越高，代表該電影的好評越多越正面）

經典恐怖角色

Leatherface
人皮面具

©flickr.com/photos/junaidrao/

🎧125 Leatherface, a serial killer who wears a mask made of human skin and a bloody butcher's apron, first appeared in the 1974 slasher film *The Texas* 1)*Chainsaw* 2)*Massacre*. 3)**Portrayed** by Gunnar Hansen in the original, the killer is played by a number of different actors in the seven other films in the series. Unlike most serial killers, who operate independently, Leatherface is part of a whole family of 4)**psychotic** cannibals. When customers arrive at their 5)**rural** Texas gas station and restaurant, they often end up dead. Leatherface does most of the killing—his favorite weapon, of course, is a chainsaw—and his brother cooks the meat, which feeds the family and is also sold as barbecue and 6)**chili** at their restaurant. Not ones to waste, the family also uses the 7)**leftover** skin and bones to make furniture for their house.

　　人皮面具是連環殺手,他戴著人皮做成的面具,穿著沾血的屠夫圍裙,第一次出場是在 1974 年的血腥恐怖片《德州電鋸殺人狂》。在原版電影中,人皮面具由貢納爾漢森飾演,在其他七部續集中則分別由不同演員飾演。人皮面具跟其他大部分獨立行動的連環殺手不同,他和他全家都是會吃人的精神病患。到他們位於德州鄉間的加油站和餐廳的顧客,通常最後都會被殺死。大部分是被人皮面具殺死,當然,他最喜歡的作案凶器就是電鋸,然後由他的哥哥煮人肉供全家食用,也做成烤肉和墨西哥辣豆醬在他們的餐廳販賣。屍體絲毫不浪費,他們家也利用剩下的人皮和骨頭做成家具。

Freddy Krueger
鬼王佛萊迪

©flickr.com/photos/r_january/

🎧126 Played by Robert Englund, Freddy Krueger is the main villain in famed horror director Wes Craven's *A* 8)*Nightmare on* 9)*Elm Street* and its many sequels. Freddy was originally a child killer, but after he was burned to death by a 10)**mob** of his victims' parents, he became an evil spirit who appears to teenagers in their dreams. When he kills them with his razor-fingered glove, they die in real life as well. Freddy is easily identified by his horribly scarred face, red-and-green

鬼王佛萊迪跟他的剃刀手套。

¹¹⁾**striped** sweater, brown ¹²⁾**fedora** and of course his deadly glove. While he is powerful and nearly ¹³⁾**invulnerable** in the dream world, he becomes ¹⁴⁾**mortal** when he enters the real world.

　　羅伯特英格蘭飾演的佛萊迪克魯格是《半夜鬼上床》和多部續集中的主要反派，由知名恐怖片導演衛斯克拉文所執導。佛萊迪本來是兒童殺手，但被一群受害人的父母燒死後變成惡靈，會出現在青少年的夢中。他在夢中用剃刀手套殺死青少年時，他們在現實中也會死亡。佛萊迪的特徵很容易辨認，臉上佈滿可怕的傷痕、穿著紅綠條紋毛衣、頭戴棕色的軟呢帽，當然，還有致命的手套。雖然他在夢境中非常強大，幾乎所向無敵，但他進入現實世界中就變成會死的凡人。

Jason Voorhees
面具傑森魔

🎧127 For murderer Jason Voorhees, who first appears in the 1980 horror ¹⁵⁾**flick** *Friday the 13th*, killing 🔵 **runs in the family**. In the original film, Jason only appears in the memories of his mother, Mrs. Voorhees, a cook at Camp Crystal Lake who seeks revenge against the camp ¹⁶⁾**counselors** she believes are responsible for her young son's drowning by killing them one by one. In *Friday the 13th Part 2*, however, Jason appears as a grown man—apparently he didn't die after all—and murders the counselor who finally killed his mother in the first movie. He then continues killing the other counselors until one stabs him with a ¹⁷⁾**machete**. It isn't until *Friday the 13th Part III* that Jason ¹⁸⁾**takes on** his familiar appearance, adopting the machete he was stabbed with as his own murder weapon, and putting on the hockey mask worn by another of his victims.

　　殺人魔傑森沃爾希斯第一次出場是在 1980 年的恐怖片《13 號星期五》，對他來說殺人是家中遺傳。在原版的電影中，傑森只出現在他母親沃爾希斯太太的回憶中，她是水晶湖夏令營地的廚師，她認為兒子溺死是夏令營輔導員害的，因此為了報復，她將輔導員一個接一個殺掉。但在《13 號星期五 2》中，傑森以成年人之姿出場，看來他沒有死，並殺死了在第一集中殺掉她母親的輔導員。然後他繼續殺害其他輔導員，直到被其中一人以開山刀刺殺他。一直到《13 號星期五 3》，傑森才以觀眾熟悉的形象出現，採用曾經殺了他的開山刀作為自己的凶器，並戴上從另一個受害人身上取下的曲棍球面具。

🔧 Language Guide

sth. runs in the family
家中遺傳，代代相傳

run 在這裡是綿延、流傳的意思。當我們說 sth. runs in the family，就表示（某種個性、特徵）在一個家族中一代傳一代。

A: Do you think John will be handsome like his father?
你覺得約翰會跟他爸爸一樣英俊嗎？

B: Yes. Good looks seem to run in the family.
會的。他們家看來有俊美的基因。

Cosplay 玩家扮演殺人魔傑森。

©Tinxi / Shutterstock.com

107

🎧 129 電影好口怕 **3**
挑選恐怖片、恐怖片類型

Chloe: What kind of movie do you want to watch today?

Robert: I wanna watch a war movie—something historical.

Chloe: Boring. I want to watch a horror flick.

Robert: Well, war movies can be scary too.

Chloe: Not as scary as a good horror flick.

Robert: But war movies are more realistic.

Chloe: I know—let's play rock-paper-scissors. The winner gets to pick.

Robert: OK. *[they play]*

Chloe: Ha, I win! Let's see, what kind of horror movie should we watch?

Robert: Does it matter? Aren't they all the same?

Chloe: No, there's all different kinds—supernatural horror like *The Conjuring* and *Annabelle*, slasher flicks like *Halloween* and *Friday the 13th*. But I like psychological horror best—*The Silence of the Lambs* is my favorite movie!

Robert: But isn't a horror movie the same as a thriller?

Chloe: Well, thrillers are more about tension and suspense. Horror movies take advantage of our deepest fears to *really* scare us—things like ghosts, demons and serial killers.

克蘿伊：你今天要看哪種電影？

羅伯特：我想看戰爭片——歷史類型的。

克蘿伊：無聊。我要看恐怖片。

羅伯特：呃，有些戰爭片也滿恐怖的。

克蘿伊：不會比正港恐怖片恐怖。

羅伯特：但戰爭片真實多了。

克蘿伊：我知道了——來玩剪刀石頭布。贏的人決定。

羅伯特：好。（猜拳）

克蘿伊：哈，我贏了！所以呢，我們要看哪種恐怖片？

羅伯特：有差嗎？還不都一個樣？

克蘿伊：才怪，種類可多了——靈異恐怖片像是《陰廳宅》、《安娜貝兒》，血腥恐怖片像是《月光光心慌慌》、《13 號星期五》。但我最喜歡心理恐怖片——《沈默的羔羊》是我最愛的電影！

羅伯特：恐怖片不就是驚悚片？

克蘿伊：呃，驚悚片比較著重精神上的壓力和懸疑。恐怖片是利用人類深層的恐懼把我們嚇個半死——像是幽魂、魔鬼、殺人魔之類的。

HORROR MOVIE FESTIVAL
31/10/18
FREE ENTRY | CINEMA CLUB

恐怖驚悚片筆記

除了對話中提到的類型之外，恐怖片還有以下常見類型：

action horror 動作恐怖片　　　　holiday horror 假期恐怖片
body horror 肢體恐怖片　　　　　natural horror 自然生物恐怖片
comedy horror 喜劇恐怖片　　　　science fiction horror 科幻恐怖片
disaster horror 災難恐怖片　　　　teen horror 青少年恐怖片
gothic horror 歌德恐怖片　　　　 zombie horror 殭屍恐怖片

© Willrow Hood / Shutterstock.com

Michael Myers在拍攝1978年電影時使用的面具，是拿《星艦迷航記》（*Star Trek*）寇克船長（Captain Kirk，左下）的面具改的。

Michael Myers

麥克邁爾斯

🎧 130 Like Leatherface and Jason, Michael Myers is a serial killer in a mask. We first meet the murderer in the 1978 slasher film *Halloween*, [1]**shot** by famous horror and science fiction director 🆖 **John Carpenter**. After six-year-old Michael murders his teenage sister with a kitchen knife on Halloween in 1963, he's committed to a mental hospital, from which he escapes 15 years later and goes on a killing [2]**spree** in his old neighborhood, also on Halloween. Stealing a white mask and knife from a local store, he kills several teenagers before being shot dead by his psychiatrist, Dr. Loomis. But Myers can't be killed. He returns for another killing spree in *Halloween II*, before again being killed at the end, a process that repeats in each sequel that follows. What's scarier than a serial killer that can't be killed?

　　跟人皮面具和傑森一樣，麥克邁爾斯也是戴著面具的連環殺手，第一次出場是在 1978 年的血腥恐怖片《月光光心慌慌》，是知名的恐怖片和科幻片導演約翰卡本特所拍攝。六歲的麥克在 1963 年萬聖節用菜刀殺死十幾歲的姊姊後，被送進精神病院，15 年後逃離醫院，回到他曾住過的社區進行瘋狂大屠殺，同樣選在萬聖節這天。他在當地一家商店偷走一個白色面具和一把刀後，殺了幾個青少年，後來被他的精神病醫生魯米斯槍斃。但邁爾斯是殺不死的。在《月光光心慌慌 2》中，他又回來進行大屠殺，最後又被殺掉，每一部續集都如此重複。還有什麼比殺不死的連環殺手更可怕呢？

🎧 Vocabulary
131

1) **shoot** [ʃut] (v.) 拍攝，過去式為 **shot** [ʃɑt]
2) **spree** [spri] (n.) 無節制的狂熱行為，**killing spree** 指「大開殺戒的瘋狂行為、大屠殺」

🐌 Language Guide

John Carpenter 約翰卡本特

約翰卡本特生於1948年，是活躍於1970及1980年代的美國電影導演，電影作品數量及類型很多，但最有名的還是恐怖片及科幻片，以《月光光心慌慌》（1978年）、《紐約大逃亡》（*Escape from New York*，1981年）、《外星戀》（*Starman*，1984年）最為賣座。約翰卡本特也是作曲家，常為自己的電影配樂，大眾耳熟能詳的《月光光心慌慌》的主旋律，就是出自他的手筆。

圖片來源：維基百科，攝影：Nathan Hartley Maas

Chucky
鬼娃恰吉

© Tinseltown / Shutterstock.com

🎧132 What's more creepy than a talking doll? A talking doll possessed by the spirit of a serial killer! In the 1988 slasher movie *Child's Play*, serial killer Charles Lee Ray is shot by a policeman and flees into a toy store, where he uses a voodoo spell to transfer his soul into a Good Guy doll before he dies. These battery-powered dolls with red hair, blue eyes and 1)**freckles** are popular with kids, and Chucky is soon given to six-year-old Andy by his mother as a birthday gift. Wanting to become human again, Chucky tries to transfer his soul into Andy's body, killing anyone who LG **gets in his way**. He doesn't succeed in possessing Andy, but he continues his efforts to become human again—as well as his killing sprees—in the six following sequels.

有什麼比會說話的娃娃還詭異？就是被連環殺手靈魂附身的說話娃娃！在 1988 年的血腥恐怖片《靈異入侵》中，連環殺手查爾斯李雷被警察槍殺，逃到一家玩具店，他臨死前用巫毒咒語將自己的靈魂轉移到好孩子恰吉娃娃上。這個用電池供電的玩偶有著紅頭髮、藍眼睛和雀斑，深受小孩歡迎。恰吉很快被一位母親當成生日禮物送給六歲的兒子安迪。想變回人類的恰吉設法將自己的靈魂轉到安迪身上，並殺害所有妨礙他的人。他沒有成功附在安迪身上，但在接下來六部續集中，他仍繼續努力讓自己變回人類，同樣持續大開殺戒。

🎧134 Vocabulary

1) **freckle** [ˋfrɛkəl] (n.) 雀斑
2) **prequel** [ˋprikwəl] (n.) 前傳
3) **conjure** [ˋkʌndʒɚ] (v.) 幻化出（影像）
4) **cinematographer** [ˌsɪnəməˋtɑgrəfɚ] (n.) 電影攝影師
5) **strangle** [ˋstræŋgəl] (v.) 勒斃，使窒息
6) **terrorize** [ˋtɛrəˌraɪz] (v.) 恐嚇，讓人恐懼

👁Language Guide

get in the way (of) 妨礙，阻止

in the way 是「擋在路上」，有個東西堵在路上當然會妨礙通行，因此 get in the way 就是「阻止，阻礙」的意思，get in sb.'s way 即「妨礙某人」。

A: It must be hard working for a boss you hate so much.
幫你那麼討厭的老闆工作一定很辛苦。

B: Yeah, but I try not to let my feelings get in the way of my work.
對啊，但我儘量不讓心裡的感覺妨礙工作。

Annabelle 安娜貝爾

© 網路圖片

🎧133 While Chucky is pretty scary, at least he's fictional. The 2014 supernatural horror film *Annabelle*, which is a 2)**prequel** to *The* 3)*Conjuring*—it was produced by James Wan, but directed by his 4)**cinematographer** John Leonetti—is based on an actual case investigated by Ed and Lorraine Warren. In real life, Annabelle was a Raggedy Ann doll given to a student nurse by her mother, and then handed over to Ed and Lorraine after a medium claimed it was possessed by the spirit of a young girl named Annabelle—and it tried to 5)**strangle** her roommate's fiancé! In the film, Annabelle is a creepy old porcelain doll possessed by an evil demon that 6)**terrorizes** a couple and their baby daughter, trying to steal their souls.

© GIO_LE / Shutterstock.com

鬼娃恰吉雖然可怕，但他至少是虛構的。而 2014 年的超自然恐怖片《安娜貝爾》則是根據艾德與羅琳華倫調查的真實案例改編而成（編註：詳見 p.115～116），由溫子仁製作，但由他的電影攝影師約翰李昂尼提執導，是《厲陰宅》的前傳。在現實生活中，安娜貝爾是一位護理學生的母親送給她的破娃娃小安（編註：見 p.116），後來有靈媒稱這個娃娃被少女安娜貝爾的亡靈附身，而且想掐死她室友的未婚夫！於是娃娃被交給艾德和羅琳華倫。在電影中，安娜貝爾是恐怖的舊陶瓷娃娃，被惡魔附身，不但恐嚇一對夫妻和他們的女嬰，還想奪走他們的靈魂。

Annabelle 在義大利參加影展。光天化日下的 Annabelle 比較不可怕。

正在看恐怖片

Rachel: Aaaah! Oh my god!

James: Ow! Stop digging your nails into my arm.

Rachel: Sorry—this movie is really scary!

James: Hey, you're the one who wanted to see a horror flick.

Rachel: Yeah, but I didn't know it was gonna be this scary. Oh no, I can't watch!

James: Seriously? Who covers their eyes during a movie?

Rachel: Is the ghost gone yet?

James: Yeah, it's gone. You can look now. And you can let go of my arm too. Here, I'll hold your hand. Is that better?

Rachel: Yeah, that's better.

James: I don't get it. Why do people pay money to be scared to death?

Rachel: OK, OK. Somebody's shushing us.

James: *[a little later]* Whoa! Whoa! Oh shit!

Rachel: Ow, you're crushing my hand! Look who's a fraidy-cat now, ha ha.

瑞　秋：啊！！媽呀媽呀媽呀！

詹姆士：噢！不要一直拿指甲掐我的手臂啦。

瑞　秋：抱歉抱歉——這部電影真的好可怕！

詹姆士：嘿，堅持要看恐怖片的人是妳耶。

瑞　秋：是啊，但我沒想到會這麼恐怖。糟了，我不敢看！

詹姆士：妳開玩笑吧？哪有人摀著眼睛看電影的啦？

瑞　秋：鬼走了沒？

詹姆士：好了走了。妳可以看了，也可以放開我的手了。來，我握著妳的手。這樣有好一點嗎？

瑞　秋：嗯，好一點了。

詹姆士：真不懂，怎麼會有人花錢把自己嚇個半死？

瑞　秋：好了，好了。有人在噓我們了。

詹姆士：（過了一會兒）厚！厚！蝦米鬼！！

瑞　秋：哎喲！你把我的手捏扁了啦！現在換誰是膽小鬼啦，哈哈。

恐怖驚悚片筆記

流行文化網站 complex.com 於 2017 年列出史上最恐怖電影名單，以下是前五名：

No. 1 《德州電鋸殺人狂》 *The Texas Chainsaw Massacre* (1974)

No. 2 《閃靈》 *The Shining* (1980)

No. 3 《活死人之夜》 *Night of the Living Dead* (1968)

No. 4 《絕命聖誕夜》 *Black Christmas* (1974)

No. 5 《失嬰記》 *Rosemary's Baby* (1968)

© spatuletail / Shutterstock.com

最恐怖導演
希區考克

Alfred Hitchcock

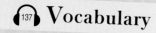

🎧 137 Vocabulary

1) **influential** [ˌɪnfluˈɛnʃəl] (a.) 有影響力的，有支配力的

2) **cinema** [ˈsɪnəmə] (n.) 電影，電影業，電影院

3) **feature** [ˈfitʃə] (n.) （電影）長片，正片，亦作 **feature motion picture / film**

4) **thriller** [ˈθrɪlə] (n.) 驚悚片，驚悚小說

5) **suspense** [səˈspɛns] (n.) 懸疑

6) **celebrity** [səˈlɛbrɪti] (n.) 名人，名氣

7) **cameo** [ˈkæmi.o] (n.) 客串演出，配角

8) **Jesuit** [ˈdʒɛzjuɪt] (n.) 耶穌會信徒

9) **lodger** [ˈlɑdʒə] (n.) 房客

10) **blackmail** [ˈblæk.mel] (n./v.) 勒索，敲詐

11) **talkie** [ˈtɔki] (n.) （口）有聲電影

12) **standout** [ˈstænd.aʊt] (n./a.) 傑出的人事物；傑出的，出色的

13) **psychological** [ˌsaɪkəˈlɑdʒɪkəl] (a.) 心理的，心理學的

14) **vertigo** [ˈvɝtɪ.go] (n.) 暈眩

15) **psycho** [ˈsaɪko] (n./a) 心理失常（者）

16) **disturbed** [dɪsˈtɝbd] (a.) 心理不正常的。動詞 **disturb** [dɪˈstɝb] 即「擾亂（心緒）」

17) **brutally** [ˈbrutəli] (adv.) 殘忍地，粗暴地

18) **slasher** [ˈslæʃə] (n.) 血淋淋的恐怖片，持刀殺人者。**slash** [slæʃ] 可當動詞和名詞，指「猛砍」

🎧 136 Born on the outskirts of London in 1899, Alfred Hitchcock is widely regarded as one of the most [1)]**influential** directors in the history of [2)]**cinema**. In his six-decade career, which began in 1919 and ended with his death in 1980—he never completed his final film—Hitchcock directed over 50 [3)]**feature** films, mostly [4)]**thrillers**. Because of his unique ability to keep audiences 🄛 **on the edge of their seats**, he became known as the "master of [5)]**suspense**." Hitchcock was also one of the few directors to become a [6)]**celebrity** 🄛 **in his own right**. Thanks to his many interviews, his [7)]**cameo** roles in most of his films, and his decade hosting the popular TV series 🄛 *Alfred Hitchcock Presents*, he became just as famous as the big stars who appeared in his movies.

亞佛烈德希區考克於 1899 年在倫敦郊區出生，是公認電影史上最具有影響力的導演之一。他自 1919 年至 1980 年過世期間的六十年職涯中，執導過逾 50 部電影（最後一部沒拍完），大部分是驚悚片。他獨特的手法總是能讓觀眾如坐針氈，因此被譽為「懸疑大師」。希區考克也是自己本身成為名人的少數導演之一。這要歸功於他接受的許多採訪、在自己執導的大部分電影中客串，並主持了十年受歡迎的電視節目《希區考克劇場》，讓他跟出演他電影的大明星一樣有名。

While Hitchcock had a normal middle-class childhood, he said that he learned about fear at a [8)]**Jesuit** 🄛 **grammar school**, where the priests punished students after class with a cane. He started his film career so early that the first movies he directed, like *The Pleasure Garden* and The [9)]***Lodger***, were silent. Hitchcock's 1929 crime thriller [10)]***Blackmail***, which was the first British [11]**talkie**, was so popular that the director began specializing in thrillers, each more successful than the last. [12]**Standouts** include spy thrillers like *The 39 Steps*, mystery thrillers like *Rear Window*, [13]**psychological** thrillers like [14]**Vertigo**, and action thrillers like *North by Northwest*.

希區考克的童年雖然跟一般中產階級一樣，但他曾說他在耶穌會大學預科學校學到恐懼，那裡的神職人員會在課後用藤條懲罰學生。他很早就展開電影生涯，所以他一開始執導的電影是默片，比如《歡樂園》和《房客》。希區考克在 1929 年執導的犯罪驚悚片《敲詐》是英國第一部有聲電影，由於大受歡迎，這位導演開始專攻驚悚片，所執導的每部片都比前一部更賣座。表現出色的電影包括《國防大機密》之類的間諜驚悚片、《後窗》之類的推理驚悚片、《迷魂記》之類心理驚悚片，以及《北西北》之類的動作驚悚片。

Hitchcock's films explore a variety of scary themes— like violence, murder and mental illness—but only two of them, [15]***Psycho*** (1960) and *The Birds* (1963), are considered horror. Based on a 1959 novel inspired by the life of serial killer Ed Gein, *Psycho* is probably Hitchcock's best-known movie. Although filmed in black and white on a low budget, this movie about a [16]**disturbed** motel manager named Norman Bates who dresses up as his mother and murders his guests, was the biggest box-office success of Hitchcock's career. And the famous shower scene, where Bates [17]**brutally** murders actress Janet Leigh with a knife, was a major inspiration for the [18]**slasher** films of the 1970s and '80s.

希區考克的電影探討了各種恐怖主題，比如暴力、謀殺和精神疾病，但其中只有兩部是真正的恐怖片，分別是《驚魂記》（1960 年）和《鳥》（1963 年）。《驚魂記》可能是希區考克最知名的電影，是根據 1959 年一本小說改編，靈感來自連環殺人犯艾德蓋恩的一生。雖然這部電影是以低成本拍成的黑白片，卻是希區考克職涯中最賣座的電影，敘述精神異常的汽車旅館經理諾曼貝茲打扮成自己母親的樣子，謀殺入住的旅客。其中最有名的淋浴戲是貝茲用刀子殘忍殺害女演員珍妮特利，這場戲成了 1970 年代和 1980 年代血腥恐怖片的主要靈感來源。

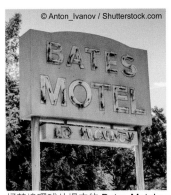

好萊塢環球片場中的 Bates Motel。　《驚魂記》當中，兇手殘殺被害者的經典畫面。

Language Guide

on the edge of one's seat
興奮焦慮，坐立難安

想形容某人非常焦慮，中文有種説法叫「坐立難安」，而英文的説法其實也很類似，只是坐立難安在中文通常表示感到緊張害怕，而英文的 on the edge of one's seat 則表示興奮緊張、屏息以待，常用來形容電影十分精采。

A: Wow, what a scary movie!
　哇，這電影真恐怖！

B: Yeah. I was on the edge of my seat the whole time!
　是啊，我整場都屏息以待！

in (one's) own right 憑本事

這個片語用在表示一個人有權利享有榮華富貴，因為都是憑自己的天份、靠自己的努力得來。

A: Why doesn't David just take over his father's company?
　大衛為什麼不接掌他父親的公司？

B: I think he wants to become a success in his own right.
　我猜他是想靠自己的努力功成名就吧。

Alfred Hitchcock Presents
《希區考克劇場》

希區考克拍攝電影超過三十年後，於1955～1965年（共7季）在美國製播主持了一系列獨立單元劇（anthology series），內容種類包括故事劇、犯罪驚悚劇及神秘推理劇。這系列節目曾被《時代雜誌》選入百大最佳電視節目。

grammar school 大學預科學校

這個名稱源自中世紀，這類學校專門教授學者使用的拉丁語及希臘語，目前則教授文史、數理各種科目。在美國，grammar school 是 elementary school（小學）的舊稱，而在英國學制中，grammar school 是為以進入大學為目標的學生而設的中學，提供大學預備課程。想入學的學生，必須在小學畢業（11歲）時參加學術能力考試（11 plus），提供成績給學校篩選。而就讀其他綜合中學及職業先修中學的孩子，大多畢業後即開始就業。

138
電影好口怕 5
中西殭屍大不同

Taylor: Have you seen *Train to Busan*? It's an awesome Korean thriller.

Megan: I've heard of it. Isn't it a zombie movie?

Taylor: Yeah. Are there zombie movies in Taiwan?

Megan: Taiwan's had some pretty good horror movies lately, but none of them are about zombies. Hong Kong put out lots of zombie movies in the '80s. The most famous one was *Mr. Vampire*. It's a horror comedy about a Taoist priest who fights zombies.

Taylor: If it's a zombie movie, why's it called *Mr. Vampire*?

Megan: Well, in Chinese they're called *jiangshi*. They're like a cross between a zombie and a vampire. They're reanimated corpses that hop around and kill the living.

Taylor: Do they drink blood and eat human flesh?

Megan: They eat flesh, but they don't drink blood. You can hide from them by holding your breath. And if you get bitten by one, the only way you can avoid turning into a zombie is by eating sticky rice.

泰勒：妳有看過《屍速列車》嗎？一部很不錯的韓國驚悚片。

梅根：我有聽說過。一部喪屍片，不是嗎？

泰勒：對。台灣也有喪屍片嗎？

梅根：台灣最近有幾部不錯的恐怖片，但都不是喪屍題材。香港在八零年代拍了不少喪屍片。最有名的是《暫時停止呼吸》（1985 年）。是一部道士打殭屍的恐怖喜劇。

泰勒：如果是殭屍電影，為什麼叫「吸血鬼先生」？

梅根：呃，中文叫他們「殭屍」。類似喪屍和吸血鬼的綜合體。他們是不會腐爛的屍體，到處跳到處殺人。

泰勒：他們也吸血、吃人肉嗎？

梅根：他們會吃人肉，但不吸血。必須摒住呼吸才能躲過殭屍。萬一被殭屍咬傷，唯一的解藥就是吃糯米，不然也會變成殭屍。

恐怖驚悚片筆記

影音娛樂網站 collider.com 於 2018 年列出史上最佳殭屍片，
以下是 2000 年後上映的片單：
《死雪禁地》*Dead Snow* (2009)
《28 週毀滅倒數：全球封閉》*28 Weeks Later* (2007)，《28 天毀滅倒數》續集
《屍樂園》*Zombieland* (2009)
《索女‧喪屍‧機關槍》*Planet Terror* (2007)（台灣未上映）
《屍速列車》*Train to Busan* (2016)
《活人生吃》*Dawn of the Dead* (2004)
《28 天毀滅倒數》*28 Days Later* (2002)
《活人甡吃》*Shaun of the Dead* (2004)

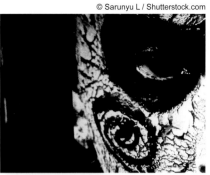
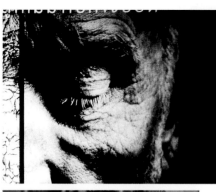

《奪魂鋸》第八集的宣傳海報。

溫子仁的搭檔編劇 Leigh Whannell。

最恐怖導演

James Wan

溫子仁

🎧139 Born into a Malaysian-Chinese family in Kuching, Sarawak in 1977, James Wan moved to Perth, Australia at the age of seven. Wan fell in love with scary movies when his mother took him to see *Poltergeist* when he was a little kid, and by the age of 11, he knew he wanted to be a [1]**filmmaker**. While attending film school at RMIT University in Melbourne, Wan met [2]**screenwriter** Leigh Whannell, and the two began writing a [3]**script** for a horror film based on their own fears and nightmares. After the script was rejected by studios in Australia, the pair decided to make a short film based on it and show it to [4]**producers** in Hollywood.

溫子仁於 1977 年生於馬來西亞砂拉越州古晉市的華裔家庭，7 歲時移居澳洲伯斯。溫子仁小時候，媽媽帶他去看電影《鬼哭神號》後，他就愛上了恐怖片，11 歲時就已立志要拍電影。他在就讀墨爾本皇家理工大學電影系時，認識了編劇雷沃納爾，兩人開始根據自己所恐懼的事情和惡夢寫成恐怖片劇本。他們的劇本遭到澳洲的製片廠拒絕後，兩人決定以這劇本拍部短片，向好萊塢的製片人推銷。

《奪魂鋸》中殺人狂用來跟受害人溝通的詭異木偶比利 Billy the Puppet。

🎧140 Vocabulary

1) **filmmaker** [ˈfɪlmˌmekə] (n.) 製片、導演等產製電影者

2) **screenwriter** [ˈskrinˌraɪtə] (n.)（電影、電視）劇本作家，編劇家

3) **script** [skrɪpt] (n.)（戲劇、電影等）劇本

4) **producer** [prəˈdusə] (n.) 製作人，製片

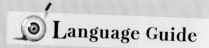
Vocabulary

1) **psychopath** [ˋsaɪkəˌpæθ] (n.) 精神病患，精神變態者

2) **jigsaw** [ˋdʒɪgˌsɔ] (n.) 線鋸，拼圖，七巧板

3) **cult** [kʌlt] (a./n.) 小眾的，非主流但有忠實粉絲的；風行，流行

4) **murderous** [ˋmɝdərəs] (a.) 蓄意謀殺的，殘忍的

5) **insidious** [ɪnˋsɪdɪəs] (a.) 陰險的，暗中危害的

Language Guide

(get sth./sb.) back on track
（將某人／某物拉）回正軌

track 表示「軌道」，當某人誤入歧途或某事走偏時其實就像火車出軌，別忘了要將它導回正途喔！

A: Sandra Bullock has been in a lot of movies lately.
珊卓布拉克最近演出不少電影。

B: Yeah. She says the nude scenes she did in *The Proposal* got her career back on track.
對啊，她說在《愛情限時簽》的裸露鏡頭讓她事業重回軌道。

Ed and Lorraine Warren 華倫夫婦
美國著名的靈異事件調查者，兩人成立了新英格蘭靈異研究協會（New England Society for Psychic Research）。許多恐怖片均取材自他們經手的調查案件，包括：《康乃狄克鬼屋事件》（*The Haunting in Connecticut*）（2009）《厲陰宅》（*The Conjuring*）第一、二集、《安娜貝爾》（*Annabelle*）第一、二集。

羅琳華倫出席《厲陰宅》的首映會。

Raggedy Ann 破娃娃小安
美國童書作家Johnny Gruelle（1880–1938）以早夭女兒心愛的舊娃娃為主角，1918年發行繪本*Raggedy Ann Stories*《破娃娃小安故事集》，同時推出同款布娃娃，在市場上大獲成功，1920年接著推出男娃娃Andy的*Raggedy Andy Stories*《破娃娃安弟故事集》。

Wan and Whannell found a producer almost immediately, and shot their film, *Saw*, on a low budget in just 18 days. The movie, about a [1]psychopath called the [2]Jigsaw Killer who kidnaps victims and puts them through "tests"—usually involving deadly mechanical traps—that they must pass if they want to survive, was released in 2004. Despite poor reviews, *Saw* soon had a [3]cult following, and ended up grossing over $100 million worldwide, over 80 times the production budget! The Jigsaw Killer and Billy the Puppet—the creepy puppet he uses to communicate with his victims—became so popular with horror fans that seven sequels have been filmed so far.

溫子仁和沃納爾幾乎是立刻找到製片人，並以低成本拍了電影《奪魂鋸》，且只花了18天。這部電影在2004年發行，敘述精神病患拼圖殺人狂綁架受害人，並要他們通過「測試」，通常是會奪命的機械陷阱，受害人若想生存下來，必須通過這些測試。儘管評價不佳，《奪魂鋸》隨即吸引到大批狂熱的支持者，最後在全世界的票房總計超過一億元，超過拍攝預算的80倍！拼圖殺人狂和木偶比利，也就是殺人狂用來跟受害人溝通的詭異木偶，非常受到恐怖片粉絲的歡迎，目前已經拍攝了七部續集。

But Wan hasn't limited his horror efforts to the *Saw* films. After directing *Dead Silence*, a 2007 movie about a [4]murderous doll that did poorly at the box office, he got back on track with [5]*Insidious* in 2010. This film, about a young boy who is possessed by an evil spirit, was also a big box office success, and inspired a sequel and two prequels. Wan has also found further horror success with *The Conjuring*, a 2013 film based on real-life paranormal investigators **Ed and Lorraine Warren** and their encounter with a possessed **Raggedy Ann** doll. The movie, and its 2016 sequel *The Conjuring 2*—about another Warren investigation involving a British poltergeist—were both critical and box office successes, and *The Conjuring 3* is currently being filmed.

但溫子仁拍的恐怖片不只有《奪魂鋸》系列。他在2007年執導的《歡迎光臨死亡小鎮》，是關於殺人的木偶，但票房表現不佳，他在2010年拍的《陰兒房》則恢復票房水準。這部電影敘述一名小男孩被邪靈附身，票房也是大賣，更推動一部續集和兩部前傳。溫子仁在2013年拍的《厲陰宅》也是成功的恐怖片，是根據真實故事改編，敘述超自然現象調查者艾德和羅琳華倫與被鬼附身的破娃娃小安交手。這部電影和2016年的續集《厲陰宅2》——另一個華倫夫婦調查英國騷靈的故事——評論和票房皆締造佳績，《厲陰宅3》目前正在拍攝中。

我才不怕看恐怖片

Emily: God, it's finally over.

Kevin: What, you didn't like it?

Emily: You liked it? My eyes were closed for half of the movie. You didn't get scared at all?

Kevin: I used to, but then I discovered the secret to not getting scared.

Emily: I'm all ears.

Kevin: The reason I used to get scared is because I identified with the characters. Now I tell myself "It's just a movie," and I don't get scared.

Emily: Easier said than done. I bet you're just numb from watching so many horror movies.

Kevin: Ha-ha. It's possible. And I don't just watch horror flicks—I play horror games too.

Emily: How do you play horror games?

Kevin: It's a little like being in a horror movie, but way more exciting! You do your best to escape the monsters, and when they attack you, you fight back!

Emily: That just sounds like your average fighting game.

Kevin: Except you're in a horror movie, which makes it more fun!

Emily: Yeah, right.

艾蜜莉：天啊，終於演完了。

凱　文：怎麼，妳不喜歡？

艾蜜莉：你喜歡？這部電影我有一半的時間都閉著眼睛。你都不會怕？

凱　文：我以前會怕，但後來我發現不讓自己害怕的秘訣。

艾蜜莉：說來聽聽。

凱　文：我以前會怕，是因為感覺自己就是劇中人。現在我會告訴自己「這只是電影」，我就不害怕了。

艾蜜莉：說得倒簡單。我看你是看太多恐怖片麻痺了吧。

凱　文：呵呵，可能喔，而且我不只看恐怖片——我還玩恐怖遊戲。

艾蜜莉：那是在玩什麼？

凱　文：有點像自己在演鬼片，但刺激多了！必須想盡辦法脫逃，被鬼攻擊的時候，還要狠狠回擊！

艾蜜莉：聽起來跟一般打鬥電玩沒兩樣。

凱　文：但情境是恐怖片啊，這樣更好玩！

艾蜜莉：真是夠了。

恐怖驚悚片筆記

電玩科技迷網站 NerdMuch.com 於 2018 年更新了一份最恐怖電玩名單，其中最新的遊戲有：：

《少數幸運兒》 *We Happy Few*（Summer 2018）

《邪靈入侵 2》 *The Evil Within 2*（October 13, 2017）

《心跳文學部！》 *Doki Doki Literature Club!*（September 22, 2017）

《痛苦之地》 *The Land of Pain*（September 13, 2017）

《侵視者》 *Observer*（August 15, 2017）

《地獄之刃：賽奴雅的獻祭》 *Hellblade: Senua's Sacrifice*（August 8, 2017）

《報復》 *Get Even*（June 23, 2017）

《十三號星期五》 *Friday The 13th: The Game*（May 26, 2017）

最恐怖作家

愛倫坡

Edgar Allan Poe

© Hethers / Shutterstock.com

愛倫坡墓，位於美國馬里蘭州巴爾的摩市。

🎧 Vocabulary

1) **macabre** [mə`kabrə] (a.) 恐怖的，關於死亡的

2) **orphan** [`ɔrfən] (v.) 失去父母，使成孤兒

3) **lasting** [`læstɪŋ] (a.) 持久的，不衰的

4) **morgue** [mɔrg] (n.) 太平間

5) **credit (with)** [`krɛdɪt] (v.) 把…歸功於

6) **detective** [dɪ`tɛktɪv] (n.)（私人）偵探，警探

7) **morbid** [`mɔrbɪd] (a.) 病態的，陰鬱可怕的

8) **ominous** [`amɪnəs] (a.) 不祥的

9) **grieve** [griv] (v.) 哀悼，悲傷

10) **genre** [`ʒanrə] (n.)（藝文作品的）類型

11) **retreat** [rɪ`trit] (v./n.) 撤退，後退

12) **abbey** [`æbi] (n.) 大修道院

13) **privilege** [`prɪvəlɪdʒ] (n.) 特權，特殊利益

14) **cask** [kæsk] (n.)（儲放液體的）桶，酒桶

15) **insult** [ɪn`sʌlt / `ɪnsʌlt] (v./n.) 侮辱，辱罵

16) **lure** [lur] (v./n.) 引誘；誘惑物

17) **cellar** [`sɛlɚ] (n.) 酒窖，地窖

18) **sherry** [`ʃɛri] (n.) 雪利酒，一種以白葡萄製成的烈酒

🎧144 Born in Boston on January 19, 1809, Edgar Allan Poe lived a short and tragic life, which may explain why he became an author of the [1]**macabre**. Poe was [2]**orphaned** at the age of two, and although a family adopted him, they later abandoned him when he went into debt from gambling. As a result, he left college and joined the army, where he began his writing career with a collection of romantic poetry, which was published in 1827. Poe married his 13-year-old cousin Virginia, and while their marriage was happy, she died just 11 years later of tuberculosis. And the author himself died two years after that of mysterious causes—some say alcohol and drugs, others heart disease or suicide.

愛倫坡在 1809 年 1 月 19 日生於美國波士頓，一生短暫且悲慘，這或許是他成為驚悚作家的原因。愛倫坡在兩歲時成了孤兒，雖然有個家庭收養他，但後來在他賭博而負債後拋棄他。於是他在大學時輟學並加入軍隊，開始寫作生涯，寫了一本詩集，於 1827 年出版。愛倫坡娶了 13 歲的表妹維吉妮亞，他們的婚姻雖然幸福，但她在 11 年後死於肺結核。這位作家則在兩年後過世，死因不明，有人說是因為酗酒和吸毒，另有人說是死於心臟病或自殺。

Poe was known mostly as an editor and critic in his lifetime—although he was fired from several jobs for drinking—but it is his Gothic horror stories that have brought him [3]**lasting** fame. With his short story *The Murders in the*

Rue [4]*Morgue*, he is [5]**credited with** inventing the [6]**detective** story. Nevertheless, it was his [7]**morbid** poem *The Raven*—about a man visited by an [8]**ominous** bird as he [9]**grieves** for his dead love—that brought him to national attention. In his early short story, *The Fall of the House of Usher*, Poe describes an evil mansion that drives its inhabitants insane, causes their deaths, and finally sinks into the lake that surrounds it.

愛倫坡生前主要以編輯和評論而聞名，儘管他因酗酒而被解雇幾次，但他因寫下哥德式恐怖故事而名留青史。他的短篇故事《莫爾格街兇殺案》被視為偵探故事的先河。不過他是以《烏鴉》這首詭異的詩受到全國矚目，這首詩描述有位男子在哀悼過世的愛人時，有一隻不祥的鳥來拜訪他。愛倫坡在早期的短篇故事《厄舍府的沒落》中，敘述一棟邪氣的宅第，把住在裡面的人逼瘋，也導致他們死亡，這棟宅第最後沉入週遭的湖中。

1960 年恐怖電影 *House of Usher* 的海報。這是導演 Roger Corman 拍攝的 8 部愛倫坡故事電影的第一部。本片於 2005 年被美國國家電影保護局收藏於美國國會圖書館。

While Poe went on to write stories in many [10]**genres**, including humor, adventure and science fiction, he kept coming back to horror. In *The Mask of the Red Death*, a group of nobles [11]**retreats** to an [12]**abbey** to escape a terrible plague, but discover that their wealth and [13]**privilege** can't protect them as they die one by one. But his creepiest story may be *The* [14]*Cask of Amontillado*, about a man who decides to take revenge against a friend who has [15]**insulted** him. [16]**Luring** his friend into a wine [17]**cellar** with the offer of a rare bottle of [18]**sherry**, he then gets the man drunk, chains him to the wall and slowly builds a brick wall around him, burying him alive!

© 《愛倫坡的奇想故事集》（*Poe's Tales of Mystery and Imagination*，1935 年）

勃培洛王子（Prince Prospero）死在紅死病下。（插畫／Arthur Rackham）

愛倫坡雖然後來寫了許多類型的故事，包括幽默、冒險和科幻，但他一直回頭寫恐怖故事。《紅死病的面具》敘述一群貴族為躲避可怕的瘟疫而隱居到修道院，卻發現他們的財富和權勢無法保護他們，並一個接一個地死去。但愛倫坡寫過最毛骨悚然的故事可能是《一桶阿蒙蒂亞度酒》，敘述一名男子決定報復羞辱他的朋友，他以一瓶稀有的雪莉酒將朋友引到一處酒窖，把他灌醉，用鎖鏈將他拴在牆上，然後慢慢在他周圍築起磚牆，將他活埋在裡面！

© 《愛倫坡的奇想故事集》

Montresor 砌牆將 Fortunato 活埋。
（插畫／Arthur Rackham）

146 電影好口怕 7
恐怖片後遺症

Karl: Hey, your TV won't turn on. Are the batteries in the remote dead?

Zoe: No. I unplugged it.

Karl: Wow, you really know how to save energy.

Zoe: Ha-ha. I did it 'cause I was afraid.

Karl: Afraid of what?

Zoe: Promise not to tell anybody?

Karl: Why are you being so mysterious?

Zoe: You can't tell anybody, OK?

Karl: OK, OK. My lips are sealed.

Zoe: It's because I watched *Ring* last week.

Karl: The Japanese horror movie? You're afraid of ghosts?

Zoe: When the ghost came out of the TV, it scared me half to death. Since then, I always unplug the TV after I turn it off. And I don't even watch TV when I'm alone.

Karl: That's silly. But have you considered something even scarier?

Zoe: What?

Karl: What if the TV turned on by itself when it wasn't plugged in?

Zoe: Aaah, stop it! I'm throwing my TV away!

卡爾：嘿，妳的電視打不開耶。是遙控器電池沒電嗎？

柔伊：沒啦，是我把插頭拔掉了。

卡爾：哇，妳真懂省電。

柔伊：呵呵，其實我是因為害怕。

卡爾：怕什麼？

柔伊：你不可以說出去喔。

卡爾：什麼事這麼神秘啊？

柔伊：你不可以跟別人說，可以嗎？

卡爾：好啦好啦。我保證守口如瓶。

柔伊：是因為上星期看了《七夜怪談》。

卡爾：那部日本恐怖片？妳是在怕鬼？

柔伊：女鬼從電視裡爬出來那一幕把我嚇死了。從那時候開始，每次看完電視我都把插頭拔掉。我現在沒人陪的時候都不看電視。

卡爾：太扯了。但妳有沒有想過更可怕的情況？

柔伊：什麼？

卡爾：要是電視沒插電的時候自己打開？

柔伊：啊！！不要再說了。我要把電視丟掉！

恐怖驚悚片筆記

根據 2004 年美國系列紀錄片 *The 100 Scariest Movie Moments*，電影製作人 Anthony Timpone、劇作家 Patrick Moses、導演 Kevin Kaufman 帶領觀眾回味影史百大最驚悚恐怖片段，以下是前 5 名：

No. 5《德州電鋸殺人狂》Leatherface 用大鎚敲破 Kirk 頭骨那一幕。

No. 4《驚魂記》私人偵探 Milton Arbogast 被殺那一幕。

No. 3《大法師》在驅魔過程中，中邪的 Regan MacNeil 頭 360 度扭轉那一幕。

No. 2《異形》（*Alien*）異形從胸腔鑽出那一幕。

No. 1《大白鯊》（*Jaws*）電影開場 Chrissie Watkins 夜裡游泳被隱身水中的鯊魚吃掉那一幕。

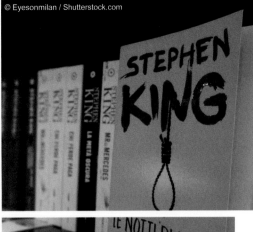

最恐怖作家

Stephen King

史蒂芬金

As you probably know, Stephen King is one of the world's most popular authors, and also one of the most [1]**prolific**. He has written 58 novels and over 200 short stories in his 50-year career, and his books have sold over 350 million copies. While King has published successful novels in the science fiction, fantasy and crime genres, he's often been called the "king of horror." Many have [2]**speculated** that his love of horror is the result of a [3]**troubled** childhood—when King was just two, his father went out to buy a pack of cigarettes and never returned—but he says his inspiration came from a collection of horror stories by **H.P. Lovecraft** that he found in the attic. "I knew that I'd found home when I read that book," says the author.

你可能知道，史蒂芬金是世上最受歡迎且產量最多的作家之一。在其 50 年的職涯中，他寫過 58 部小說和兩百多篇短篇小說，並售出逾三億五千萬本書。史蒂芬金雖然成功出版過科幻、奇幻和犯罪類型的小說，但常被稱為「恐怖小說之王」。許多人猜測他對恐怖故事的熱愛是源自坎坷的童年，史蒂芬金兩歲時，他父親出門買香菸後再也沒有回家，但他說他的靈感來自他在閣樓找到的霍華德洛夫克拉夫特的恐怖故事集。這位作家說：「我在讀那本書時，我知道我找到了歸屬。」

Vocabulary

1) **prolific** [prəˋlɪfɪk] (a.) 多產的，富有創造力的
2) **speculate** [ˋspɛkjəˌlet] (v.) 推測，揣測
3) **troubled** [ˋtrʌbəld] (a.) 困難重重的，困頓的

Language Guide

H.P. Lovecraft 霍華德洛夫克拉夫特

洛夫克拉夫特（1890～1937）的聲望在他過世後才慢慢打開，現在已被視為繼19世紀的愛倫坡之後，20世紀對恐怖小說家影響最大的作家。他稱自己寫作的主題是宇宙主義（Cosmicism），善良邪惡、喜悲哀懼在無限的時間、空間當中根本沒有意義，人不論再怎麼努力理解所處的世界，也只不過是活在無處不在且隨機的巨大惡意當中。

洛夫克拉夫特所著的《克魯蘇的呼喚》（*The Call of Cthulhu*）後來演變出架空神話體系「克蘇魯神話」（Cthulhu Mythos），其中的恐怖元素可見於現代各類恐怖作品（小說、電影、音樂甚至動漫、遊戲）當中。

🎧150 Vocabulary

1) **telekinesis** [ˌtɛləkəˈnisɪs] (n.) 念力，
心靈傳動能力

2) **bestselling** [ˈbɛstˈsɛlɪŋ] (a.) 暢銷的；
名詞為 **bestseller** [ˈbɛstˈsɛlə] 暢銷作品

3) **alcoholic** [ˌælkəˈhɔlɪk] (n./a.) 酒鬼，酗酒者；
含酒精的

4) **prey (on)** [pre] (v./n.) 捕食；獵物，
被捕食的動物

🐌 Language Guide

prom 高中舞會

美國高中每年都會舉辦的舞會，被視為高中生的
重要活動之一。一般來說，參加者都會穿著正式
服裝，並與事先找好的舞伴（date）一起赴會。
重頭戲是公佈大家選出的最受歡迎男生與女生，
加冕為舞會國王與皇后（prom king / queen）。

© Sarunyu L / Shutterstock.com

🎧149 King's first novel, *Carrie*, about a high school girl who uses her psychic powers to get revenge against the students who bully her, is one of his most successful novels—and also one of the scariest. After some of the students dump pig's blood on her at the 🔊 **prom**, she uses [1]**telekinesis** to lock everyone inside the gym and burn it down! First published in 1974, *Carrie* was made into a very scary horror film two years later by Brian De Palma. But apparently people liked being scared—*Carrie* was turned into a Broadway musical in 1988, a sequel was filmed in 1999, and a new film version came out in 2013.

史蒂芬金的第一本小說《魔女嘉莉》是他最成功的小說之一，也是最驚悚的，敘述女高中生利用自己的超能力來報復霸凌她的同學。有幾個同學在學校舞會上將豬血灑在嘉莉身上後，她用念力將所有人鎖在體育館內，並將體育館燒毀！《魔女嘉莉》在 1974 年首次出版，兩年後由布萊恩狄帕瑪拍成格外可怕的恐怖片。顯然大家都喜歡被嚇到，《魔女嘉莉》在 1988 年改編成百老匯音樂劇，1999 年拍續集電影，2013 年又推出新的電影版。

Since *Carrie*, King has written a long string of [2]**bestselling** horror novels, many of which have also been turned into popular movies. One of these is *The Shining*, a 1977 novel about an [3]**alcoholic** author who gets driven insane by a haunted hotel. Not only was the novel a [2]**bestseller**—the 1980 movie version, starring Jack Nicholson and directed by Stanley Kubrick, is considered one of the greatest horror films ever made. Another of King's biggest horror successes is *It*, his 1986 novel about an evil clown named Pennywise that [4]**preys on** children. *It* was made into a successful 1990 miniseries and an award-winning 2017 movie, which is the highest-grossing horror film of all time.

自《魔女嘉莉》後，史蒂芬金寫了大量的暢銷恐怖小說，其中有許多拍成受歡迎的電影。其中一本是 1977 年的小說《鬼店》，敘述酗酒的作家在一間鬧鬼的旅館被逼瘋。這本小說不但暢銷，1980 年的電影版也被認為是史上最棒的恐怖電影之一，是由傑克尼克遜主演，史丹利庫柏力克執導。史蒂芬金另一本成功的恐怖小說是 1986 年的《牠》，敘述會吃小孩的邪惡小丑潘尼懷斯，在 1990 年改編為成功的迷你劇，2017 年改編成獲獎電影，也是史上最賣座的恐怖電影。

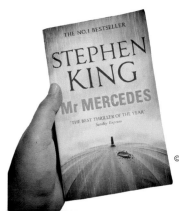

© Raihana Asral / Shutterstock.com

最美的女鬼

Grace: What's the most famous Chinese-language horror movie?

Lewis: Hmm, interesting question. In Chinese, we often call horror movies "ghost movies," but the most famous ghost movie isn't really that scary.

Grace: Oh? What is it?

Lewis: I think if you ask people in Hong Kong or Taiwan what the most famous Chinese-language horror movie is, most of them will say *A Chinese Ghost Story*. It's a love story about a man and a ghost set in ancient China.

Grace: So it's a romance?

Lewis: Yeah. It's based on a story from a Qing Dynasty collection called *Strange tales from a Chinese Studio*. It has the fighting and comedy of an old ghost movie, but also uses a lot of innovative techniques. It won a lot of awards, and was a big hit at the box office too.

Grace: Was the ghost the man fell in love with scary?

Lewis: No, and she was beautiful. The Taiwanese actress who played her ended up becoming a sex symbol.

葛瑞絲：中文電影當中，最有名的恐怖片是哪部？

路易斯：嗯…很有意思的問題。在中文裡，我們經常會用「鬼片」稱呼恐怖片。但最有名的「鬼片」不怎麼恐怖。

葛瑞絲：哦？是哪部？

路易斯：如果去問香港人或台灣人中文最有名的恐怖片，我想大多數的人會說《倩女幽魂》。一個發生在中國古代，人鬼相戀的故事。

葛瑞絲：所以是浪漫愛情片？

路易斯：沒錯。這部電影取材自中國清代故事集《聊齋誌異》。這部有老式鬼片的武打和詼諧成分，但也採用了許多創新技術，得了很多獎，而且非常叫座。

葛瑞絲：那個人愛上的鬼很可怕嗎？

路易斯：不可怕，她非常美。扮演女鬼的台灣女星還成為性感偶像。

恐怖驚悚片筆記

扮演《倩女幽魂》聶小倩的女星王祖賢，不論在陰陽兩界都有榮獲選美冠軍的實力。如果想要一邊看恐怖片，一邊欣賞美女，以下是恐怖片最性感女性（不一定是鬼）前 5 名：

No. 5 《德州電鋸殺人狂：從頭開始》*Texas Chainsaw Massacre: The Beginning*（2006）的 Jordana Brewster

No. 4 《3D 食人魚》*Piranha 3D*（2010）Kelly Brook

No. 3 《德州電鋸殺人狂》*The Texas Chainsaw Massacre*（2003）Jessica Biel

No. 2 《詭屋》*The Cabin in the Woods*（2012）Anna Hutchison

No. 1 《辣的要命》*Jennifer's Body*（2009）Megan Fox

Spirits East and West

東西鬼怪大不同

文／ **Madeleine** 以熙國際創辦人

紐約出生長大，經劍橋、聯合國任職，回台歷任經濟部、教育部、國會、商業司、資策會、中小企總…等前三百大企業的國際化顧問，同時主持近 20 個國內主要數位與平面媒體專欄。創立以熙國際，致力於協助渴望站上世界舞台的華人與世界接軌，帶領華人說世界的語言，圓自己的夢想。

Preface

In watching Asian and Western horror films, by comparing how the plots are designed to scare audiences, we can easily find that there are significant differences in how Asians and Westerners view ghosts and the concept of horror. This stark contrast can be explained by differences in history, culture, and religion.

前言

當我們在看亞洲恐怖片和西方恐怖片時，透過比較雙方如何設計影片劇情讓觀眾覺得恐怖，我們可以輕易地觀察出，東西方對鬼以及「恐怖」的概念有明顯的不同。這份顯著的差異，可以從雙方的歷史、文化與宗教來說明。

Ghosts vs. Serial Killers

When talking about horror films, Asians immediately think of long-haired female ghosts or child ghosts with big black eyes like the one in The Grudge. Whereas Asian horror films are almost always about ghosts, many Western horror films—like The Silence of the Lambs—feature serial killers.

For Asians, the fear they feel arises from certain folk beliefs. Even today, traditional taboos are still followed by many Asians. Violating taboos is usually the last thing an Asian would want to do, and this is used to create an atmosphere of dread in Asian horror movies.

The serial killers in Western horror movies, on the other hand, can be seen as an extreme expression of the individualism that has long prevailed in the West. These serial killers are sometimes even seen as a representation of self-empowerment. Since folklore and taboos no longer play a large role in Western culture, horror films rely more on graphic violence and gore to evoke fear in audiences.

鬼vs.連環殺手：什麼是人心中最深的恐懼？

說起恐怖片，亞洲人可能會立刻想到長髮女鬼或如《咒怨》裡有雙黑色大眼睛的小鬼。一般來說亞洲恐怖片的主題通常都是鬼，相反地，西方恐怖片往往以連環殺手為主角，如《沉默的羔羊》。

對亞洲人而言，他們的恐懼源自於特定民俗。許多傳統的禁忌至今被許多亞洲人遵從。一般而言，亞洲人絕對不會想去觸犯禁忌，這是亞洲恐怖片驚悚氛圍的根源。

西方恐怖片裡的連環殺手，則被視作西方長期以來盛行個人主義的極端表現方式。有時連環殺手的主題也被視作一種自我賦權的形式。由於在西方文化裡，民俗和各種禁忌已不再被看重，觀眾的恐懼也因此較倚靠寫實的暴力和血腥畫面。

How Do Asians And Westerners View Spirits Differently?

The differing views Asians and Westerners have about ghosts are strongly affected by their religions. Westerners believe that the spirits of the dead are immaterial. They don't need food and usually don't have any connection with living people anymore. This definition is a reflection of the Christian concept of Heaven, where the spirits of the dead reside in immaterial form for eternity.

In Asia, however, the conception of ghosts is completely different. People tend to believe that the dead have the same material and emotional needs as the living, and that they can be found all around us in our lives. The Chinese believe that when people die, their spirits split into three parts: one goes to the underworld to pay the debts they accumulated in life (in accordance with the Buddhist concept of karma); one remains in the tomb; and one resides in an ancestral tablet in the family home. Unlike the West, in Asia the spirits of the dead remain a part of people's daily lives.

亞洲人與西方人對鬼魂有什麼不同看法？

亞洲人與西方人對鬼魂所持有的不同觀點深受各自的宗教影響。西方人相信死人的靈魂是非物質的。這些靈魂不需要飲食，通常也不再和活人有任何干係。這個定義基本上反映了基督教裡「天堂」的概念，死者的靈（鬼）魂在天堂是全然超脫於物質，並只會待在死後的世界，即天堂裡。

在亞洲，鬼的概念則截然不同。人們傾向於認為鬼魂和活人一樣有物質和情感需求，而且鬼魂就存在於我們生活的周遭。中國人相信，當人們死了，靈魂會分作三個部份——一到地獄償還生前的債（源自佛教裡因果報應的觀念）；一留在墳墓裡；一則會在人們家中的祖先牌位，顯示鬼魂被視作亞洲生活的一部分，西方則不然。

Halloween vs. the Ghost Festival

Observing festivals is another way to understand how Asians and Westerners view ghosts. On Halloween, people dress up in scary costumes and carve jack-o'-lanterns to keep ghosts away, suggesting that in the West ghosts are generally unwelcome and seen as intruders in the lives of the living.

Today, Halloween has evolved into a lighthearted, festive occasion that is celebrated around the world, while the Ghost Festival has retained its traditional form and can only be found it countries with the same folk beliefs.

During the Ghost Festival, instead of chasing ghosts away, the Chinese do their best to please them by burning spirit money and making offerings of food or daily necessities for the spirits to enjoy in the afterlife. The Chinese also place water lanterns in rivers to guide ghosts so they can visit their living relatives. What's interesting is that Chinese people please ghosts because they're afraid of them and believe they may be punished if they lack sincerity, whereas Westerners see Halloween as a festive occasion because they're less scared of ghosts.

萬聖節vs.中元節

觀察中西鬼節是另一種瞭解亞洲人和西方人認知鬼的方式。在萬聖節，人們為了把鬼嚇走而喬裝打扮，並製作南瓜燈籠以將鬼趕走，意味著鬼在西方基本上不被歡迎，被視為人類生活的入侵者。

萬聖節如今已演變為歡樂且全球化的節慶；另一方面，中元節則保持傳統，仍只在有同樣信仰的國家慶祝。

中國人很強調在中元節時要討好鬼，而非一味將鬼趕走，比如燒紙錢、獻祭食物或日常用品，好讓鬼在死後也能享受到這些。中國人也會將水燈放入河，引導鬼魂找到正確的方向以拜訪活著的親人。有趣的是，中國人討好鬼魂是因為怕鬼，他們認為如果沒有誠心祭拜，可能會有報應，然而西方人將萬聖節視為一個歡樂的節日，則正是因為他們較不怕鬼。

More Fun Facts about the Ghost Festival

Unlike Halloween, which is only one day, the Ghost Festival lasts for a month—the seventh month of the lunar calendar. During this month, people are discouraged from hanging clothes outside to dry, whistling, getting married, buying a house, and even sleeping in.

According to legend and historical record, the festival can be traced back to a tale from the third century. A Buddhist monk named Mulian was looking for a way to rescue his mother, who had been turned into a hungry ghost as punishment for her sins in life. The Buddha told Mulian that his mother could only have food on certain days, and this is how the Ghost Festival came to be.

During China's Cultural Revolution, the festival was seen as something to be destroyed. But luckily, it has survived to the present day. When we examine the various aspects of the festival today, we can see many beliefs unique to Asia, and then compare them to the beliefs held in Western cultures.

以熙國際官網

更多關於中元節的趣事

不同於萬聖節只有一天,中元節為期足足一個月,在農曆的七月這一個月中,人們最好不要在戶外晾衣服、吹口哨、嫁娶、買房,甚至是晚起。

根據傳說和歷史記載,中元節最早可以被追溯到西元三世紀的一則故事:有一名叫目連的佛教徒,為了解救因生前的惡行而被懲罰作餓死鬼的母親,四處尋求解決辦法。佛祖告訴目連,他的母親只能在特定的日子進食,這在日後成為了中元節的由來。

在中國的文化大革命期間,中元節有一度被認為是應被除去的事物。幸運的是它成功留存到了今日。今天,當我們仔細檢視這個節日的許多細節,能從中看見許多關於亞洲的獨特信仰,並把它和西方文化做比較。

Spirit Festivals
You May
Not Know About

你。可。能。不。知。道。的。鬼。節

Qingming Festival

台灣清明節

[152] [1]**Ancestor** worship has been an important part of Chinese culture for thousands of years. In China, Taiwan and Chinese-speaking [2]**communities** all over the world, families visit cemeteries each April during Qingming Festival, also known as Tomb-sweeping Day, to clean their ancestors' graves and pay their respects. And during Ghost Month (the seventh month of the Chinese calendar), when the gates of hell open and spirits return to visit the living, the Ghost Festival is held at [3]**Buddhist** and Taoist temples to appease hungry ghosts with [4]**offerings** of food, drink and spirit money. But the Chinese aren't the only ones to hold festivals in honor of the dead. Other countries where Buddhism is [5]**practiced** have similar festivals, and other cultures around the world have their own unique rituals and [5]**practices** for honoring the dead.

　　幾千年來，祭祖一直是重要的中華文化。在中國、臺灣和世界各地的華語族群，每年四月清明節，又稱掃墓節時，家人會一起去掃墓，清理祖先的墳墓和祭拜祖先。在鬼月（農曆七月）鬼門開時，鬼魂會回到陽間探望生者，佛寺和廟宇會舉行中元節法會，以飯菜、水酒和冥紙等祭品超渡餓鬼。但華人不是唯一會舉辦祭典紀念亡靈的民族。其他信奉佛教的國家也有類似祭典，世界各地其他文化也有自己獨特的儀式和習俗以紀念亡靈。

農曆七月城隍廟遊行當中的
七爺、八爺。

[153] **Vocabulary**

1) **ancestor** [ˈænsɛstə] (n.) 祖先，祖宗

2) **community** [kəˈmjunəti] (n.) 社群，社區，社會

3) **Buddhist** [ˈbudɪst] (a./n.) 佛教的；佛教徒。**Buddhism** [ˈbudɪzəm] 為「佛教」

4) **offering** [ˈɔfərɪŋ] (n.) 供品，供奉

5) **practice** [ˈpræktɪs] (v./n.) 實行，信奉；習慣，常規

© julianne.hide / Shutterstock.com

Obon 日本御盆節

© julianne.hide / Shutterstock.com

154 Like the Ghost Festival, the Japanese festival of Obon is a Buddhist tradition that takes place during the summer months. It was originally held in the seventh month of the lunar calendar, but now takes place at different times in different regions—usually in mid-July or mid-August. It's believed that during the three days of Obon, the spirits of the dead return home to visit their living [1]**relatives**. Although Obon started out as a strictly religious festival, nowadays it has become a holiday where people return to their hometowns and spend time with family. People prepare for Obon by cleaning their homes, as well as their family tombs, and placing offerings of fruit, vegetables and sweets in front of [2]**household** [3]**altars** called *butsudan*, which are decorated with flowers and *chouchin* (paper lanterns).

　　就如同中元節，日本的御盆節是在夏季舉辦的佛教傳統祭典。原本是在農曆七月舉行，但現在各地區舉行時間互異，通常是七月中或八月中。在為期三天的御盆節，人們相信亡靈會回家探望陽間的親人。雖然御盆節一開始僅僅是宗教祭典，但現在已變成大家回到家鄉與家人團聚的節日。為了準備過御盆節，大家會打掃住處和家族墳墓，在家裡的佛壇前擺放蔬果和甜食等祭品，佛壇會用花和紙燈籠裝飾。

On the first day of Obon, people light the *chochin*—and sometimes bring them to the family tomb—to call their ancestors' spirits back home. This is called *mukae-bon*. In some regions, fires called *mukae-bi* are lit at the entrances of houses to help guide the spirits home. The second day is spent celebrating the spirits' return. Stages are built at parks and temples, and a dance called the Bon Odori is performed to the beat of taiko drums. People often wear light cotton [4]**kimonos** called *yukata* to these performances, and afterwards enjoy traditional games and snacks at [5]**booths** set up nearby. On the final day, families say goodbye to their ancestors and again light the *chochin* to guide them back to the afterlife in the ritual of *okuri-bon*. Sometimes, fires called *okuri-bi* are lit to help them find their way. And some people place floating lanterns called *toro nagashi* in rivers, lakes or the sea to send their ancestors off.

在御盆節第一天，大家會點亮紙燈籠，有時會把紙燈籠帶到家族墳墓，好召喚祖先靈魂回家，稱為迎魂盆。某些地區的人會在家門口點燃火堆，稱為迎魂火，以引導亡靈回家。第二天會慶祝亡靈歸來。公園和寺廟會搭起舞臺，人們會跟著太鼓的節拍表演盆舞。大家會穿著輕便的棉質和服，稱為浴衣，去看盆舞表演，之後在附近的攤位玩傳統遊戲和享用傳統點心。在最後一天，家人會告別祖先，再次點亮紙燈籠，以送魂盆儀式引導祂們回到陰間。有些時候會點燃火堆幫亡靈指路，稱為送魂火，有些人是在河邊、湖邊或海邊放燈籠送走祖先的靈魂，稱為放河燈。

🎧 155 **Vocabulary**

1) **relative** [ˈrɛlətɪv] (n.) 親屬
2) **household** [ˈhaʊs‚hold] (a.) 家庭的，家用的
3) **altar** [ˈɔltə] (n.) 祭壇，供桌
4) **kimono** [kɪˋmono] (n.)（日本）和服
5) **booth** [buθ] (n.) 攤位

© MAHATHIR MOHD YASIN / Shutterstock.com

© icosha / Shutterstock.com

圖片來源：維基百科

浮世繪當中，江戶時期家庭過御盆節的情景，屋前的紙燈籠就是 *chochin*。

Phi Ta Khon

泰國鬼臉節

© topten22photo / Shutterstock.com

© topten22photo / Shutterstock.com

156 Dan Sai is a [1)]sleepy farming town in Thailand's [2)]mountainous Loei [3)]Province, but once a year it LG comes to life with one of the country's most colorful festivals. Phi Ta Khon, also known as the Ghost Mask Festival, has its roots in an ancient Buddhist story. According to legend, in a past life the Buddha went on a long journey in the [4)]wilderness, and was gone so long that his followers thought he was dead. When he finally returned, the [5)]celebrations were so wild that they woke the spirits of the dead. This three-day festival was originally held sometime between March and July, with the dates selected annually by the town's mediums, but it now takes place on the first weekend following the sixth full moon of the year.

　　丹賽是泰國山區黎府一座寂靜的農業小鎮，但每年在全國最多采繽紛的節慶時會變得熱鬧滾滾。皮搭空節，又稱鬼臉節，源自古代的佛教故事。根據傳說，佛陀的其中一世在荒野中長途跋涉時，因久久沒有消息，他的弟子以為他死了。他最後回來時，因舉辦的慶祝活動太過盛大而驚動亡靈。為期三天的鬼臉節原本是在三月到七月間舉行，每年的舉辦日子由鎮上的靈媒挑選，但現在都在每年第六個滿月後第一個週末舉行。

© Jarun Tedjaem / Shutterstock.com

Phi Ta Khon begins before dawn with the town's
[6]**residents** gathering to ask Phra U-pakut, the spirit of the
Mun River, for protection. Next, the young men parade
through town in ghost [7]**costumes** [8]**consisting of** scary
masks and clothes sewn from brightly colored cloth. The
wooden masks have long noses and are painted with
rows of long, sharp teeth. The "ghosts," often drunk
on rice wine, dance through the streets to traditional
Isaan music and wave large wooden [9]**phalluses**—
symbols of [10]**fertility**—at the crowds. On the second
day, another parade takes place, with locals carrying a
[11]**sacred** Buddha image through the streets to the town's
main temple, where they set off bamboo rockets, which
are believed to bring the rains needed for a good harvest.
On the final day, people throw their ghost masks into the
river—or sell them to tourists—and return to the temple
to listen to Buddhist [12]**sermons**.

鬼臉節是在黎明前開始，小鎮居民會聚集在一起，向穆河的
河神—水財佛烏巴庫尊者祈求庇佑。接下來，年輕男子會打扮成
鬼，戴上可怕的鬼臉面具，穿上色彩鮮豔布料縫製而成的衣服，在
小鎮上結隊遊行。木製面具有長鼻子，上面塗著兩排又長又銳利的
牙齒。這群「鬼」通常因為喝了米酒而醉醺醺，在街上跟著傳統的
東北音樂跳舞，並朝群眾揮舞巨大的木製陽具，象徵生育力。第二
天會舉行另一種遊行活動，當地人會扛著佛像穿越大街小巷，遊行
到小鎮上的主要寺廟，並在那裡發射竹製火箭，他們相信這能帶來
豐收所需的豐沛雨量。在最後一天，大家會將鬼臉面具扔進河裡，
或賣給觀光客，然後回到寺廟聽佛教講道。

157 🎧 Vocabulary

1) **sleepy** [ˋslipɪ] (a.) 寂靜的，冷清的
2) **mountainous** [ˋmaʊntənəs] (a.) 多山的
3) **province** [ˋprɑvɪns] (n.) 地區，省，州
4) **wilderness** [ˋwɪldənɪs] (n.) 荒野
5) **celebration** [͵sɛləˋbreʃən] (n.) 慶祝活動，慶典
6) **resident** [ˋrɛzɪdənt] (n.) 居民
7) **costume** [ˋkɑstum] (n.) 戲服，道具服
8) **consist (of)** [kənˋsɪst] (v.) 組成，構成
9) **phallus** [ˋfæləs] (n.) 陰莖
10) **fertility** [fəˋtɪləti] (n.) 生育，繁殖（力）
11) **sacred** [ˋsekrɪd] (a.) 神聖的，供神用的
12) **sermon** [ˋsɜmən] (n.) 佈道，說教

💿 Language Guide

come to life 活起來，熱鬧起來

字面上是「活起來」的意思，也用來表示在一段沈
寂之後，重新熱鬧起來。

A: This place is pretty dead for a resort town.
以度假小鎮來說，這裡滿死氣沉沉的。

**B: That's because it's the low season. It really
<u>comes to life</u> in the summer.**
那是因為現在是淡季。夏天一到就整個熱鬧起
來。

© Jarun Tedjaem / Shutterstock.com

Día de los Muertos

墨西哥亡靈節

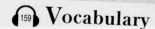

🎧 159 Vocabulary

1) **in common (with)** [ɪn `kɑmən] (phr.)
（與……）有共同處

2) **trick-or-treating** [trɪk ɔr `tritɪŋ] (n.) 玩不
給糖就搗蛋遊戲

3) **prank** [præŋk] (n.) 惡作劇

4) **dedicate (to)** [`dɛdɪ, ket] (v.) 以……獻給

5) **blend** [blɛnd] (n./v.) 混合（物）

6) **reunion** [ri`junjən] (n.)（親友）團聚

7) **marigold** [`mærə, gold] (n.) 萬壽菊，金盞
花

8) **tequila** [tə`kilə] (n.) 龍舌蘭酒

9) **essence** [`ɛsns] (n.) 精華，精髓

10) **beverage** [`bɛvərɪdʒ] (n.) 飲料

11) **mourning** [`mɔrnɪŋ] (n.) 哀悼，哀痛。動
詞為 **mourn** [mɔrn]

🎧 158 Although Día de los Muertos, or Day of the Dead, begins on October 31, it doesn't have much else ¹⁾**in common with** Halloween. Instead of ²⁾**trick-or-treating** and ³⁾**pranks**, this Mexican holiday is a time when families gather to express their love and respect for loved ones who have passed away. The origins of Día de los Muertos lie in the ancient traditions of the 🔠 **Aztec** people, who held a month-long summer festival ⁴⁾**dedicated to** Mictecacihuatl, Goddess of the Underworld, in which they honored their ancestors. When the Spanish arrived, they combined this celebration with the similar Catholic holidays of 🔠 **All Saints' Day** and 🔠 **All Souls' Day**, held on the 1st and 2nd of November. In modern Mexico, Día de los Muertos has become a national holiday that is a unique ⁵⁾**blend** of Catholic and Aztec religious practices.

　　雖然亡靈節是在 10 月 31 日開始，但跟萬聖節沒有什麼共同之處。墨西哥的亡靈節不討糖果也不搗蛋，而是家人團聚並緬懷過世親人的日子。亡靈節源自古阿茲特克人的傳統，他們曾舉行為期一個月的夏季慶典以獻給死亡女神，米克特提卡希瓦，並紀念自己的祖先。西班牙人來時，結合了類似的天主教諸聖節和萬靈節，分別是 11 月 1 日和 2 日。在現代的墨西哥，亡靈節已成為國定假日，是結合天主教和阿茲特克宗教習俗的獨特節日。

亡靈麵包 pan de muerto

The celebration begins at midnight on October 31, when *angelitos*—the spirits of dead children—return to earth for 24 hours to visit their living relatives. Then, on November 2, the spirits of adults return for a family [6]**reunion**. To guide their relatives back home, families build altars called *ofrendas* at the cemeteries where they're buried. The *ofrendas* are decorated with photos of the dead, candles and Mexican [7]**marigolds**, known as the flowers of the dead. And as the spirits get hungry on their long journey, some families also bring their loved ones' favorite foods. Toys and candy are brought for the *angelitos*, and [8]**tequila** and cigarettes for the adult spirits. It's believed that the deceased eat the [9]**essence** of the food, so the families enjoy a picnic after the spirits have finished their meal. Some families also set up *ofrendas* in their homes, usually with foods like *pan de muerto* (sweet bread shaped like bones) and *calaveras* (skulls made of sugar) and [10]**beverages** like *atole* (a sweet corn drink) and hot chocolate. As you may have guessed, Día de los Muertos isn't a time for [11]**mourning**, but for celebrating the memory of relatives who have passed away.

慶祝活動從 10 月 31 日午夜開始，小天使——過世兒童的亡靈——回到人間停留 24 小時探訪親人。然後在 11 月 2 日，成年人的亡靈回到人間與家人團聚。為了引導親人的亡靈回家，家人會在埋葬死者的墓園搭建祭壇。祭壇會用死者照片、蠟燭和墨西哥萬壽菊，又稱死亡之花裝飾。由於亡靈在長途旅行到人間後會飢餓，所以家人會帶來死者最喜愛的食物。他們會幫小天使準備玩具和糖果，幫成年亡靈準備龍舌蘭酒和香菸。他們相信亡靈會吃食物的靈氣，所以在亡靈吃完後，家人就會享用野餐。有些家人也會在家裡布置祭壇，通常會擺放亡靈麵包（骨頭形狀的甜麵包）和骷髏頭糖（用糖做成的骷髏頭），以及玉米粥（甜玉米熱飲）和熱可可等飲料。你或許已經猜到亡靈節不是哀傷的日子，而是紀念與過世親人的回憶。

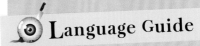

Language Guide

Maya 馬雅與 Aztec 阿茲特克古文明

馬雅和阿茲特克為中南美三大古文明之二。馬雅文明（Mayan civilization）始於西元前 2000 年左右，使用獨特的象形文字，在數學、曆法方面有極高的成就。西元 900 年後，馬雅文明突然神秘消失，只留下許多巨型神殿的遺跡。阿茲特克文明（Aztec civilization）接而承襲馬雅文明，信奉太陽神 Huitzilopochtli（因為相傳阿茲特克人是受到太陽神的指示才得以脫離原統治者而建國），於西元 1325 年落腳於現今的墨西哥城。

All Saints' Day and All Souls' Day 諸聖節和萬靈節

諸聖節顧名思義就是紀念所有天主教聖徒的日子，各處習俗不同，有的會到死者的墳前獻花或點蠟燭，有的則是吟唱詩歌。諸聖節的隔天是萬靈節（All Souls' Day）也稱為 Feast of All Souls，是紀念亡者的日子，通常會到親友墳前灑聖水、獻上鮮花及點蠟燭或為其誦經祈禱。在中世紀的英國及愛爾蘭人會為這兩個節日準備代表死者靈魂的 soul cake，送給挨家挨戶為死者祈禱或吟唱詩歌的小孩或窮人，每吃掉一塊蛋糕便代表有一個靈魂被拯救。

© Jose Gil / Shutterstock.com

© Quetzalcoatl1 / Shutterstock.com

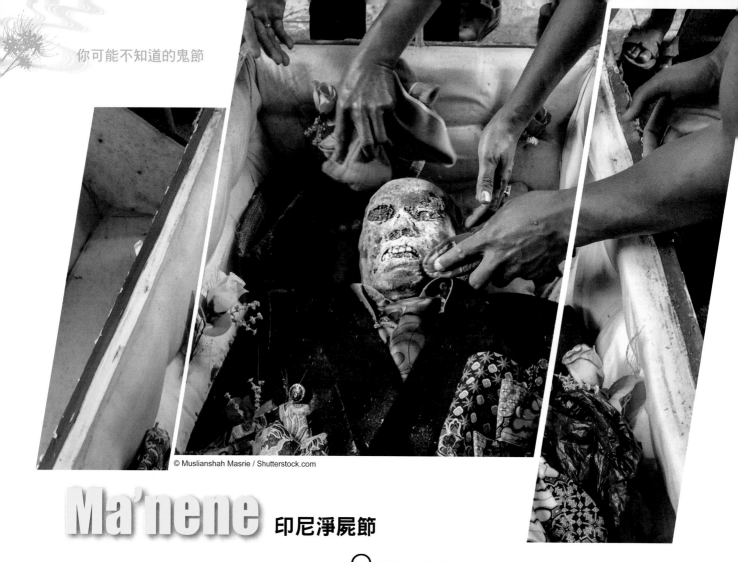

© Muslianshah Masrie / Shutterstock.com

Ma'nene 印尼淨屍節

🎧160 Although the people of Tana Toraja, a remote region in the [1]**highlands** of Sulawesi in Indonesia, are mostly Christians, they still follow traditional beliefs known as *Aluk To Dolo*, or Way of the Ancestors. This is especially true when it comes to funeral practices. For the Torajans, death is not a sudden event, but a gradual process. When family members die, they're kept at home while money is saved for the funeral, which may take months or even years! Naturally, the bodies need to be preserved. This was done in the past with special [2]**herbs**, but now [3]**formaldehyde** is used. Living relatives treat the dead—who are said to be "sick" or "sleeping"—as members of the family, talking to them and bringing them meals.

　　位於印尼蘇拉威西島高地的偏遠塔納托拉查地區，其居民雖然多數是基督徒，但仍遵循稱為「祖先之道」的傳統信仰，尤其是涉及喪葬習俗時。對托拉查人來說，死亡不是突如其來的事，而是漸進的過程。家中有人死亡時，他們會將屍體放在家中一陣子，直到存夠喪葬費，這可能需要幾個月甚至幾年！屍體理所當然需要保存。過去是用特殊藥草，但現在用甲醛。親人仍會以家人的方式對待死者，會說死者是「生病」或「睡著」，並跟他們說話，為他們準備飯菜。

The funerals, when they finally happen, are grand events. The whole village gathers, and water buffalos—which are believed to carry the dead to the afterlife—are [4)]**sacrificed**, sometimes dozens. The meat is cooked for a feast, which is a lively event with dancing, music and laughter. The deceased are then placed in wooden coffins along with the possessions they'll need in the afterlife, and the coffins are placed in caves [5)]**carved** into the sides of [6)]**cliffs**. The entrances of some caves are guarded by *tau taus*, which are wooden images of the deceased.

等到終於要辦葬禮時，他們會隆重舉辦。所有村民都會來參加，相信能帶領死者到來世的水牛會被當成祭品，有時會殺十幾隻。牛肉會在盛宴上烹調，盛宴上充滿歡樂氣氛，有舞蹈、音樂和笑聲。死者這時會被放入木製棺材，還有死者來世需要的隨身物品，然後將棺材放進懸崖峭壁的洞穴中。有些洞穴入口會放置叫做「陶陶」的雕像守護，那是木製的死者肖像。

If you think that's the last time families see their loved ones, you're wrong. In a ritual called Ma'nene, which takes place every three years in August, families are again united with their dead relatives. After prayers are said, the bodies of the dead are removed from their coffins and laid in the sun to dry. Relatives then clean the corpses with brushes, dress them in brand new clothes and take them for a walk around the village before returning them to their coffins. The Torajans believe that honoring their ancestors this way will bring good luck and [7)]**abundant** harvests.

你若以為那是家人最後一次見到死者，那你就猜錯了。在每隔三年在八月舉行的淨屍節，家人會再次與過世親人團聚。在祈禱過後，棺材中的屍體會移出來，放在太陽底下曝曬。然後親人會用刷子清理屍體，替屍體換上新衣服，帶著死者在村子裡散步，然後放回棺材。托拉查人相信用這種方式紀念祖先能帶來好運和豐收。

托拉查人居住的高腳屋造型極具特色。

**淨屍節
流程**

❶ 每隔幾年舉辦一次的淨屍節到來，當地民眾聚集墓穴進行準備工作。

❷ 淨屍節當天， 亡者的家屬將棺木移出墓穴，準備淨屍。

❸ 屍體曝曬清理之後，親屬替亡者換上新衣服到村裡散步。

塔納托拉查的葬禮

© Elena Odareeva / Shutterstock.com

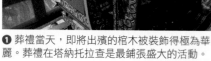
© Oscar Espinosa / Shutterstock.com

❶ 葬禮當天，即將出殯的棺木被裝飾得極為華麗。葬禮在塔納托拉查是最鋪張盛大的活動。

❷ 棺木被移出靈堂，開始出殯。

❹ 棺木被安放在托拉查人居住的高腳屋造型轎子裡，由許多壯漢抬著在村子裡遊行。

© Ade Jukmanul hakimm / Shutterstock.com

❸ 穿著黑衣的喪家列隊準備展開出殯遊行。

© emran / Shutterstock.com

❺ 葬禮上屠宰許多水牛宴請賓客。當地人相信水牛能將亡魂帶到來世。

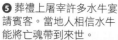
© John Crux / Shutterstock.com

© Luisa Puccini / Shutterstock.com

©flickr.com/photos/nh53/

❻ 葬禮結束四天後，棺木由壯丁拉上陡峭岩壁的洞穴安置。

❼ 有些墓穴口有稱作 tau tau 的木製人偶守護。

皇家墓穴入口有大量骷髏。

🎧163 Vocabulary

1) **ceremony** [ˈsɛrəˌmoni] (n.) 儀式，典禮
2) **exhume** [ɪɡˈzum] (v.)（從墳墓）挖出
3) **decompose** [ˌdikəmˈpoz] (v.) 分解，腐爛
4) **meantime** [ˈminˌtaɪm] (adv.) 同時。
   in the meantime 即「在此同時」
5) **bond** [bɑnd] (n.)（人之間的）關係，聯繫
6) **rum** [rʌm] (n.) 蘭姆酒
7) **procession** [prəˈsɛʃən] (n.)（人、車）行列，隊伍，遊行
8) **shroud** [ʃraʊd] (n.) 壽衣，裹屍布
9) **perfume** [pɚˈfjum] (n.) 香水
10) **alcohol** [ˈælkəˌhɔl] (n.) 酒，酒精

Famadihana

馬達加斯加翻屍節

All the way across the Indian Ocean on the island of Madagascar, the Malagasy people practice a burial ritual similar to Ma'nene. This could be because the ancestors of the Malagasy are believed to have come from Indonesia over 1,000 years ago. Known as Famadihana, or the "turning of the bones," this ritual takes place in the central highlands of Madagascar five to seven years after a loved one has passed away. Like Ma'nene, Famadihana is a [1]**ceremony** where deceased relatives are [2]**exhumed** for a family reunion before being returned to their graves. The custom is based on a belief that the spirits of the dead enter the afterlife only after the body [3]**decomposes** completely—a process that may take years—and that in the [4]**meantime**, family [5]**bonds** must be maintained.

> 遠在印度洋對岸的馬達加斯加島，馬拉加斯人的喪葬習俗跟淨屍節類似。這可能是因為馬拉加斯人的祖先據說是一千多年前從印尼過來的。Famadihana 的意思是「翻轉屍骨」，這個儀式是在親人過世後五到七年，在馬達加斯加中部高地舉行。就像淨屍節，在翻屍節的儀式中，家人會在團聚時將過世親人的屍體挖出來，然後放回墳墓。他們相信死者靈魂只能在屍體完全腐化後才能進入來世，因此才有這種習俗，腐化過程可能需要幾年時間，所以這段期間他們要維持家庭關係。

On the day of the Famadihana, the family and friends of the deceased—some who have traveled great distances on foot—gather for a feast of roast meat, rice and [6]**rum**. When everyone is full, and many drunk, they march in a [7]**procession** to the family tomb to the beat of a brass band. The bodies of the dead are removed from the tomb and placed on mats on the ground, where the silk [8]**shrouds** they were buried in are removed and replaced with fresh ones. As the bodies are sprinkled with rum or [9]**perfume**, the living relatives talk to the deceased, telling them the latest news and family gossip. The family members then wrap the bodies in mats, and as the band begins playing, they lift the bodies above their shoulders and carry them in circles around the tomb, dancing and singing. As sunset approaches, the deceased are returned to the tomb, along with gifts of money and [10]**alcohol**, and the ceremony comes to an end.

> 在翻屍節這天，死者的親友 —— 有些人是長途徒步而來 —— 會團聚在一起享用烤肉、米飯和蘭姆酒。大家吃飽後，會一起跟著銅管樂團的節拍行進到家族墓園，而其中有不少人會喝醉。他們接著把死者的屍體從墳墓中移出，放在地上的草席上，將包裹屍體的絲質壽衣脫下並換上新的。他們一邊在屍體上灑上蘭姆酒或香水，一邊跟死者說話，聊最近的消息和家族八卦。然後家人用草席包裹屍體，樂隊開始演奏時，他們將屍體扛在肩上繞著墳墓跳舞和唱歌。在日落將至時，將屍體連同錢和酒一起放回墳墓，這場儀式就這樣結束了。

© beibaoke / Shutterstock.com

Sky [1]Burial

西藏天葬

165 **Vocabulary**

1) **burial** [ˋbɛrɪəl] (n.) 埋葬，葬禮，動詞為 **bury** [ˋbɛri] 埋藏

2) **cremate** [ˋkrimet] (v.) 火葬，焚化。名詞為 **cremation** [ˌkriˋmeʃən]

3) **part** [pɑrt] (v.) 分離

4) **vulture** [ˋvʌltʃɚ] (n.) 禿鷹

5) **gruesome** [ˋgrusəm] (a.) 可怕的，令人毛骨悚然的

6) **outsider** [ˋaʊtˋsaɪdɚ] (n.) 外人，局外人

7) **compassion** [kəmˋpæʃən] (n.) 同情，憐憫

8) **lama** [ˋlɑmə] (n.) （西藏、蒙古僧侶）喇嘛

9) **monastery** [ˋmɑnəˌstɛri] (n.) 僧院

10) **juniper** [ˋdʒunəpɚ] (n.) 杜松

11) **grind (up)** [graɪnd] (v.) 磨（碎），碾（碎）

12) **barley** [ˋbɑrli] (n.) 大麥

164 While Christians [1]**bury** their dead and Buddhists generally [2]**cremate** them, the Tibetan Buddhists have a more unique method of [3]**parting** with their loved ones— sky burial. Known in Tibetan as *jhator*, this funeral practice involves leaving the body of the deceased outdoors to be eaten by [4]**vultures**. This tradition may seem [5]**gruesome** to [6]**outsiders**, but to Tibetan Buddhists it's perfectly natural. In a land where the ground is too hard for grave digging and wood too **scarce** for [2]**cremation**, sky burial is a practical solution. And because Buddhists believe that the body is just an empty shell once the soul leaves, giving it to the vultures as food is seen as an act of [7]**compassion**.

基督徒通常用土葬的方式埋葬死者，佛教徒通常用火葬，而西藏佛教徒告別親人的方式更獨特，是天葬。天葬在西藏語叫「札陀」，這種喪葬習俗是將屍體放在野外讓禿鷹啃食。這種傳統對外人來說或許很可怕，但對西藏佛教徒來說是很自然的。在這塊由於土壤太硬，而難以挖掘造墳的土地上，可用於焚燒的木材也很稀有，天葬是很務實的辦法。而且由於佛教徒相信靈魂離開後，肉體只是個空殼，讓禿鷹吃掉屍體是一種慈悲的表現。

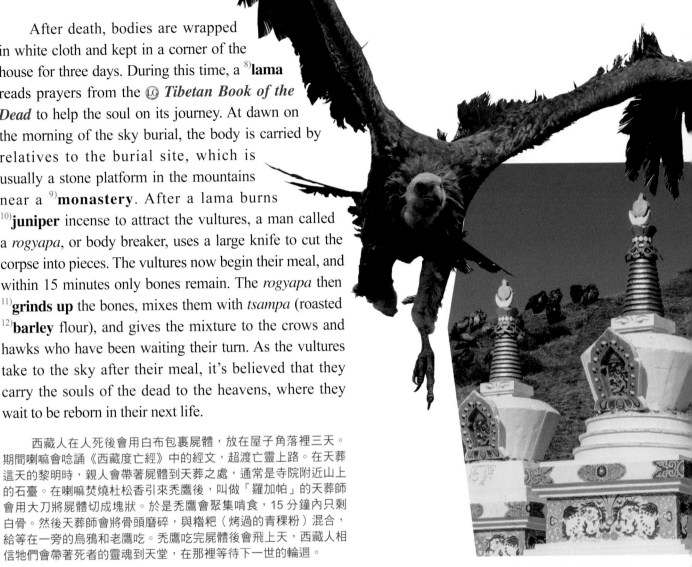

After death, bodies are wrapped in white cloth and kept in a corner of the house for three days. During this time, a [8]**lama** reads prayers from the Ⓛ *Tibetan Book of the Dead* to help the soul on its journey. At dawn on the morning of the sky burial, the body is carried by relatives to the burial site, which is usually a stone platform in the mountains near a [9]**monastery**. After a lama burns [10]**juniper** incense to attract the vultures, a man called a *rogyapa*, or body breaker, uses a large knife to cut the corpse into pieces. The vultures now begin their meal, and within 15 minutes only bones remain. The *rogyapa* then [11]**grinds up** the bones, mixes them with *tsampa* (roasted [12]**barley** flour), and gives the mixture to the crows and hawks who have been waiting their turn. As the vultures take to the sky after their meal, it's believed that they carry the souls of the dead to the heavens, where they wait to be reborn in their next life.

西藏人在人死後會用白布包裹屍體，放在屋子角落裡三天。期間喇嘛會唸誦《西藏度亡經》中的經文，超渡亡靈上路。在天葬這天的黎明時，親人會帶著屍體到天葬之處，通常是寺院附近山上的石臺。在喇嘛焚燒杜松香引來禿鷹後，叫做「羅加帕」的天葬師會用大刀將屍體切成塊狀。於是禿鷹會聚集啃食，15 分鐘內只剩白骨。然後天葬師會將骨頭磨碎，與糌粑（烤過的青稞粉）混合，給等在一旁的烏鴉和老鷹吃。禿鷹吃完屍體後會飛上天，西藏人相信牠們會帶著死者的靈魂到天堂，在那裡等待下一世的輪迴。

圖片來源：維基百科，攝影／FishOil

最讓人發毛的鬼話英文：EZ TALK 總編嚴選特刊 /
EZ 叢書館編輯部作 . -- 初版 . -- 臺北市：日月文化，
2018.09
　　面；　公分 . -- (EZ 叢書館；32)
ISBN 978-986-248-746-4 (平裝附光碟片)

1. 英語　2. 讀本

805.18　　　　　　　　　　　　　　　107011489

EZ 叢書館 32

最讓人發毛的鬼話英文
EZ TALK 總編嚴選特刊

總　編　審：Judd Piggott
專案企劃執行：陳思容
主　　　編：潘亭軒
資　深　編　輯：鄭莉璇
校　　　對：潘亭軒、鄭莉璇
封　面　設　計：徐歷弘
版　型　設　計：蕭彥伶
內　頁　排　版：簡單瑛設、蕭彥伶
錄　音　後　製：純粹錄音後製有限公司
錄　音　員：Jacob Roth、Leah Zimmermann

發　行　人：洪祺祥
副　總　經　理：洪偉傑
副　總　編　輯：曹仲堯
法　律　顧　問：建大法律事務所
財　務　顧　問：高威會計師事務所
出　　　版：日月文化出版股份有限公司
製　　　作：EZ 叢書館
地　　　址：臺北市信義路三段151號8樓
電　　　話：(02)2708-5509
傳　　　真：(02)2708-6157
客　服　信　箱：service@heliopolis.com.tw
網　　　址：www.heliopolis.com.tw
郵　撥　帳　號：19716071日月文化出版股份有限公司

總　經　銷：聯合發行股份有限公司
電　　　話：(02)2917-8022
傳　　　真：(02)2915-7212
印　　　刷：中原造像股份有限公司
初　版　一　刷：2018 年 9 月
定　　　價：350 元
I　S　B　N：978-986-248-746-4

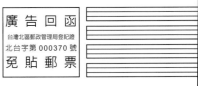

日月文化集團
HELIOPOLIS
CULTURE GROUP

感謝您購買 最讓人發毛的鬼話英文　　　　EZ TALK 總編嚴選特刊

為提供完整服務與快速資訊，請詳細填寫以下資料，傳真至02-2708-6157或免貼郵票寄回，我們將不定期提供您最新資訊及最新優惠。

1. 姓名：＿＿＿＿＿＿＿＿＿＿＿＿　　　　性別：□男　　　□女

2. 生日：＿＿＿＿年＿＿＿＿月＿＿＿＿日　　職業：

3. 電話：（請務必填寫一種聯絡方式）

　（日）＿＿＿＿＿＿＿＿　（夜）＿＿＿＿＿＿＿＿　（手機）＿＿＿＿＿＿＿

4. 地址：□□□＿＿＿＿＿＿＿＿＿＿＿＿＿＿＿＿＿＿＿＿

5. 電子信箱：＿＿＿＿＿＿＿＿＿＿＿＿＿＿＿＿＿＿＿

6. 您從何處購買此書？□＿＿＿＿＿＿＿縣/市＿＿＿＿＿＿＿書店/量販超商

　□＿＿＿＿＿＿＿網路書店　□書展　□郵購　□其他

7. 您何時購買此書？　　年　　月　　日

8. 您購買此書的原因：（可複選）

　□對書的主題有興趣　　□作者　□出版社　□工作所需　　□生活所需

　□資訊豐富　　　□價格合理（若不合理，您覺得合理價格應為＿＿＿＿＿＿）

　□封面/版面編排　□其他＿＿＿＿＿＿＿＿＿＿＿＿＿＿

9. 您從何處得知這本書的消息：　□書店　□網路／電子報　□量販超商　□報紙

　□雜誌　□廣播　□電視　□他人推薦　□其他

10. 您對本書的評價：（1.非常滿意 2.滿意 3.普通 4.不滿意 5.非常不滿意）

　書名＿＿＿＿　內容＿＿＿＿　封面設計＿＿＿＿　版面編排＿＿＿＿　文/譯筆＿＿＿＿

11. 您通常以何種方式購書？□書店　□網路　□傳真訂購　□郵政劃撥　□其他

12. 您最喜歡在何處買書？

　□＿＿＿＿＿＿＿縣/市＿＿＿＿＿＿＿書店/量販超商　□網路書店

13. 您希望我們未來出版何種主題的書？＿＿＿＿＿＿＿＿＿＿＿＿＿＿

14. 您認為本書還須改進的地方？提供我們的建議？

＿＿＿＿＿＿＿＿＿＿＿＿＿＿＿＿＿＿＿＿＿＿＿＿＿＿＿＿＿

＿＿＿＿＿＿＿＿＿＿＿＿＿＿＿＿＿＿＿＿＿＿＿＿＿＿＿＿＿

＿＿＿＿＿＿＿＿＿＿＿＿＿＿＿＿＿＿＿＿＿＿＿＿＿＿＿＿＿

＿＿＿＿＿＿＿＿＿＿＿＿＿＿＿＿＿＿＿＿＿＿＿＿＿＿＿＿＿